Hear Me Roar

Rhonda Parrish

All copyright for individual stories remains with original authors
Anthology Copyright © 2020 by **Rhonda Parrish**

All rights reserved. No part of this publication may be reproduced, distributed or transmitted in any form or by any means, without prior written permission.

www.poiseandpen.com

Publisher's Note: This is a work of fiction. Names, characters, places, and incidents are a product of the author's imagination. Locales and public names are sometimes used for atmospheric purposes. Any resemblance to actual people, living or dead, or to businesses, companies, events, institutions, or locales is completely coincidental.

Book Layout based on one © 2014 BookDesignTemplates.com
Edited by Rhonda Parrish
Cover design by Andreea Elena Vraciu

Hear Me Roar / Rhonda Parrish.—1st ed.
ISBN 978-1-988233-74-1 (Physical)
ISBN 978-1-988233-75-8 (Electronic)

Dedicated to everyone, everywhere who fights—in any way—for equality.

CONTENTS

INTRODUCTION 1
THE PRINCESS OF DRAGONS...3
LIGHT CHASER, DARK HUNTER 7
DEFEND US IN BATTLE 33
BLACKTOOTH 500..47
FATHER CHRISTMAS, MOTHER HUBBARD, THE DRAGON (AND OTHER SELECTED SCENES FROM THE END OF THE WORLD)..65
THE NAGA'S MIRROR 87
MADAM LIBRARIAN 95
OF DRAGON GENES AND PRETTY GIRLS 103
BLACKOUT..113
GINNY AND THE OUROBOROS 131
RED IN TOOTH AND MAW 145
SERPENT IN PARADISE..169
TIA TIME 193
FOR THE GLORY OF GOLD 203
THE RISE OF THE DRAGONBLOOD QUEEN 217
A NIGHT IN THE PHILOSOPHER'S CAVE....................243

RHONDA PARRISH

INTRODUCTION

I have a weakness for premade covers. It's a real thing. It started as a love for stock art and has evolved into its current incarnation over several years. Premade book covers feature the cover art and some sort of placeholder title and author name. When you buy a premade cover, the artist changes the text to match your book and voila! You've got a cover.

I find premade covers incredibly inspiring and often fall in love with covers long before I have anything written to go with them. That was sort of the case with this cover... and sort of not.

I belong to several premade cover Facebook groups and one of them was having an auction. This was one of the covers available and as soon as I saw it I knew I had to have it. Of course, after I'd purchased it I had to figure out what to do with it. I didn't have time to write a novel to match so I thought I'd use it for an anthology.

As soon as I made that decision everything else clicked into place. The topic? Empowered women and dragons. The title? *Hear Me Roar*.

To make things a little bit different from my usual anthologies I only opened this one up to submissions from people who were subscribed to my mailing list. I was a little nervous about that—it's always a risk when you limit the number of people sending you work to consider—but I needn't have worried. As it turns out my mailing list subscribers are a talented bunch.

This anthology begins with a story by an author who is in elementary school and ends with one who teaches undergrads. I really liked the idea of using those two pieces as bookends and then carefully placing all the rest in between.

The stories which fill these pages span spectrums. They vary in voice and genre. Some of the dragons are easily recognized as such, some not so much but each story has a unique and interesting take on the 'empowered women and dragons' theme.

As an anthologist I often try to guess which stories will be people's favourites. Will it be the one about a unique dragon hoard or the one about girls finding friendship in unlikely circumstances? The story with deep roots in math and science or one of the ones about a princess leading her people?

I hope every reader finds at least one gem of a story in this collection which they want to lay on top of Smaug-style and treasure forever.

Rhonda Parrish
Edmonton
4/1/20

AURORA B.C. DONEV

THE PRINCESS OF DRAGONS

So much for invading Fulton! Princess Marsha had been stuck in the tower for seven weeks and she was tired of just sitting there.

"I'm done with this," said Marsha, and turned into a Galaxy-Tail—one of the five kinds of dragons that lived in Magistonia. They are fierce, bold dragons! A Galaxy-Tail is jet black with a purple tail and purple eyes, and can shoot stars. Really sharp stars.

Naturally, she smashed the tower. It turned into a billion pebbles.

Marsha glided down to the ground and alerted her guard-dragon, who was also a Galaxy-Tail.

"Nightmare, find all the dragons in Magistonia, and say they are invited to my polls. It's for ruler of dragons. Understand?"

"Yes, Princess," agreed Nightmare.

At the voting, it was chaos. Absolute discord! All the dragons wanted to sit in the front row. Finally, they settled down to hear Marsha speak. This is what she said:

"So, dragons of Magistonia! We need more land. I can help you get more land. I tried to invade Fulton, but my stupid dad grounded me. We can succeed if we work together and win a war! A war against unicorns!"

A young Flame-Wing in the audience stood up. "Talons up to vote for this girl!" he said, pointing to Marsha.

All of the dragons raised their talons and cheered.

"Yay!"

"War on the unicorns!"

"I'm so glad you're the princess!"

"Fulton was too small of a goal for you."

In the Armory, Nightmare was thinking. "If there are one hundred eighty-nine dragons in Magistonia, and they each need plates and tail clubs... Hmm..." Nightmare thought and thought about it. "I've got it! I'll tell Marsha!" The Galaxy-Tail wrote something on a piece of paper, and then rushed off excitedly.

When Nightmare arrived at the Throne Room, Marsha stood up suddenly and cried, "You're early, Nightmare! How much armour do we need?"

"It's a bit of a mouthful, so I wrote it down." replied Nightmare, handing Marsha the paper.

"Thanks! I'll go tell the blacksmith!"

"Welcome, Princess."

"All right, guys!" said Marsha. "The unicorns will come to get their coffee in three... two... one... Where are they?" In twelve minutes (that seemed like twelve hours) the herds arrived and the princess of dragons confronted the princess of unicorns who was... her twin sister Princess Darla?!

Darla was quite surprised to see Marsha. "Marsha! 'Sup?"

"The sky," said Marsha, sarcastically. Then, she lunged at her sister. Darla parried and dove, but Marsha blocked it.

Just then, Princess Marsha tripped over a hole. "Darn gnomes," she said. Princess Darla saw her chance. She sprang at her twin. Marsha scrambled away to avoid death, but her left leg didn't make it. *Whoosh!* Instead of cutting off Marsha's head, Darla's sword struck her knee.

"Ow!" screamed Princess Marsha.

That was it. The war was cancelled.

The unicorns gave the dragons a humongous forest and nine lakes to add to their kingdom.

Darla ran all the way back home to Finichesit, crying, "I nearly killed my sister! I'm a terrible person!" and Marsha turned into a Galaxy-Tail and flew to the blacksmith. When she got there, she said, "I need a metal leg. Left, from knee down. Size twenty."

Lizzie Smith, the blacksmith's daughter, said, "'Kay, they're in the cabinet marked '20.'"

"Thanks!" Marsha hopped to the cabinet and searched the drawers. "Metal arms, metal legs! Right, left! Thigh, whole, shin!" She grabbed the shin piece.

"Where is the attachment room?"

Lizzie pointed to the back.

"Thanks!"

The princess of the dragons grabbed a screwdriver. Whistle, clink, screech, click. "Phew," she said. "Done."

Marsha sat at the beach, smiling at two Lake-Talons racing in a lake. She was proud of what her subjects had done against the unicorns, and she was giving them what they needed: peace. Suddenly, a Wind-Scale swooped by.

"Princess Marsha!" she cried. "Princess Gabrielle of the phoenixes is here—and she wants an audience with you!"

Marsha sighed, and wished the peace was hers, too. "I'm coming, Breeze."

> ***Aurora B. C. Donev*** *is an extravagant reader and excited to contribute to others' bookshelves. When she is not reading (which isn't often), she is acting or coding. She is currently living with two adults, two guinea pigs, one fish, and many, many, many books.*

JOSEPH HALDEN

LIGHT CHASER, DARK HUNTER

The land was young, traces were left
  Before the cleft, a single people
  The sundering began from famine
  Failing plants, lamb and dwindled sun.
  The solve temporary, focused on stability
  Left a rift stuck firmly as a claw in a perch.

-From Persalia's Lichtfan Canto 8:15

Zerianne

Arrest the old crone, the men said.

They abuse their power by tasking me with the most base of chores: sweeping away an old Dunkellian who had probably gotten lost wandering to watch the nearest bloodsport. My only solace is that this work will protect the fertile land I hold so dear.

The sheer-faced mountains surrounding our lands hold a bright halo of light above everything. In the ruined grey-black of the sky, there is but a narrow gap where the light can shine without being hindered by either dense smog or the tall peaks. On the treelines of the encircling mountains, heliostat mirrors reflect sunlight onto crops far below. They are the only way we can stay alive in our otherwise dark-walled nook, but this life is far better than the world outside.

A minute down the narrow path and I set eyes on the old Dunkellian. She's wearing a cloak with the uneven grey weave of mycelium, and a mottled grey felt hat.

Mushrooms. The Dunkellians use them for everything, like poorly trained carpenters who use nothing but hammers.

"You're under arrest," I tell her, unsheathing my sabre. I feel a fool for acting this way against such a non-threat, but I will be darkened before I let the men get rid of me for lacking procedural rigour. Eventually, they will have to accept a woman in their ranks.

The old woman peeks with narrow eyes around a thin-limbed spruce. Her face is etched with cavernous wrinkles carrying the shadow of her home everywhere she goes.

She wraps her cloak around her lumpy body and nods.

"Have you an explanation for your trespass?" I ask. "It might ease your sentence."

She yawns and steps onto the path, waiting. She is two-thirds my height and twice as wide. She couldn't have hidden even if she were twenty years younger with the blessing of a year's sunlight.

Standing right behind her, I am assaulted by the familiar Dunkellian stench of compost and decay. Mixed in, however, are the scent of dried autumn leaves and petrichor after rainfall.

Strange. Although I had only ever been close to a handful of arrested Dunkellians, none of them ever smelled like this.

I search her for weapons and unseen threats, but of course she hasn't any. I would be shocked to discover any Dunkellian of her age who posed more threat than philistinism.

It is unpleasant for both of us as I pat her down. She refuses to look at me, and when I finish she starts without me down the mountain toward the castle base. I catch up to her easily, but it still annoys me.

So I loudly proclaim all the laws she has broken by wandering up here, and go into great detail outlining the severity and duration of her punishments.

Nothing I say elicits so much as a grunt from her, and my blood froths in spite of the chill air. Maybe the old woman is in shock, but her demeanour says she is placating me until she can get on to something better.

The trees and the air thicken, which normally lift my spirits, but the silence between me and the woman is a thin wire cutting through it all.

We pass three tower checkpoints and I am forced to report to smug-looking, stubble-faced men whom I can tell are biting back slurs.

We are within sight of the stark fortress, two tall ramparts bordering a jagged-topped wall. The battlements are dotted with patrolling archers.

They are only partly protecting our lush fields. More importantly, they prevent anyone from getting out to the heliostats, which makes the old woman's presence even more mystifying. How could she have snuck by them?

Maybe the woman has not understood a word I have spoken.

"Do you even speak Hellezunge?"

She snorts and chuckles, the first noise she has made beyond breath.

Her derisive attitude feels too much like that of the men, who only acknowledge my existence when they are about play their nasty tricks: hiding embarrassing Dunkellian mushrooms in my bunk, weighting my armour so I move like an oak, and soaking my clothing in rotten butter that takes months to wash out.

I feel the urge to lash out. Deep down, though, I know I would feel the same as when I had knelt as a child beside my mother in the dirt, her hands tracing the corn stalks I had broken by running angrily through our fields.

I could not even remember what I had been angry about. All my mother had done was look at me with the sadness of a frozen harvest and said, "When you hurt them, you hurt us all."

I would not lash out. I would follow the proper conduct with my prisoner. Light shines where you cast it.

The portcullis raises and I usher the woman through. Torches flicker. Moans echo from the walls.

We enter the warden's chamber. He is a moustached man with his gut half-supported on his desk.

"Name?" he asks, picking up a quill and barely looking at us.

This is it. Now the old bag will get it for being insolent.

She answers, to my astonishment. "Silreena Wesolek." Her voice is as rough as an avalanche.

"Crime?"

"Failure to present to checkpoints Gluhen, Spiegeln, and Anstrahlen," I say. "Failure to produce proper identification. Finally, trespassing in the hallowed light."

My last words make the warden stop.

"Twelve years," I say, and he nods.

She is led away so quickly I am robbed of my chance to gloat in her face.

Silreena

Tired. Whole thing took too long. Nowhere unwatched in hallowed light. Will have to find another strategy.

Cell mates look starved. Feel bad for them. If I could save them too I would.

Guards never found pouches tucked under breasts. So different from when I was young.

Pour out powder into floor cracks. Smells strong, like pantry mould. Barely enough to overpower stench of urine.

Work powder into earth. Masonry ready to collapse. Dungeon upkeep not priority for guards. I inspected tunnels beforehand.

Should never try to avoid decay. Lichtfans normally fight it; glad they didn't this time.

Rumble takes hours to come. Tunnel-grubs are here now, and they want powder.

Floor gives way. Dust fills air, and guards with torches are blind.

Light is only for what cannot endure.

Reunited with tunnel-grubs, I collapse tunnel behind me, and make way home.

Zerianne

"Please let me go after her, sir," I say to the high commander, in his gorgeous office with floor-to-ceiling faceted crystal windows reflecting off mirrored walls.

The tall high commander pokes a lit fireplace with an iron. The top of his head, like all of the upper class, is shaved with the skin showing a dark tan.

I am aghast at the waste of beautiful birch to make a fire he does not need.

The high commander pulls out the glowing tip and inspects it.

"No," he replies. "The tunnels lead back into Dunkelherrscht. You have neither the rank nor the experience."

I must sway him. If I do not, the men will spread lies that I cannot succeed at any assignment, even one as simple as locking up a harmless old woman. They will recommence their refrain that a lady should never be allowed to join the guard.

"Sir, I am the best person to track her down. I arrested her. I recall the way she smells, the way she moves."

The high commander smiles at me like I am a child who has just attempted something adorable.

May darkness take him.

"You in Dunkelherrscht? No. You wouldn't last a few hours in their endless night."

His smile vanishes and the fire poker becomes a weapon in his grip. "You are dismissed, Ensign."

I salute and march out of the room, my palms as hot as his fire poker.

Silreena

Sneak through hidden tunnels. Tunnel-grubs wriggle happily behind. They know what's coming.

Seems like I'm only one who recognizes tunnel-grubs need light. Lichtfans say, "We need light the most," but they don't. Makes them soft. Blind. Lazy.

Tunnel-grubs grow in light. Soothes their hunger. No one trusts Silreena the Strange with much, but they should trust as caretaker.

I recognize what things need. Give it to them.

I shovel through dirt now. Tunnel grubs see, start to help. They're much better diggers, but still a lot of work. I could have used more help, but would have had to ask.

And no one wants to hear. Silreena the Strange is for laughs, maybe, but never for listening.

Better to show through action. Easier than pretending importance before work is done.

Finally break through surface. Extra surprise of carrots, tumbling down in web of roots.

Tunnel-grubs don't care about carrots. They scuttle straight into beams of light.

They bathe.

I encourage them to keep quiet. Hard to do with five of them.

Teep and Rov grow eyes. They break open like mushroom caps out of mycelium.

Tunnel-grubs have complex life-cycle. Changing. Growing happier. Becoming what they could be when finally given what they need.

Farmers going to make rounds soon. I need to get out. Hard to get tunnel-grubs back. They would stay here forever. Wish I could let them.

Coax four of them back into tunnel, but Rov won't come. I have to climb up out of hole and pry him away. He's bigger. Can barely get arms around him.

On way back down, cloak catches on stray root and tears. Better than getting caught—I can hear workers making rounds through fields.

Rov and Teep help steer way back with new eyes. They're better than me underground now. Never expected it.

I can't believe people call them pests.

Zerianne

They have gotten my locker. Wood chips from its ruin line the floor, and for the first time, the smell of wood fibres makes me nauseous. How dare they turn the smell of nature into something horrid?

A message is carved into the remaining piece of my locker door:

Woman can't even police a woman.

It is an absurdity. There is no one around to laugh at me. No one for me to blame. This way, it becomes a message from everyone.

My chest hitches every time I breathe. I feel foolish as my hands shake putting the iron key into the lock. I have been through worse. I have sworn so many times they would never stop me.

I change into my uniform, brushing a tear away that should be used on a plant, not wasted on these scoundrels.

Why do I so long for their acceptance?

Exiting the barracks, I walk along the dirt path at the edge of the Lichtfall fields.

There is still no one around. They have planned for no accountability. If I complain, they could say someone outside the guard did it.

Bathed in the reflected sunset, I gaze longingly at the beautiful daisy and pine-coloured concentric circles. They are aligned with the patterns of the sun's radiance, those crops most in need of light at the centre.

Somewhere at the far side is my family's homestead. I drink in the fresh air, life and pollen of a life I once knew. If I am strong enough, perhaps one day I will be able to return and nurture the land.

The farther I get from the hate-filled locker, the easier it is to breathe. However, the insults tangle into a knot I cannot untie.

I see a dark spot in the brilliant patterns of the field, and I look around for the farmer. Are they not aware of this wasted land?

Perhaps I can help. It is the closest I have come to farming for a while.

Closer to the dark patch, I see the earth has caved in. The tilting crops jut in like the teeth of a beast.

This was intentional vandalism, and my heart aches the same as it did years ago.

It had been the end of the year, close to harvest, when a Dunkellian man broke in. He gorged himself on our crops, trampling and tearing up the harvest as though the sun were at its end.

Then he torched everything.

My mother sobbed in the soot, her tears channeling down the black on her face as she brought one mutilated plant after another up to her lips and kissed them. We could not get her out of the field for hours.

Although we scraped through the next few seasons, mother developed incessant stomach pains.

Now she cannot work the fields, and is shunned for it.

As am I, for the work I had to take up thereafter.

I am paid far better on the guard, enough to hire mother the help she needs. It was and still is a struggle, but I know if I am strong enough, I can bear the burden.

The light shines where we cast it.

The only light the hole in front of me deserves, however, is the light of clarity, in order to find out who would do such a thing.

Then I see a piece of grey fabric caught on one of the roots farther into the hole.

Crouching down, I pick up the mycelium weave. A Dunkellian, of course.

Lifting the fabric to my nose, my grip tightens as I recognize the mix of compost, dried autumn leaves and petrichor.

Silreena. Recognition burns a dizzying mixture of inadequacy and rage. Insults and repeated injuries against what remains of my dignity.

Can't even police a woman.

My fist shakes. I will catch her. Blacken the fact I am not permitted.

Deeper into the hole, I can see the way is blocked. There will be no following her that way.

That will not stop me, though. I will sneak into Dunkelherrscht and make sure Silreena can never hurt another Lichtfan crop ever again.

High on the wall separating Lichtfan and Dunkelherrscht, I am but a distant observer to all life. No one would expect me to jump down.

I pass a few guards who grunt but do not meet my gaze.

At the far end where the wall meets the cliff is the massive heap of compost that Lichtfans dump onto the Dunkellian side. It is normally a blight on the landscape, but today it is my gateway to redemption.

I have timed my arrival with the guard change, so when there is a gap, I jump.

I impact and the putrefaction flows up and over my head. I cannot breathe, and thrash until I see the grey light of air again.

Soon I am hiding in a dark alley—every alley here is dark—changing into a confiscated mycelium cloak. As I walk away, tufts of compost fall off and join into a blanket on the mud.

The compost is soon replaced by mushrooms in every nook. Bright spotted mushrooms provide the only colour next to the tight-packed grey and brown buildings.

Where there is brightness here, there is death.

I come upon two boys and their mother. They strike at one other with staves while the mother watches. When one of them falls into the mud, the other pauses his attacks. That gets him cuffed by his mother.

"Stop being soft!" she yells.

She demonstrates what she wants him to do by kicking the downed boy.

"Again!" she snaps.

The boys get up and set upon each other again. I bite my tongue. I have seen similar scenes in my time guarding the wall, but never so close that I can smell the blood coming down lips.

When one of the boys starts weeping, the mother's voice rings at them to stop.

She crouches down and cradles the weeping boy in her arms. "I know you hurt, my child," she says.

Her voice has shifted as abruptly as a flowing stream darting around winter's grasp in the last throes of fall.

"You remember why we do this?" she says, beckoning to the other boy to join them.

"So we can win."

"Why?"

"So we can taste light and fruit."

"I had part of a strawberry once," the standing boy brags.

"Hush now," the mother says as she finally sees me.

I have been entranced by the unexpected tenderness. I have not the time to sift through what I have seen, however, because my intrusion brings the hard edge back to the mother's features.

My only relief is the fact that their accent is not strong, so I may pass for one of them.

"Excuse me, do you happen to know where Silreena Wesolek is?"

The mother squints. "Don't know."

"Silreena the Strange! Silreena the Strange!" the boys parrot, laughing. "That's her real name."

"Hush," the mother snaps. "I don't know where she is, but it's likely she'll be with everyone else at the arena for the daylight glory. Not that you could find someone in the masses, though. You headed that way, too?"

I nod, grateful my disguise is working. The arena seems as good a place as any to continue my search, so I follow the mother and boys through the dense, dirty streets, aware I am inhaling spores with every breath.

They do not smell as badly as I had imagined, and for a moment, if I close my eyes, I feel as though it is spring.

Silreena

Tunnel-grubs are restless in dripping caverns. Developing faster. The more light I give them, the more they want. The bigger they are.

Cursed Lichtfans. Took everything, and now I can't give mine what they need. Every trip across wall is dangerous.

Today, though, has other option. Even Lichtfans know spectacle requires light and so for these tournaments, they give it to us.

Everyone will be there. Could take grubs into patch of sun without being noticed.

Running late. Grandmother said she used to keep schedule with sun cycle. Must have been nice.

Give mushrooms quick water, then whistle to tunnel-grubs. Could carry them once—no more. All five have eyes now.

Setting buckets to catch water, I hurry out toward arena, the grubs wriggling behind.

Zerianne

I am walking shoulder to shoulder in crowds of Dunkellians, regretting my hasty decision to partake. I cannot turn back now, though, as I am swept into an enormous, foul-smelling coliseum.

Every surface is spongy, a weave of wood fibres with a crackling web of thick white tendrils wrapped around everything. The Dunkellians carved the entirety out of a fungal network.

I am ushered to a seat in the first rows just behind a mob of men and boys twitching with bloodlust.

Someone claps me on the shoulder: a woman with the face of a young lady, and the eyes and grey hair of a crone.

"Glad I'm not the only woman sprouting for this," she says, grinning with wide-gapped teeth.

"I don't know why there aren't more of us here," I say, hoping not to stand out.

"That's what I'm always thinking," the woman says. "I don't understand why they haven't opened the competition up to us. Every year I hope—hope we'll get our chance at the light, eh?"

I nod and smile.

"Name's Plorath," she says.

I am saved the trouble of replying by a collective silence that steals over the crowd.

One of the heliostat mirrors walks sunlight toward us. Although it is not nearly as bright as the light in Lichtfall, in the oppressive darkness it is a sight to behold.

The beam from the mountains splits the Dunkellian world open and offers a glimpse into heaven.

The light reaches the centre to shine on a man in a mycelium robe so long it blends into the web around him. He holds the huge cap of a carved, dried mushroom. He holds it up to his lips and his voice echoes across the coliseum.

"Welcome. The light graces this day of struggle and triumph. Though we need it not, we are grateful, as it freshens the darkness hereafter.

"In the light, the best warriors will battle for the honour to be front guard in the sacred tunnel routing. May every drop of blood spilled today bear new life tomorrow in the grand cycle. May our bodies bring bounty."

"May our bodies bring bounty," the crowd echoes.

The man walks to the side, where he is raised by guards onto a stage adorned with giant mushrooms. He sits in a shadowy throne, and nods to a hooded man with a maul.

The hooded man lifts his maul above one of the enormous mushrooms, and smashes it. A cloud of spores erupts.

The crowd roars, and two bare-chested men rush into the arena.

For the first fifteen minutes, they kick, punch and throw mud in each other's faces.

It is what I imagined Dunkellian bloodsport to be, but I feel like I have dug and found roots of a plant infected with an unknown parasite. I cannot shake the words of the boy from earlier:

So we can taste light and fruit.

Staves and clubs push up out of the ground, and I hope the men do not kill each other.

I scan the crowd for any sign of Silreena, but the mist of spores makes distant figures hazy. Despite the violence that surrounded my guard training, I do not want to watch it today.

"Will the winner really get to be on... the first guard?" I ask.

Plorath is all too happy to answer. "Yes! They get to be the front warriors to fight the mountain worms when they next attack. Can you imagine being lucky enough to win?"

"No," I reply honestly.

"I dream that sometimes. To be retired, have as much food and drink as I want. To be able to go into the light when I want to. The killing I'm not so sure about, but if it gets me there, I'll do it, you know?"

Plorath holds up her arms and sways as if drunk off illumination. This is the second mention of a competition for light, but I've never heard of any of it. Certainly not Dunkellians being allowed to come into Lichtfall whenever they pleased.

"That cannot be true," I say.

"I didn't believe it for a while, either, but then my friend's husband speared a mountain worm. I watched with my own eyes as he got promoted and got fatter than an armillaria mushroom. Of course he didn't share with poor Betty, who works just as hard as she did before."

I gape at the bloodied men still fighting and immersed in the raucous cheers of the crowd. Are they really killing each other to have a slice of life in light?

One of them collapses, and the chants grow deafening.

"Finish! Finish! Finish!"

My stomach turns. I look away.

The crowd boos, and reluctant clapping slowly spreads. I hazard a glance back to see one man helping the other up.

Thank the light for that.

The robed man presents the victor with a mushroom wreath, then announces the next match.

The light greys as the next match begins, and I feel I am the only one who thinks it strange. The high mountaintops are free and clear of clouds. There is no activity around the heliostats.

Wait... there is something, a bright cloth waving, is there not? It is so thin it is hardly noticeable, and the Dunkellians probably ignore it because they know not what appearance the reflected light is meant to take.

Someone is waving a thin flag in the beam. It must be to scatter the light, steal a bit of it.

Could it be Silreena?

She was sneaking about in the hallowed light when first I met her. Later, she tunnelled into the fields. Was she merely trying to sneak into Lichtfall? No, if that were the case then she would have stayed in once she had dug the tunnel. Instead, she fled and collapsed it behind her without a care to how much damage she did along the way.

No, Silreena must be after light.

I am soon back out on the streets.

The ramshackle buildings grow more dense and tall, so I lose sight of the waving flag. Every Dunkellian seems to be reaching for the light in some way, whether it be by fighting or by building tall and wobbly mud structures.

I guess at the building where the flag-waver is, an entry with the door ajar. The residents have no worry of theft; there is little to steal.

Up narrow, uneven stairs, I slow near the top, quieting my footsteps. I brush past a rough curtain and onto a roof with a short ledge the only barrier to the wind and a dizzying height.

Across from me, in the neighbouring hovel, is Silreena.

She waves a translucent white cloth. Below her, brown, glistening creatures growl softly. What in the dark are they?

Never mind that. I guessed the wrong building, and the gap is wider than I dare jump.

Silreena stops waving as she sees me.

She whistles loudly and scurries down the steps. I follow suit. We both race to the bottom, and I am convinced I will beat the old crone.

When I rush out the front door, Silreena is fleeing on a catwalk between the levels. I go up after her, and the stairs in her building are slimy. Did those creatures do this? The secretion reeks of rancid cooking oil.

I run as fast as I can through the network of mud buildings. The awful slime slows my pace.

Eventually I reach the edge of Dunkelherrscht, a sheer cliff wall. Silreena must have gone somewhere, and after a minute of scanning I see it.

The opening is small, a dimple that would normally go unnoticed. The trail of slime goes up to the wall and into the caverns.

Fine. Farther into the darkness I go. The light shines where we cast it.

The tunnels are dark, wet and filthy with slime, the only thing that allows me to navigate the echoing maze.

I hear sobbing and wonder if Silreena has some poor soul captive in her dark lair. I hasten.

I slide down a slope and around a corner to find Silreena's grubs there to greet me with glowing eyes. Up close, they are less repulsive than I had imagined, but that I will not let that fool me into thinking them docile. They growl but—thank the light—they do not approach.

Behind them, glowing mushrooms illuminate a scene of destruction. Pots, containers and furniture are knocked over and trampled. A barkskin note propped against the glowing wall reads, "Even your corpse should not sustain new life."

In the corner, Silreena cries, cradling a large fragment of what I think is a red reishi mushroom.

I am about to claim victory, to proclaim revenge over the crops she destroyed in Lichtfall, when she lifts the fragment to her lips and kisses it.

Then another. And another. I faintly see her tears splash on the red-brown skin of the fungus.

I am stuck, my heart barely able to keep pumping.

"You making arrest?" Silreena asks without looking up.

The grubs block my way even if I could move.

My heart aches. I crouch and take slow breaths. I can smell my mother's burnt crops, and taste the ash of yesteryear.

"Who did this to you?" I whisper after a minute.

"Does it matter?" Silreena replies. "Damage done now."

The words stab like the daggers of anxiety that ruined my mother's stomach. "Nobody deserves such cruelty."

Silreena snorts. "How can Lichtfan say that? Woman in guard—aren't used to this by now? Can't imagine men will let you go much longer without making you suffer."

I sag against the side of the tunnel. "You are astute. They do not."

"Then quiet," Silreena spits. "Arrest, or let me mourn."

I watch Silreena conduct a funeral over all she has lost, and am stricken by how I have managed to keep my head in the weeds for so long. The lost mushrooms are as dear to her as peaches.

Silreena could be within a few years of my mother's age.

I am that same child I once was, having trampled through a great field with no understanding of what lay underfoot.

Shining light can astonish.

"I am sorry, Silreena," I say at last, when she has lain the last mushroom down. The words come out like I am wrestling limbs out of a thicket. "I am trying to say... I understand better than you might expect."

"You understand nothing. You came to arrest."

"I will not arrest you," I say, my voice catching. "You have lost enough already, and... I did not know. Can you... I want to understand."

Silreena turns to me, her lined face glowing from the few mushrooms remaining after the slaughter.

"No one listens to Silreena. No one ever wants to hear Silreena."

I see the echoes of these words etched deep like the scars of invading beetles beneath tree bark. The same cruel words I may have uttered in the past.

Darken me. I have to do better.

"I am listening. I want to hear."

Silreena stares at me for a long time. The grubs growl, still on edge.

"To what end? Steal Silreena's story, thoughts? Haven't you taken enough?"

My mind flees to defend itself. It is who I am, is it not? I feel cornered, hunted. As a boiling reply flits at the end of my tongue, I pull back, and let the energy shudder through me.

I deserve this, and yet, this is not about me.

This is about a gnarled branch growing in the darkest pits of ourselves, planted by hands that want us to blame each other.

"You work hard for your grubs," I say. The words sound absurd in the open.

"Of course," she snaps. "They deserve better."

"You work very hard," I say, and again feel my words failing me.

"No other option," Silreena says.

"Yet... you suffer."

Silreena looks at me, and for a moment, her pain and anger are replaced by bewilderment. "Of course. Silreena is the Strange. What you want? Understand obvious?"

"I thought hard work should be enough… for anyone. Till the soil well enough and sprouts will grow after any storm."

"Not often sprouts after such destruction," Silreena says. "Mushrooms, yes… sometimes."

I close my eyes. Of course.

"My mother… always said to nurture a plant's roots, which meant understanding where it came from. Please, Silreena. Let me hear your story."

Silreena pauses. "I am no plant," she says at last.

"No, I did not suggest—what I meant to say was—"

"Enough," Silreena says, putting up her hand.

She scans each of my eyes, searching for something only she can see. She whistles, beckoning and calling her grubs away from their guard post.

"Your name?" she asks.

Silreena

Strange. Someone is finally curious for story, but I struggle to find words. Tongue held too long; words slipped off long ago and scurried to dark corner.

Zerianne sits beside, grubs curled in nooks all around.

"They need light," I say. Words ready to tumble. Yes, story buried, but its foundations in every mutter. Should have known.

"They need light. It not yours to control. Light needs sharing."

Dangerous. Have been called a heretic for less. But I hurt, and the hurt lessens the more shared. Words make seem like damage can be fixed.

Zerianne nods. Purses lips. Even if she'll arrest me, call me names, Silreena the Strange has already lost too much. World is flipped: actions have not been enough, and someone wants to listen.

Tongue wags like Lichtfan aspen in wind.

"Mother told story when I was child. Said it was most important for me to remember. Tell others.

"Mother's great-grandmother knew a time when light was shared between all. Was no wall. Was one land.

"Famine threatened everything. Emergency. Had to prioritize. Decision made to focus light on most fertile land.

"Not all agreed. Were riots. Had to build wall. Temporary, they said. But divisions lasted. Created Lichtfall and Dunkelherrscht.

"Silreena followed after mom and dad. Told history to everyone. In school, got whipped and told no one wants to hear stories. Mom and dad got it much worse.

"Guards went easy on me as child, but… still lost everything. Have nothing. Since then, focus on action instead of talk."

Zerianne moves mouth. I imagine words struggle on tongue tip, wrestle between what's heard and what's believed. I give time, hope for understanding. But ready for anger.

So familiar with anger.

"But… we are so different," Zerianne says.

Shake head. "You have light. We have none. That's all."

She covers mouth. Words rush out of me to fill gap. Need them as much as they need hearing.

"Lichtfans want to keep high status. No matter what. Rituals put in place stopped riots after wall built. Worst ritual is murder of tunnel-grubs. They mistreated by Lichtfans, then pushed toward Dunkelherrscht. Cruel. Grubs deserve better, so much better. Instead they're starved, angered. So they come to Dunkelherrscht and attack. All Dunkellians think them cruel beasts, pests to be wiped out in ceremonies. All helps to distract from trampling foot of Lichtfall."

I give Zerianne more time. Then she says, "No. I do not believe it. I cannot believe it."

Shrug. "Silreena cannot show you proof. Lichtfans clever, hide evidence. Change tunnel locations. Some of it buried for years, and no one left alive who remembers. But I've seen parts, hints. Not surprised you don't accept. No one has ever believed Silreena the Strange. If it isn't you arresting, the

Dunkellians will kill Silreena for keeping tunnel grubs as pets. Or for talking to you tonight. Down any path, I lose."

Zerianne quiets for a long time.

"Have you heard enough?" I ask, hating the thick judging air. "Life too short to waste time explaining again. If that all, then Silreena has grubs to care for. Mushrooms to… start again."

Do not cry. Too much water wasted already. Start again. Mycelium not fully destroyed. Can salvage.

"It is… horrendous," Zerianne says at last. "I feel so… so helpless. What is there to do against such… deep forces?"

Poor one. Unloaded on her. She's handling. Letting it root. Taking seriously.

Makes words matter. Makes the hurt less.

Instincts kick in. This is what Silreena does, and always will do: care and nurture the needy.

Push over to her, rest a hand on shoulder. "Start small, bit by bit."

She looks with glistening eyes. "Start with what?"

Smile. Easy. "By helping Silreena with grubs."

Zerianne

I know not if any lasting benefit will come from helping Silreena with her grubs. I only know we have to help one another.

We sneak back in through Silreena's tunnels. The tunnel-grubs take a liking to me, huddling into my side and nearly knocking me over when we hear noises.

Back at the castle base, I request a shift on the heliostats, something routine enough the high commander grants it. Thankfully my foray into Dunkelherrscht did not make me miss a shift, and nothing looks awry.

We devise hand signals for telling Silreena and the grubs when to move through checkpoints. The tunnel-grubs are intelligent, quick studies.

The guards at the checkpoints sneer as I go through. It is perhaps a blessing they stare so much at me rather than the surroundings where Silreena and the grubs slink.

Finally, we cross the threshold into the hallowed light and reach the massive heliostat.

I tag off the guard on duty, then a few minutes later call Silreena out of the bushes. Just as she steps out, another guard emerges yawning from a bunk in the guard tower.

"Hey!" he shouts, snapping alert beside me. "Dunkellian!"

Curses. Why did no one tell me about increased security?

I will not—cannot—use violence.

"Please," I say, raising my hands. "Stand down, and let us be."

The man frowns. "You led her here. Do you know how many laws you've broken?"

"All too well."

"I have to arrest you both," he says, stepping away from me and unsheathing his sabre. He holds it levelly, not threatening, but not wavering either.

He is not a bad man. He is probably one of the good ones, who played no part in the pranks against me.

But there is not enough time to debate, and certainly not at the point of a sword.

I duck and weave, using the proximity of the wall to make it hard for him to swing. I knock him off balance and put him in a headlock.

"I'm sorry," I mutter.

He drops his sabre and wheezes, "They're waiting for me at... checkpoint. They will follow up when I... don't arrive."

With my foot, I brush his sabre beneath me, then push him away. I snatch the weapon up quickly and lift it warily.

"Then go, if you must," I say. "Report to the checkpoint. I will not stop you."

He stares at me, then scans the grubs and Silreena. "What are they?"

"Tunnel-grubs. They need sunlight."

"I... will be thrown in a cell if I let you be."

"As I said, do what you must. Go get reinforcements to arrest us, or stay and leave us alone." I know too well what this will cost if I lose my job and can no longer send mother money for help.

Mother, forgive me.

The man turns and jogs down the hill.

"How much longer do they need?" I call to Silreena who is ushering the tunnel-grubs onto the brightest patch of ground.

"Don't know," she says.

The grubs bask in the sun at the base of the heliostat. Their skin undulates and they let out rumbling purrs so loud they echo across the plains below.

I pray I have not been misled, as I have been my whole life.

Fissures cascade up and down the length of the grubs' bodies. They twitch and shudder.

Below, guards gaze at us through spy glasses. They exclaim and rush off. A moment later, they are armed and heading up the hill.

Darken it all. "They are coming for us, Silreena."

She nods, crouching near the writhing grubs. After a moment she says, "Can't move them until they're done. Will hurt them too much. Look."

The grubs are writhing, in the thralls of an intense transformation. On some level I know she is right. I respect and understand how much she values their life like the sanctity of a carrot patch. But those values will mean nothing if they catch us.

"They're going to be killed as soon as the guards get here!" I shout. "Come on, Silreena. Let us go."

"No."

"This is insane! If we both get arrested, how does that change anything?"

Silreena sits beside her grubs and glowers at me. "I appreciate all your help. If we do not take care of the small, we have no hope of rectifying the big. This I know."

Darken it all.

I close my eyes, a few tears streaming down my cheeks. I thought I had prepared myself for all outcomes, but I had not. The full reality of never seeing another spring, never plucking another fresh raspberry with my mother, is as dark as the dungeon that awaits me.

"Zerianne!" Silreena calls suddenly. "Come, need your help!"

Silreena is struggling to keep a grip on the leathery skin of two large grubs each wider than her torso. They twitch so violently that the three she is not holding slide down the mountainside.

"Stop them!" she shouts.

I run and block two with my legs while I reach out and barely grab the third. They are far heavier than I thought, and I gasp from the effort to hold them back.

Their skin is a mottled brown and red. The smell is a mixture of sweat and burnt vegetation. Hard mounds poke out of their body and jab me.

"Silreena, what in the dark… is happening?"

"Complex… lifecycle," she wheezes. "Like mushrooms."

A wet bubble bursts and splashes my neck. One of the grubs has a foot with five digits, each lengthening into claws.

I scramble up and out of the way as they flex and thrash.

Moments later, I gape at four-legged grubs who can now stabilize themselves. The cracks on their skin have formed scales that pulse open and close, flickering light. With limbs, they are three times the size of any Lichtfan or Dunkellian.

A short distance away, a group of guards jogs up the mountain toward us.

"Are they done now?" I ask Silreena. "Because they are going to be soon."

Silreena calls to the grubs but all their eyes are closed, their backs flexed.

"Almost done," Silreena says. "Must be. Just need to protect… bit longer."

"Light give me strength."

I have trained against multiple assailants, but never as many as five.

And I cannot use violence against them. I will not.

"Stop!" I shout at the approaching group. "Leave us be!"

"You're under arrest!" shouts the leading square-jawed captain.

I unsheathe my sabre and run down the hill toward them. If I cannot stop them, then I can at least stall them.

I throw my sabre high into the air, which makes them slow and follow with their eyes. The sabre plants into the ground a few metres in front of me, and I stand with my hands raised.

"Take me," I say, "but you do not want to go near *them*."

The guards stare, eyes wide, at the grubs behind me.

The captain is the only one unfazed. "Seize her," he snaps. "And kill those... lizards."

I hear bestial roars, and hot light wraps suddenly around me. All the guards shield their eyes, and I turn to see the grubs—the lizards—flying toward me.

They have grown wings longer than any bird I have ever seen. Their bodies pulse with light through the slits of their scales opening and closing as they breathe. When they open their mouths, brilliant beams of light cast out like the sun breaking through cloud cover, and it blinds all the guards.

The captain swings furiously and I dart out of the way, grateful the beams are not shining directly in my eyes, too.

He continues swinging and approaching the lizards, grunting and shouting in determination.

"Stop!" I shout, but he ignores me.

He gets close to one of the lizards, Rov, I think, and his blade nicks the skin before Rov bats him to the ground, knocking him unconscious. I wince.

I do not know what Silreena was thinking. These lizards are *nothing* like mushrooms.

The other guards drop their sabres. Some turn and run away. Some stay still, hands raised, squinting in the blinding light of the lizards.

Silreena calls to the lizards, and they trot happily up to her. She pets them and with each stroke they grow brighter.

"Can go now. They're done," she says.

Teep curiously sniffs the petrified guards, then launches into the sky with the rest of his brothers and sisters, descending on the great wall dividing Lichtfan and Dunkelherrscht.

They tear it apart until I can no longer tell where the crops end and the compost begins. I gasp at the broken plants. Are they going to doom all Lichtfans for our sins? Or worse—doom all that lives and grows?

They dig frantically through the rubble, and I think back to the dense network of tunnels we had traveled through.

Tunnel-grubs wriggle their way out into the light cast by the lizards, basking and growing. Dunkellians and Lichtfans wander toward the destroyed boundary, faces lit by strobing lights.

"This is... this is going to change everything," I say.

Silreena grins at me. "Told you. Take care of small, take care of big. Change everything."

The light shines where we cast it.

The lizards were casting it everywhere.

The dragons transformed out of dark
   Made their mark on the land
   Casting light into the shadows
   Bodies aglow with potential
   They flew and bridged the rift
   Caused a drift in a split society
   Light was now available for all
   No thralls could be, nor lords
   The women who brought this change
   Silreena the Strange and Zerianne
   Set an example that spread
   Prosperity bred when walls were torn down
   That is how our land grew lush
   And the sky flush with dancing dragons

-From Persalia's Lichtfan Canto 10:21

JOSEPH HALDEN

__Joseph Halden__ is a wizard in search of magic, an astronaut in need of space, and a hopeless enthusiast of frivolity. He's shot things with giant lasers, worn an astronaut costume for over 100 days to try and get into space, and made his own soap. A graduate of the Odyssey Writing Workshop, he writes science fiction and fantasy in the Canadian prairies.

JENNIFER R. DONOHUE

DEFEND US IN BATTLE

I'm ten when Dad pulls me out of school right after lunchtime. It's one of those hot days on the edge of spring and summer, heat shimmers coming up off the parking lot as I follow him to the motorcycle. The back of his neck already has the beginnings of a tan, and I wonder how we'll play hooky today: fishing, or Great Adventure, or what.

"It's time you learned what this family does," he says, handing me his old leather jacket, too big, soft and buttery, smelling like the memory of his aftershave. It has darker, unwrinkled spots where his patches used to be. The twelve-pointed star is the only one left, in the middle of the back, matching the back patch on the jacket he wears now.

"Does Mom know?" I ask, reaching for the spare helmet.

"Your mother doesn't understand. We don't discuss it." He takes something else off the side of the bike, then turns and plants the tip of a sheathed sword on the asphalt between us. "Sandy, pray with me."

"We're going to get in trouble," I say. Any minute the principal will burst out here with the hall monitor, yelling angrily. There'll be police sirens and flashing lights, cops with guns.

"We won't." Dad waits, and I step in closer, putting my free hand on the warm crossguard. The sword is almost as tall as me, and the air smells like rain and exhaust and honeysuckles. He closes his eyes and bows his head. We almost never to go church, but we pray a lot. "Michael the Archangel, defend us in battle, be our protection against the malice and snares of the devil. May God rebuke him we humbly pray; and do thou, O Prince of the Heavenly host, by power of God, cast into hell Satan and all evil spirits who wander through the world for the ruin of souls. Amen."

"Amen."

"Do you see that?" Dad asks, pointing to the south. I squint and look, and just see hazy sky and far-away storm clouds, the sudden spring greening of all the trees around us. I don't want to disappoint him by saying no.

"I don't know."

"You will soon. Get on."

I've been on the back of the motorcycle before, but not like this. Dad drives fast, cuts corners, and once rides on the line in between a bus and an SUV. I grip the handles under my seat and pray some more on my own, too scared to close my eyes, flinching as bugs ping against the helmet's face shield. Somebody honks at us, and the sound zooms and fades like in a cartoon.

We pull off the highway on an exit that isn't numbered, and pass a collapsed gate with a rusted away sign. The broken-up road grinds and pops beneath the tires, trees and bushes shouldering in closer until the asphalt peters out. Dad stops and cuts the engine.

"Keep your helmet on," he says, waiting for me to get down before stepping off the bike and fastening the sword belt around his waist. He opens one of the saddle bags and takes out an axe, the wooden handle dark, the head smooth and unmarked. "Take this."

It's heavier than I expect, and I almost drop it. "Dad, what are we doing?"

He jerks his head for me to follow, and walks off through the trees. The axe feels like a solid piece of Mom's voice saying "you're going to hurt yourself" but the weight of it settles in my hands, welcome in a way I don't have words for. It feels right, and comforting, even though my stomach is all knotted up with fear and excitement, and I think I might throw up. My heart struggles in my throat like a bait fish trapped in the cage of my fingers, right before it goes on the hook.

The wind picks up and the trees all sway together, the leaves whispering in a furious chorus. The air stretches taut, like a storm is rolling in, and I look up at the sky to check for those dark clouds. Ahead, Dad breaks the tree line and stops, drawing his sword with a ringing flourish. "Stay out of sight," he says, voice muffled by the helmet.

A rusty crane lists over the edge of the sudden cliff, hooked chain dangling over nothing, the landscape stony and barren. The air is oily and thunder-charged, and there's a noise like a rising wind, or an approaching train, a heavy roaring in my ears. I can't see anything, but I feel hot breath, and the storm squall of beating wings. For the first time since I was little, I pee my pants.

Dad strides forward, both hands gripping the sword, and I crouch damply in the tree line, fingers still wrapped around the axe because I forget how to let go. I want to run, but Dad is here. Dad is fighting, head thrown back, swinging the sword in mighty arcs as the dust and leaves roil up from the ground. I can only look, and then can only look away, when I remember how to turn my head. He has to be okay, I think, he has to win. I don't know what to do if he doesn't. Find his phone on the bike? Run back to the highway?

"Sandy! Sandy, bring the axe!"

The world is a sudden stillness like having my head in the biggest seashell ever, and it grows quieter even as I stumble towards him, carrying the axe carefully, my wet jeans bunching and clinging, feeling cold even though it's warm out. He holds his hand out and I shove the axe handle into it and start to back away except he reaches across and yanks me forward, closing both our hands on the handle of the axe and raising it. I scream as we bring the axe down together, burying it into nothingness. Then the hot blood spills on my hands and I see the dragon.

It's bigger than a school bus, gray, spade-headed, whitish scales over its eyes. Some of the hooked claws are broken off bloody, and the edges of the pointed wings are tattered like if you tied a kite off and left it to fly all day. It shudders and kicks a back leg a few times as black blood flows from its neck onto the broken stones.

I stare at it and Dad pulls his helmet off, and then mine. He dips his hands in the blood and says, "This is what we do," as he draws his fingertips across my cheeks and forehead. "This is what the family has done for hundreds of years. We can still see the dragons, and we fight them."

"Why?" I feel like throwing up, my chin wobbles with building tears, and my skin tightens under the drying blood. "Why can't the police do it?"

"Because we are soldiers of God, and this is a sacred duty." Dad picks up the sword and axe. "Let's go."

"Does Mom know?"

"No. She wouldn't understand."

"Like how she doesn't understand the club?" In the summer, Dad's friends come to town on their roaring motorcycles and camp in the backyard for a week. They make bonfires and drink a lot of beer and talk all night. Mom stays away as much as she can without completely leaving, and tries to keep me away, but nobody ever tells me why. Dad's friends are big and loud, but they're nice to us. They're fun.

"Kind of like that."

"I'm really scared, Dad."

"It's all right. A dragon is a scary thing."

"Were you scared?"

"Yes. If you aren't scared anymore, it's too dangerous."

"Did your dad do this?"

"Yes, and his dad. Since before there was America, even. Back to the Crusades." He pulls a rumpled pack of wet naps out of a saddlebag and leans down to wipe the blood off my face before cleaning his.

"How did they know?"

"An angel told them. Like Michael."

"Are we the only ones?"

"I can call the club sometimes, but they're not always close enough. And they have a different calling. There's more in the world than dragons that most people won't be able to understand. You'll see what I mean."

"I'm scared," I say again. Dad crouches down and hugs me for a long time before he takes me home.

I'm thirteen the next time we kill a dragon. In a way, I almost forgot the first time, like maybe it was a dream. I'd tried looking in the house and garage for the sword and axe, and couldn't find them. If they existed, they were hidden better than the Christmas presents ever were.

Dad wakes me up just before noon; it's summer and Mom's at work. "Get dressed," he says. "We're going hunting."

"I'm tired." I was up late raiding.

"I don't care."

I shuffle around my room, pull on jeans and a t-shirt. I carry my boots out to the living room, yawning. "So where are we going?"

Dad hands me a sword. "See how that feels."

I almost drop it. Shocked wide awake, I bring my left hand in to steady the pommel. It's plain, no engravings, the handle wrapped in leather, and I take a experimental swing amongst our plants and furniture. The air sings softly over the edge. "It feels great."

Dad nods. "Good. Now let's suit up and get going."

I have riding gear of my own, leather jacket with removable Kevlar panels, helmet with gold and white angel wings painted on it, new from Christmas. Another couple of years and I'll have my own license, my own bike.

On the back of the motorcycle, I almost know where Dad's going. It isn't anything I can focus on, just a sense of the air being different, or a sound just outside my hearing. I remember how scared I was the first time, and I'm scared again, but excited too.

We park the bike halfway up a brush-tangled driveway and walk the rest of the way on cracked asphalt with bushes and grass forcing their way up through it. I try to carry my sword confidently, my heart roaring in my ears. My skin is electrified, every hair standing on end. "Dad, I can feel—"

Dad holds up a gloved hand, looking straight ahead. I look, and this time, I see it. Kind of. I can see a shape in the air where I think the dragon is, branches bending away from it. Its choking sulfur exhalations are just bearable inside the helmet. Does it see us? Did the other dragon *stink* like that? I see movement off to the side, try to track it. The first one was so *big*, and this one can only be the same. Maybe its head is over—

Then I hear it roar—really hear it this time—and it comes into shimmery focus. Dad's drawn the first blood, ducking underneath the furious swipe of claws, the rattlesnake dart of its huge head. At first I think I can't move, that I'm frozen like in a nightmare, and then I run forward and, two handed, drive my sword into its side.

It roars hot stinking subway breath, the air filling with heat shimmers, and Dad tackles me from the side, just in time to avoid a volcanic spume of flame from its mouth, leaving the sword stuck into the dragon.

The dragon rears back, snarling and shaking its head furiously, paws at the sword, then ducks its head to try and pull it out with its teeth, fully distracted. Dad's on it again in an instant, ramming his sword through its eye straight up to the cross guard.

The dragon collapses, more flame drooling from its mouth and onto the ground, where some leaves catch fire for a second and go out again. Wisps of smoke rise up from the ground around us.

I get up shakily, my stomach flutter flopping over and over, and Dad just looks at me. I go and grip the sword, *my* sword, and put my boot against the side of the dragon for leverage, pulling it out like King Arthur taking the sword from the stone.

"I'm sorry," I say, turning with the black-slicked blade dripping in my hand. My voice is too loud inside the helmet in the sudden quiet. The dragon ticks as it cools, like a car engine in the winter.

"You were perfect," Dad says, grinning behind his face plate. "Now let's get out of here before the fire department shows up."

We get ice cream on the way home, sitting in the too hot shade licking our cones, leaving our leather jackets draped on the bike. "I'm thinking about joining fencing club at school," I say, somehow shy after what we've just done. I don't always know what Dad will think about something.

"It's a good idea."

Mom doesn't think so, of course. Me and Dad practice in the backyard, long, sweaty, sunburnt hours, when Mom isn't home. In the fall, I join the fencing club. I come home bruised and exhausted and happy, and my grades are good so there's no excuse Mom can give. A fencing sabre isn't really like the sword Dad gave me, but it's the closest I can get here. There's no European martial arts club nearby.

Dad and I kill two more dragons before my senior year of high school, and that summer I get my motorcycle license and my own bike. The club comes out to celebrate with their normal bonfire out in the backyard and this time when Mom tries to leave with me, I stay.

I have my first beer with those guys—Big John, Paul, Santiago—and hear their stories of the things they'd faced. Dad concentrates on dragons; the club, sometimes, faces worse. Actual demons. Hellhounds. Magic beyond what they'll even explain to me.

At the kitchen table—and Mom's maybe going to *murder* me—Paul tattoos a Saint Benedict's cross on the inside of my right wrist.

The next dragon is different. It's younger, maybe, or angrier. I wake up at dawn and the sky is bloody with the rising sun. I make coffee and get the gear ready. Mom's still asleep when we leave, side by side on the highway, riding into the day.

We turn down yet another overgrown road that's the same and different from the others. The asphalt's maybe more intact, and there are more signs, bleached blank from years in the sun. I catch sight of a structure through the trees and realize it's a little amusement park, with a roller coaster and one of those freefall rides, not close enough to the beach to really get the tourists, or maybe not big enough or exciting enough. The road opens up into the big cracked apart parking lot, and then it all goes dark.

I have dreamlike flashes, impressions.

Red hot pain up one leg and arm like from going down a metal playground slide at noon in the summertime.

Roaring like the ocean or a train, first muffled by my helmet and then loud and uninterrupted.

The high wail of a siren, ambulance or police or fire truck.

Then my veins are cold, so cold, but nothing hurts anymore.

It's so hard to open my eyes again, and when I do everything is so white and bright. Then I remember the dragon and give a jerk, and hands hold me back, Mom's perfume all around me. "Stop, stop. Sandy, honey, you're going to hurt yourself. You were in an accident."

"Dad?" I croak. My throat is drier than it has ever been. What I want to say was *Is Dad okay? Did he kill it?*

"Your father," Mom says and stops. Machines in the room beep. The loudspeaker in the hallway says something, muffled worse than a drive thru. "I never wanted you to get that motorcycle," she says. I drag my eyes open all the way, look at Mom's red face, her wet eyes.

"It was an accident," I ask, or say.

"On the highway," Mom says, her voice all wavery. "You could've been killed."

It seems like a ridiculous and obvious thing to say, but I don't know how to answer, and anyway Mom starts crying again. I turn my head just a little, moving my eyes further, but can't see Dad. "Is Dad?"

"Your father is fine," Mom says firmly, angry suddenly, or more angry. "He called the ambulance and then called one of his *buddies* to come and get the bikes." Mom keeps talking, but my eyes grind shut again and I float away in a dream of a summer day that smells like salt and honeysuckles and the heavy metallic reek of dragon's blood.

The next time I wake up, Mom isn't there, but the creak of a leather jacket and the smell of motor oil, sweat and old coffee says Dad is. "I'm sorry, kiddo."

"It's not your fault."

"I should've known to look out for you better," he says. His eyes are wet and red, but his cheeks are dry. "Your mother is divorcing me."

"Because of this?"

"No, but this was the last straw. At least the club will always take me."

"Dad, you're leaving? Like this? With me like this?" I try to sit up, fall back against the pillow with my vision blurring, the room doing a slow tilting spin away from me.

"I'm sorry."

"I don't want you to go."

"I know." He carefully reaches across and takes my hand, the one with the IV taped to the back. "You can call me or text me when you want. I'll get back here when I can."

"But did you kill the dragon?" I ask urgently, quietly.

"I did," he says in a tight, fuzzy voice. "And it almost killed you."

"But you killed it," I say, and I'm asleep again without wanting to be.

And when I wake up again, he's gone, just like that. His stuff out of the house. My motorcycle is gone too, but he leaves his car, signed over to me.

I heal throughout the summer, slow and angry in front of a window AC, watching everything on Netflix. I've got road rash up my left side, arm, leg, and a puncture through my wrist that must've been from a claw and broke a bunch of the little bones so I can't hold a controller, type on a keyboard. My leg isn't broken but the tendons are all wrenched around, so trips to the bathroom are a big event.

The fencing team visits me once when I'm still in the hospital, but that's it. And without Dad anymore I realize I didn't really have friends that weren't school friends. I've never hung out with anybody, or gone to movies, or parties. I've trained. I've tried to research, learn more about dragons and their history, but finding anything in the school library is impossible. What's online is mostly on tinfoil hat websites that are mostly about chemtrails and surveillance. All I know is what Dad and the club members told me and now I'm alone.

Well, alone with Mom, who knows nothing about the only thing I'm interested in doing. Who loves me but doesn't really know how to connect with me, other than to sit on the other couch and watch what I'm watching. Other than to talk to me about what we should have for lunch, or dinner.

Mom never talks about Dad. If she was so unhappy, I don't know why she hung on for so long. She could've left ages ago, and it might've made a lot of things easier. Eventually, I heal up, get off the couch and get a job at the convenience store near the house, to get into the world, start acting like a grown up. Sometimes I can feel a dragon, and it almost drives me crazy. I have no sword, no way to kill it even if I did go to it. And I'm not bad off enough to want to go and let one kill me, finish the job.

I try to ignore the feeling, the smell of them, the itch between my shoulder blades. I try to ignore it when I see the sky change with their presence. I try to ignore them, and after a while, I drink to ignore them, going to bonfires at the beach with my coworkers, finally making acquaintances if not friends. And after a while, I don't feel them anymore, or maybe they don't come around there anymore, or are drawn off by somebody else. I have no way to know.

Dad rarely answers my texts. When I call, he's distracted, doesn't talk much, doesn't answer my questions. Changes the subject if I ask him to come get me. Sometimes he texts me pictures, nothing supernatural, nothing dragon-y, no swords. Just camera phone pictures from Dad on a road trip that never ends. His tattoos, or somebody's tattoos, the Corn Palace, a pretty sunset. A line of parked motorcycles. New boots.

I sell Dad's car and get a motorcycle again and me and Mom have a big fight about it. I think I want her to kick me out. She doesn't kick me out. We cry and then we have dinner together and we sort of talk but still don't know what to talk about. She's really trying, though, and so am I. I don't work for a convenience store anymore, I work at a bar, and she worries about me but doesn't kick me out. She argues on the phone with Dad sometimes.

I pay rent that Mom doesn't ask for, and I stay out all night, and I pray a lot. At first it's the normal everyday kind, praying for a green light, praying for a cop to not pull me over, praying for my period to come. That last one is what doesn't happen. And I'm paralyzed for a couple of days; I don't know what to do, or who to talk to. I'm ashamed to admit, I don't really know who the father is, either. One of two guys.

I make an appointment with Planned Parenthood to have a pregnancy test, just to be really sure, and to discuss my options. I can't be a mom right now. But I don't know if I can go with the alternative either.

I sit in the waiting room filling out the clipboard they give me. There's a TV on a cart, like it's movie day in high school, and the volume is just a little too loud. Some morning show with some celebrity chef making macaroni and cheese. A stack of plastic toys in the corner, but no kids here, just me and two other women, all not looking at each other.

A nurse calls me in the back and hands me a cup to pee in. I've never had to do this before, that I remember, and I read the instructions on the little wrapped wipe she gives me too. I do my best, and am then ushered to an exam room to wait, where there are three magazines in the rack that are five years old, and posters about birth control. It's not like I didn't use anything. I made sure I had condoms with me. Just in that percentage that failed, I guess, because the nurse comes back in a little while and tells me it's positive.

"We have a counselor who can talk do you about your options," she says carefully, looking at my face. "You'll have to schedule an appointment, though."

"I'll make the appointment to talk, yeah," I say. "I have a lot to think about." Which guy is the father? Does it even matter? I fucked somebody from the bar, that doesn't mean I want to spend my life with them, marry them, parent a child with them. I always thought a lot more consideration went into such a thing. Nothing ever goes the way I think it's supposed to.

"Okay, just stop at the desk there when you walk out. We'll help you figure out what you need." I wonder if she's a mom. She doesn't look old enough, but I'm only a good judge of age if I'm trying to figure out whether somebody's twenty-one.

I get a weird feeling, though, the same tension like a dragon's nearby and I walk straight outside. I call Dad on the sidewalk in front of the clinic and his phone rings and rings until it hits voicemail. I hang up, a knot in my stomach. Nervousness or the baby? It's only been six weeks probably, what's it even called right now? A zygote? Not an embryo yet. Then I call Mom. "Are you home? I need to talk to you."

"I'll be home in about an hour," she says. Wanting to be happy, apprehensive instead.

"I'll see you then," I say, hang up. I drop my phone in my jacket pocket, get on my bike. For the first time in a while, I wish I was still wearing Dad's old jacket, the one that used to have his club patches on it. The sky doesn't look like there's a dragon around, and the air doesn't smell like it, just the salt of the ocean, the green of somebody nearby cutting their grass. I pull my helmet on and ride home, looking for signs, reasons to feel the way I feel.

I beat Mom home and I pace around the house, looking again for anything Dad might've left me, any sign. There's a bible on the bookshelf, next to an old dictionary, some paperbacks. I pull it off the shelf, open it and put my finger down on the page. "And you will know the truth, and the truth will set you free," John 8:32. I wasn't sure what further truth I needed, and what free meant. That's what I get for trying to tell fortunes with the Bible.

Mom walks in the door right as my phone rings. I pull it out, expecting Dad, but the screen says Big John, and that knot in my stomach turns into a cannonball. Big John has never called me. I've barely said hello when he's saying, "Hey, kiddo. There's been an accident."

"Is he okay?" I ask, Mom staring at my face, still holding her keys and purse, but I know he isn't. If he's okay, Big John wouldn't have called.

"I'm sorry," Big John says.

"Are you…going to bury him?" I ask. My lips feel kind of numb, and the world around me very distant.

"We're not doing anything until you get here, Sandy. We'll pay for your ticket, whatever you need."

"Okay," I say. He says more, and I do too, and I guess we come up with a plan.

They were out in the Southwest somewhere, Arizona. I can be there as soon as tomorrow. The bar is just going to have to deal. I don't start to cry until I hang up, and Mom tries to catch me up in a hug as I drop the phone clattering to the floor, stumble to the bathroom on liquid legs. My stomach bottoms out, then everything comes up, and I manage to flap the toilet lid and seat up in time, tears streaming down my face, my throat burning.

Mom holds my hair and rubs my back as I throw up, cough, choke, throw up some more, and finally there isn't anything left, just the terrible, husked-out acidic feeling. "There was an accident," I finally say, and she nods. I can't stop wondering. Was it a dragon? Was it something worse? Was it just the motorcycle? Big John will tell me once I'm there. Either the rest of the club got the thing already, or they didn't.

"I'll see about your flight," she says. "Was it Big John?" I nod, and that old look is on her face, her lips a thin line, and I wonder how much she knows. Dad always just said she wouldn't understand. "I'll call him back. You get cleaned up."

I take a hot shower, just standing there, watching the water swirl around the drain. Thinking of times I'd done this with dragon's blood sluicing off me, almost black and still carrying its own heat. After, I rub the steam off of the mirror and peer into my eyes. Experimentally, I lay my hands on my belly the way you always see pregnant women do. "You're going to grow up knowing what we do in this family," I say softly. It's far too early to feel a response but somehow, I know it hears. And it'll hear when I tell Mom the truth, and face whatever that ends up meaning between us. I don't know how else to reconcile everything that's happened. I don't know how else to move forward. Especially without Dad.

But I will. We will. And Big John better have a sword for me.

Jennifer R. Donohue *grew up at the Jersey Shore and now lives in New York with her husband and her Doberman. Though she got a bachelor's degree in psychology, she has always wanted to write. She currently works at her local public library, where she also facilitates a writing workshop. Her work has appeared in Daily Science Fiction, Mythic Delirium, Syntax & Salt, and elsewhere.*

GWEN C. KATZ

BLACKTOOTH 500

The air is filled with screams and trills as two hundred dragons strain against their harnesses. Beaked jaws snap in frustration. Scythed claws scrape the ground. Two big males break free of their traces and attack each other, putting down their heads to rake each other's bellies with their horns until their drivers manage to tear them apart.

It's punishingly hot and the sunlight reflects off the black volcanic rock in waves of shimmering heat. Yet thousands have gathered to watch the start of the Blacktooth 500.

Amid the chaos, I examine our team's harnesses while Amelia looks the dragons over and coos gently to calm them. They nuzzle her arms. At fifteen, Amelia already has a way with the beasts. If only she had more discipline, she would be the finest up-and-coming driver in the league.

And I'm not just saying that because she's my daughter.

I check our cart's brakes and each of its six wheels. It's blue with "Angel Peaks Rookery" blazoned on the side in big yellow letters. I give the name one last polish. I want it everyone to be able to read it as we blaze across the finish line.

All the best racing teams in the country are here. Ray Freedman, my old rival, is hitching up his team next to me. He beat me on our last sprint, and he won't let me forget it. Across the valley I spot Sanjay Singh with his famous team of hexapods. Quiet and methodical, he's never failed to complete a race.

And there's Arianna Cross. Last year's champion. She stands perched on her deep red cart, her smile a slash across her face. The other teams give her wide berth. Rumors about her dirty tricks and brutal training methods follow her everywhere and she's been investigated twice for animal cruelty. But she wins races.

The nervousness prickling in my stomach makes me feel like a rookie. I've driven many races, but this is Amelia's first. What if there's an accident? What if there's an eruption? What if a dragon gets hurt? What if Amelia gets hurt?

I glance at Amelia to see how she's holding up. But, minutes away from the start, I find her sitting with her back against the cart, holding a backpack against her chest and apparently not thinking about the race at all.

"Go put that backpack in the truck. It's time to get in position," I tell her.

"Oh, um, I was going to bring this with me," says Amelia.

"Don't be silly," I say. "It'll throw off your balance, and there's no room in the cart."

She tightens her grip on the backpack and glares at me.

I want to tell her to stop being ridiculous and put down the backpack this instant if she wants to race, but there isn't time for an argument.

"All right, you can keep it in the cart," I tell her. "But you can't wear it during the race. I don't want it snagging on something."

She carefully tucks the backpack into the corner of the cart. Then she takes Goldface by the harness and we lead the team to the starting line. Her mind still seems to be elsewhere. I look at her, wondering what she's thinking about. We used to understand each other so well.

I hold out the reins to Amelia. "Would you like to drive the start?"

Her eyes widen. "Really?"

"Why not?" I say, as though giving her complete control of the team is no big deal. "It's your race as well as mine."

She takes the reins and grins.

Ray Freedman queues up his team of guirs next to us. He smirks at our team. "Weavers? That's adorable."

Amelia bristles. She says, "I can't wait to see your guirs flat on their butts."

"Amelia!" I say sharply, though I've wanted to say the same thing to Freedman many times.

Freedman isn't the only driver looking askance at our mismatched team. While most rookeries specialize on one or two types of dragon, Angel Peaks Rookery breeds all four of the major dragon lineages, and today we're running them all.

Closest to the cart are our two hexapods. Big, muscular dragons with six legs and no wings at all, hexapods are the slowest, but the strongest and most reliable, and a favorite on long races.

Next come our pair of guirs. Guirs, two-legged dragons capable of fluttering short distances, are the most popular type of racing dragon thanks to their sprinting speed.

Ahead of the guirs we're running two weavers, Sylph and Spark. Weavers are long, lithe dragons with webbed back ridges. Most teams shun them in favor of faster breeds, but I stand by our choice. Weavers excel at navigating difficult terrain, and the Blacktooth 500 is exceptionally difficult. Sylph is a pearly white dragon with bright blue eyes. Spark is our smallest dragon, but she's tough for her size and agile on the tricky parts of the course.

In front of them all run our lead pair of drakes, Goldface and Thunder. Drakes are spiny quadrupeds with small vestigial wings. They were once prized for their intelligence and heat vision, but the trend now is to breed them for size and speed instead. Nowadays many drakes have lost their heat vision altogether. But not ours. Thunder is gray and stocky and never loses focus. Goldface, with her bright yellow mask, is sharp-eyed and clever.

There was a fifth lineage once, the true fliers. When I was a child you could still spot their trainers releasing them into the sky on fine days. But they were small and couldn't pull carts so few rookeries bothered to raise them, and fewer dragon fanciers kept them. They dwindled, and then disappeared. Every so often a rumor goes around that someone has found true fliers on some little farm in the tundra. But it always turns out to be baseless gossip.

Ahead of us, a barren salt flat stretches as far as the eye can see. Mindless of the forbidding landscape, the dragons strain against their harnesses, held back only by their carts' claw brakes.

The race marshal fires his pistol with a resounding crack.

Twenty drivers release the brakes.

Forty lead dragons leap ahead and surge across the starting line.

The crowd jumps to their feet, cheering us on.

Cross's team takes a quick lead, with Freedman right on her tail. The rest of the pack, our team among them, runs nearly neck to neck.

"Let's go, let's go!" calls Amelia, flicking the whip over the dragons' heads. Goldface and Thunder scream with delight, happy to be in motion. The cart's wheels clatter over the cracked ground. Wind lashes our faces.

The 500-mile racecourse follows the treacherous volcanic Blacktooth Range. The first leg of the journey passes through the salt flats that run beside the mountains. This is the easiest stretch. Every team will be running flat-out, trying to gain time to make up for anything that might slow them down later in the race.

The second leg of the race covers the foothills and the plateau. Lava flows turn this part of the course into a treacherous maze, but they're nothing compared to the threat posed by the ignipedes that make their dens in the crags.

On the last leg, the teams have to traverse the mountains and then make it all the way back down to the finish line in the valley. It's tempting to put on a burst of speed on the downhill, but the slopes are crisscrossed with crevices and drop-offs. Whole teams have been lost on the descent.

But there's no use worrying about any of that just yet. For now, we just have to keep pace and make it to the first checkpoint.

Amelia's face glows as she clutches the whip. Her exhilaration lifts my spirits. The world rushing past in a blur, the thunder of the dragons' feet. I fell in love with this feeling when I first raced as a child. I want so badly to pass my love of dragons on to her, and yet for years I've worried that she doesn't feel as I do.

The pack spreads out and we begin to fall behind. Amelia's forehead creases and she cracks the whip again. "Come on, Goldface! We can do better than that!"

"Don't push them too hard," I warn her. "Here on the straightaway, we can't beat the guir-heavy teams. But we'll show our strength in the third leg."

She slacks off the whip, but I can tell she doesn't want to.

By the time we reach the first camp, the sky is deep purple and everyone except Singh is already there. Amelia jumps off the cart and stretches gratefully.

"Go into the station and get the dragons some straw to sleep on," I tell her. "I'll mix up their food."

I unpack the kerosene stove and mix up some gruel from water, meat, and kibble. The dragons greedily shove their muzzles into their dishes, splashing gruel all over the salty ground in their eagerness. Soon they're licking the bowls clean. But there's no bedding.

"Amelia, where's that straw?" I call.

Amelia pops her head out of the cart. She's holding her backpack. "Oh—I'll get it in a minute."

"Get it now. The more time we waste, the more tired the dragons will be tomorrow."

She sighs and trudges into the station.

When the dragons are bedded down and we're drinking our soup, I tell her, "You have to remember this is a real race, not a joyride. Every minute matters. Anything we do could be the difference between winning and losing."

Amelia sighs and rolls her eyes. "I'm sorry I'm not perfect."

I try to keep the frustration out of my voice. "I don't expect you to be perfect. But you do want to win, don't you?"

"Sure I do," says Amelia. But her voice is distracted.

My heart aches at the distance that has grown between us. When she was a toddler, she rolled around on the floor with the new hatchlings. At six, she was dressing up our guirs and bringing them to show and tell. By twelve she was breeding her own clutch of dragons.

She threw herself into the project, memorizing family trees and poring over books of dragon biology. But when they hatched, I discovered that she'd done the unthinkable and crossed two different lineages, allowing dangerous recessive genes come to the surface. The hatchlings came out too small, top-heavy, burdened with overlarge wings that got in their way but couldn't carry them aloft. I yelled at Amelia when I saw what she'd done. I shouldn't have, but those were real living creatures she'd condemned to suffer.

The kind thing would have been to euthanize them on the spot, but Amelia begged me not to. She loved the poor creatures and she promised to be responsible for them. They still live at the far end of the stable. Amelia visits them every day.

The dragon-breeding incident opened a rift between us that has never closed. Amelia used to tell me everything, but now she's cagey and spends all her time by herself. I never know what she's up to. And it's only getting worse.

Even now, in the middle of her first race, all she can pay attention to is that backpack. She has it on her lap.

"What's in there, anyway?" I ask.

Amelia's face colors a little. Reluctantly she pulls out a battered, once-white teddy bear.

I smile. "Johnny Bear! I haven't seen him in a while."

"I just wanted to bring him. For luck or whatever."

I chuckle. "You'll fit right in with the other drivers. I hear Freedman won't race without his lucky underwear."

That gets a snicker out of her.

It's a warm night, and the dragons snuffle soothingly in their sleep around us. As we crawl into our sleeping bags, I feel I've made the right choice in bringing Amelia along.

The next day, the sun comes out in force. Heat shimmers over the sparkling surface of the salt flat and our shirts stick to our backs. Only the dragons are delighted. Their blood running hot, they charge ahead, kicking up clumps of salt.

By now the teams are so spread out that I can't see any more than a faint trail of white dust far in the distance. All around us is still. The sharp basalt peaks of the Blacktooth Range jut up to our left while to our right, the crystalline plain seems to extend forever. The team needs no direction and I fall into a trance, listening to the clack of the wheels and the jingle of the harnesses.

A piercing whistle cuts through the air.

I stiffen and look around. "Did you hear that?"

Amelia nods. The whistle is how dragon drivers let each other know there's danger. It isn't reliable; plenty of drivers will happily let another team drive into a sinkhole or lava flow, so if the team ahead is warning us, something must be really wrong.

I put up a hand to shield my eyes from the glare and squint at the dust cloud ahead of us. There's something funny about it. After a moment I realize it's going the wrong way. Someone's team is coming back towards us. Farther off, I spot a second dust cloud, a larger one. There's something on the course. Something that isn't a cart.

"Stop the team," I say abruptly.

"What? No! We're making good time!" says Amelia.

"Stop the team. Now. There's an ignipede ahead."

She slams the brake. The claw digs into the salt. The dragons come skidding to a halt, huffing in annoyance.

"How can there be an ignipede?" asks Amelia. "I thought they only lived in the mountains!"

"They come down into the lowlands to hunt. Now keep your voice down. They have very sharp hearing. Hush, Sylph! There's a good dragon."

We hunker down in the cart and watch the dust cloud. Amelia is biting her lip, her eyes wide. She's never encountered an ignipede before, but she's heard the stories.

I can recognize Ray Freedman's guirs by their blue backs. They're headed toward us at full tilt. And behind them, undulating through the salt, is the ignipede.

Its scales are glossy black, the skin between them fiery orange. It slithers on dozens of tiny legs, its head perched on top of a long, curved neck. Rapier-sharp teeth line its open jaws.

Ray Freedman plies his whip and shouts at his team. Foolish man. Not even a team of guirs can hope to outrun an ignipede. If you're unlucky enough to attract its attention, common wisdom says to cut the traces of your lead dragon and release it as a decoy. Better to lose one dragon than your whole team and yourself as well. But Freedman is clearly not willing to do that.

The ignipede tilts its head this way and that, sizing up whether a human or a guir would make a better first bite. Then it lunges. It catches the cart by one wheel and flips it on its side, sending Freedman flying out onto the rough salt and his team plowing to a halt in a tangle of harnesses.

Sylph trills.

"Amelia, keep her quiet!" I whisper.

Amelia jumps off the cart and slips forward to stroke Sylph's neck. "Shh, shh, girl. Easy."

But it's too late. The ignipede's head jerks up. It stares straight at us.

"Amelia!" I hiss. "Shut her up or we both die!"

"I can't! She's trying to help!" Amelia whispers back.

The ignipede swerves away from Freedman and slithers towards us. Sylph is still trilling. If I cut her traces now, we might still survive. I flick open my pocketknife and leap from the cart.

I reach Sylph and grab hold of the trace. As I'm about to cut, Amelia grabs my hand.

"No!" she says. "Sylph's the only one who can protect us."

The ignipede is upon us. I can smell the charred-meat smell of its breath. I can see the claws on each of the countless rippling legs.

Sylph rises on her hind legs and trills again.

The ignipede trills back.

It slows and bends its head toward the weaver, blinking its tiny half-blind eyes. It's barely five feet away from Amelia. I can hardly suppress my urge to throw myself between her and it, even though that would be a death sentence for both of us. Amelia is trembling, but she stays still.

Sylph and the ignipede sniff each other. Then the ignipede raises its head again and slithers away, leaving a shallow channel through the salt in its wake.

We stay frozen in place, not daring to breathe, until it's out of sight. Then I throw my arms around Amelia. "Are you all right? Did it hurt you?"

"N...no, I'm fine," she says in a shaky voice. Slowly she rises to her feet.

"I'm not sure what just happened," I admit.

"She's a weaver," says Amelia, stroking Sylph's head. "That lineage—they have ignipede blood in them. When she started trilling... I think she was calling to it. Telling it not to attack."

I look at Amelia in astonishment. "How do you know that?"

She shrugs. "It was in a book, I guess. I've read a lot about dragon lineages."

Pride and surprise mingle within me. When I try to teach Amelia about our dragons, she always seems like she's not paying attention. But somehow she knows more about weavers than I do.

We drive over to Freedman, who lies sprawled on the ground beside his overturned cart. Amelia checks on his dragons while I kneel beside him, trying to size up his injuries. The coarse salt crystals ripped his forearms and the side of his face raw.

"Are you all right? Anything broken?" I ask.

"Just bruised, I think," he says, wincing as he tries to get up.

"His dragons are fine," says Amelia, coming to my side.

"Should we get the medical team?" We'd have to give up the race, but it would be low to leave an injured driver stranded out here.

He shakes his head. "If my guirs are all right, we can make it back to camp. You've done enough. Whatever you did back there... it saved my life."

"I didn't do anything," I say truthfully, putting my hand on my daughter's shoulder. "It was Amelia."

The foothills rise around us, black and rugged. The dragons put their heads down to haul the cart up the rocky slope. One step, then another. Our hexapods huff and strain. Amelia and I get off the cart to lighten its load.

The encounter with the ignipede left us dead last out of the teams that were still running. But we pass one or two during the ascent. Drakes and guirs skid and stumble while our weavers confidently navigate the steep trail.

At last the trail levels out as we reach the plateau. But as soon as we crest the ridge, we find half the teams bunched up ahead of us, the dragons huffing and screaming in frustration.

As I crane my neck to try to spot the source of the disturbance, a smell like hot asphalt hits me. Lava.

I call a halt and our dragons flop onto their bellies to rest. Leaving the team with Amelia, I thread through the crowd. An expanse of ripply, corded black rock greets me. A few patches still glow reddish-orange. A fresh lava flow.

"It happened an hour ago," says one of the drivers. "Covers half the plateau. No one can get across."

"Wait—Singh's going for it!" calls someone else.

Everyone swings around to look. There he is, slowly driving his hexapods onto the still-hot flow. I tense up. Hexapods are tough, but even they can't step directly onto lava—and the cart can't handle it either. If he gets lucky and manages to stick to the patches where the crust is coolest and thickest, he might make it, but one false step and that dragon will never race again.

"Haw, Kamala!" he calls, steering his team to the left. "Whoa—slower, slower. Now gee!"

"He's insane," laughs Arianna Cross. She's standing on her cart with her arms crossed. "He'll never make it."

Singh's lead dragon picks her way forward step by step. Then, a crack. Her leg breaks through the crust. There's a hiss and an agonized squeal as her scaly skin contacts molten rock. Singh runs forward to pull her free and release her from the traces. Eventually seven dragons pull the cart back to safety while the eighth—the wounded hexapod—whimpers in the cart.

The rest of the drivers decide to wait.

A spiny head rubs against my leg. Goldface is next to me, dragging her traces. The rest of the team meanders aimlessly behind her, threatening to get tangled. Behind them they pull the unattended cart. There's no sign of Amelia.

"We've got a loose team," someone calls.

Arianna smirks. "You need to keep better control of your dragons."

Letting your dragons wander off while stopped is a beginner mistake. Cheeks burning with embarrassment, I take Goldface by her harness and lead the team away, muttering apologies to the other drivers.

I stake down the team—more securely than Amelia did, hopefully—and go to look for her. Some of the other drivers have unpacked their stoves to heat up a snack while they wait, but Amelia isn't among them. Could she be lost? The mountains can be treacherous. Echoes bounce from one cliff face to the other, leading the unwary astray. There are cliffs and unstable slopes.

I pick up my pace. The mountains suddenly seem unfathomably vast. Every rock taunts me. What was I thinking, bringing a fifteen-year-old out here?

At last I come around a bend and find her in a secluded cleft in the rocks. She's sitting on the ground, her backpack open beside her, holding something in her hands. Johnny Bear lies abandoned on the ground beside her.

"Amelia!" I cry, rushing up to her. "You can't just wander off like that! You scared me! I thought something had happened to you!"

"I'm fine," she says.

"Well, the team wasn't. They got loose while you weren't watching them," I say, my nervousness bubbling over into frustration.

Then I spy what's in her hands. It's a smooth, oblong object speckled with green. A dragon egg.

"What are you doing with that egg?" I demand.

"I wanted to keep an eye on them," says Amelia quietly.

I look at the open backpack. There are two more eggs inside, carefully swaddled in rags.

"You stole eggs out of the hatchery and brought them on the race?" I say incredulously. "What were you thinking? They'll get broken!"

"They won't! I'm being careful!" Amelia insists, cradling the egg to her chest.

"Wait a minute." I pick up one of the other eggs from the backpack and study the pattern of speckles. "This egg isn't from any of the purebred lineages. You've been crossbreeding dragons behind my back!"

"I had to keep it a secret!" says Amelia. "You wouldn't have let me if I'd asked."

"There's a good reason for that! Don't you remember what happened last time? Those poor beasts in the stable?"

"They're not poor! They're… special."

In the distance, Goldface screams.

"We'll discuss this later," I say. "Pack up those eggs and get back to the team. We've got a bigger problem right now."

Our dragons are fluttering their wings and pulling against their harnesses—they want to race. Amelia moves from one dragon to the next, making soothing noises.

"They'll be eating each other alive at this rate," I say. "And the worst part is that half the course is probably safe. If we could only tell which part!"

"Goldface could," says Amelia.

"What?"

"Goldface could tell which path is safe. With her heat vision. Remember those obstacle courses we used to do where she had to find the hot objects?"

In a flash I see that she's right. Goldface can see the temperature of the ground ahead, and she'll instinctively pick the safest path. The weavers will keep the other dragons following her trail.

It's astoundingly risky. But if we can pull it off, we could gain hours of advantage while the other teams wait for the lava to cool.

My first instinct is that I can't try something so dangerous with Amelia here. It's one thing to risk my own safety. Putting her life on the line is something else entirely. She's never raced before. She's never seen someone's flesh melted by molten rock. She has no idea what she's risking.

I can't tell Amelia that, of course. She'd roll her eyes and tell me to stop treating her like a baby.

But then it strikes me: Trying to protect her is what's driving her away. If I want her to respect me, I have to show that I'm willing to let her take risks.

"Let's do it," I say.

Amelia grins.

I make a path through the crowd and lead our team to the edge of the lava. Goldface and Thunder sniff the fresh black rock experimentally.

"Another contender!" says Cross. "This should be fun."

"Ignore her," I whisper to Amelia as I take my place in the cart. "She likes to get under your skin."

Amelia gives Cross a withering look. Few looks are as withering as Amelia's.

"All right now, Goldface, slowly," I say. The drake sets one forefoot onto the hardened lava, then the other. She sniffs. She looks this way and that, peering into the distance with her large black eyes. Then she begins to cross the flow.

The rest of the team is unsure. I can feel their fear as they begin to move. The traces pull taut. With a bump, the cart rides up onto the surface of the lava. My muscles tense as I wait for the heavy cart to break through, but the surface holds.

"She's doing it," whispers one of the other drivers.

Painfully slowly we creep across the lava flow. The wheels rattle and jolt over the bumpy surface. Heat rises off it, making sweat drip down our faces and plaster our hair to our foreheads. Beside me, Amelia grips the edge of the cart, her knuckles white.

Goldface steps, looks around, steps again. Sometimes she changes direction for no apparent reason. The other dragons huff in confusion. They want to run straight ahead and get off the lava flow as soon as possible. But Thunder and the weavers keep them in line.

Behind us comes the crunch of another set of wheels. I look over my shoulder. Cross is driving her team onto the lava, following our trail. Where our team jagged to the left, so does hers. Where we swerved to the right, so does she. And she's gaining on us.

"Get lost!" says Amelia. "Find your own way across."

"This is a race, you know," says Cross.

As the plateau stretches on, Goldface grows more confident. She's up to a regular walking pace, though she still carefully scopes out the path in front of her. Cross is right on our tail by now. Her drake screams and snaps his teeth at the back of our cart. It's an extra level of pressure that we don't need right now.

The edge of the lava flow comes into sight. Goldface perks up when she spies the cool ground ahead, and with her, so does the rest of the team. The last few steps go quickly, and then, at last, the cart trundles over the edge of the flow and we're back on safe ground. Amelia and I both let out a sigh of relief.

From behind us comes the crack of a whip. "On your left!" shouts Cross as she beats her team into a full gallop and surges past us, throwing a cocky grin over her shoulder.

"I'm beginning to hate her," says Amelia.

"You're not the only one," I reply through clenched teeth.

There's no time to rest. The other teams have no doubt already begun to cross the lava behind us. I hand the whip over to Amelia. "Want to drive this next bit?"

She nods, glaring at Cross's cart vanishing into the distance. Amelia cracks our whip and our team is off.

It's the last night of the race and I'm trying to keep Amelia from noticing how keyed up I am. Angel Peaks Rookery has never won the Blacktooth 500.

There's prize money on the line, but that's not what I care about. I want to prove that we can do it. That our dragons can do it. That being like Arianna Cross is not the only way.

Amelia is sitting up with her arms wrapped around her knees. I know what it's like to have insomnia during a race. In training they always tell you the importance of getting enough sleep. They don't tell you how on earth you're supposed to do that while adrenaline courses through your veins.

A movement makes me look up, startled. Arianna Cross is sitting on the edge of our cart, her legs hanging over the side.

"Nice stunt with the lava," she says. "Looking forward to tomorrow?"

"We are, actually," I say tartly.

"As am I. It promises to be a most exciting day." Before either Amelia or I can think of a retort, Cross slips off the cart and disappears into the darkness.

The air itself is betraying us. We gasp, desperately seeking oxygen in the thin alpine atmosphere, which is tainted by the sulfurous fumes that pour out of vents in the mountainside. Our heads pound. Our limbs are heavy. The dragons are feeling the same effects, but they trudge on, pulling the cart step after agonizing step up the steep trail through Blacktooth Pass.

Spires of stone jut up nearly vertical on either side of us. True fliers once roosted on these peaks hundreds of years ago when they were still found in the wild. Or anywhere.

We're ahead of most of the other teams, but Cross is still in the lead. I'd hoped that our hexapods' strength would give us an advantage over her on the climb, but somehow, every time we come around a bend, she's farther ahead. Her dragons run like they fear for their lives and, not for the first time, I wonder what she does to them.

We reach the crest and look around, surveying the view from the top of the world.

"Wow," is all Amelia can say.

Though the air is hazy with volcanic gases, we can still see for miles. The world spreads out around us on every side, the Blacktooth Range running north and south, the plateau with its fresh layer of lava, the salt flats spreading out clean and white to the east. It's harsh and stark and breathtakingly beautiful.

Behind us, the other teams zigzag slowly up the ridge, but there's only one spot of movement amid the still landscape ahead. Cross.

I say, "Let's get her."

Amelia nods, a big smile on her face.

"Whoa, whoa, slowly now, Thunder," I call as we begin down the slope. The dragons, happy to be on the downhill, want to gallop. They don't know how quickly the cart could get out of control. But they trust me and allow me to hold them back.

We pass truck-sized boulders and wide cracks threatening to swallow us into the fiery bowels of the mountain range. Our guirs skid several times and even Goldface loses her footing once, but Slyph and Spark keep the team steady.

Cross is still putting more distance between us, letting her team run with reckless disregard for either their lives or her own. Goldface screams. She doesn't like seeing Cross in the lead any more than I do.

We're past the hardest part of the descent. So I ease up and let the team go a little faster. Now we're matching pace with Cross, but it's not enough. She'll outstrip us again in the final sprint.

I let the dragons pick up just a little more speed. Cross's bright red cart grows larger ahead of us. We're doing it. We're really doing it. We're going to catch her.

And then I notice the traces going slack. The dragons are still gleefully galloping down the hillside when the prow of the cart nudges the hexapods' tails. Then it bumps the back of their legs. The cart is no longer being pulled. It's rolling on its own, and it's picking up speed.

"We're jackknifing. Set the brake!" I call to Amelia.

She lowers the claw brake, only to watch in horror as it snaps off and tumbles away.

Someone must have loosened the screws. Cross. She was on our cart last night. But there's no time to dwell on that. The cart is still gathering speed. If I call the dragons to a halt, it will ram into them and drag them after it. The only thing to do is ride it out and try to steer onto flatter ground where we can slow down.

The cart goes over a bump, throwing me and Amelia around and scattering our gear. Amelia's backpack goes flying and lands on the mountainside.

"The eggs!" she cries, leaping from the careening cart.

"Amelia!" I scream.

She hits the ground. I flinch at the crunch of the sharp lava rocks. She rolls, then scrambles to her feet and grabs for the backpack. Is she all right? Or, in the heat of the moment, is she just not feeling her injuries?

I look around for a way to stop. There's a narrow crevice in the ground beside me, not wide enough for the cart to fall into but wide enough to catch the wheel. It'll be a hard crash, but it'll stop the cart.

I call, "Thunder, Goldface, haw!"

The dragons swerve, jerking the cart off its runaway course. As the wheel lodges in the crack, the cart comes to a stop with a neck-wrenching jerk that nearly throws me onto the ground. I slam into the side of the cart, wrenching my shoulder. Stars burst across my vision. The wheel snaps off and the dragons are yanked to a sudden halt, yelping and screeching.

Mindless of my throbbing shoulder, I jump from the cart and rush to Amelia's side. She's got bits of gravel lodged in both arms and a bleeding cut on her cheek, but she doesn't even notice. She opens the backpack and checks the eggs for damage.

"Amelia, how could you do something like that?" I say. "You could have died and you just lost us the race!"

Amelia picks up the largest egg. She whispers, "It's hatching."

The egg trembles in her hands. A tiny crack forms at one end, then another. The web of cracks bulges as the baby dragon tries to push its way out. Then, all at once, the shell splits in two and the hatchling lies in Amelia's arms, wet and sticky with albumen.

I brace myself for a twisted body and misshapen limbs, but the creature in front of me is nothing like that. It's small and sleek, with two delicate clawed feet, a long tail, and two broad, membranous wings that it stretches and folds as it lies there on its back, trilling at us.

I know this dragon. I saw them soaring and wheeling across the sky when I was a little girl.

"A true flier," I whisper.

Amelia nods. She cleans off the hatchling with the edge of her shirt.

"How?"

"I read about it when I was studying dragon lineages. All those recessive genes: They're true flier genes. They're not gone, just hidden. All I had to do was crossbreed the right dragons."

"Amelia," I say in awe, "you're a genius."

The hatchling sits up on Amelia's hand and flaps its wings experimentally.

"I think she's ready to fly," says Amelia. She offers the baby dragon to me. I'm filled with awe for the delicate creature in my hands and for the brilliant, amazing girl beside me who saw what I couldn't see even when it was right in front of me.

The dragon is so light. I can feel it trembling as it looks around at this strange new world. I raise it on one hand and release it.

Far below, Arianna Cross drives across the finish line. And the baby dragon takes off into the sky.

Gwen Katz is an author, artist, game designer, and retired mad scientist who lives in Altadena, CA with her husband and a revolving door of transient animals. Her first novel, Among the Red Stars, *tells the story of Russia's famed all-female bomber squadron, the Night Witches. When she's not writing, she can often be found in her garden or at the local nature center, teaching kids about wildlife.*

DAMASCUS MINCEMEYER

FATHER CHRISTMAS, MOTHER HUBBARD, THE DRAGON (AND OTHER SELECTED SCENES FROM THE END OF THE WORLD)

You know, when it was all said and done, the apocalypse kinda sucked.

Okay, I'm being a bit melodramatic. I mean, it hasn't *all* been bad. Sure, there's never enough to eat, there's no fresh bubblegum, drinking a glass of water is akin to playing Russian roulette with Cholera and you're more likely to die from accidentally scratching yourself on a rusty nail than Before, but what the hell do you expect when a solar flare fries the entire Eastern Hemisphere and causes the collapse of modern civilization? Roses and sweet honey? At least it's not like all those movies and video games and comic books where there's, like, hordes of mutated-giant-mohawked-zombie-cockroaches terrorizing the remnants of mankind in a deserted wasteland.

I'm a glass-half-full kind of girl, so the plus side of total worldwide destruction is that the petty bureaucratic bullshit that caused most of humanity's daily stress kinda got pushed aside. No cops to bust you for carrying an open container or hitting the bong, no annoying neighbors in the apartment upstairs vacuuming at three in the morning, and definitely no catty, busy-bodied bitches at the workplace constantly asking, "So, when *are* you going to get married?"

The best way to sum it up is to quote John: *It's like a cosmic reset button was hit, Chia, and there's a sign in the window that says No Law, No Religion, No Problem.*

John's my buddy, my boy-toy, my let's-get-it-on-right-here-in-the-ruins best friend with benefits. If I were a different sort of woman, I'd say he's my soul mate, but I'm not, and he isn't. I didn't even know him Before. We met when we were both scavenging through the canned goods aisle of a Wal-Mart outside Tallahassee. I traded him two cans of chicken noodle soup for a roll of toilet paper and we've been together ever since.

Soul mate or not, John's a sweetheart. He told me once he was a sanitation worker (read: garbage man) back in the day, and that's why he's so good at sifting through the wreckage of old stores and identifying what's prime stuff and what's irradiated crap. He's pretty scrappy in a fight, too. Once he took on three armed gang bangers with only a garden trowel when they tried to shake us down for our supplies. That's when we decided to head up north, which proved to be a good idea because not long after I heard the Southern Militia Confederation started raiding the area and racking up the body count.

Now, I've seen some strange shit with John, like the time we ran afoul of those cultists who gathered under the Gateway Arch in St. Louis to worship a giant Ronald McDonald statue as their god, or when we spent two days trapped by a flash flood at the top of an abandoned roller coaster, or that night we *accidentally* tipped over a kerosene lamp that caught half of Des Moines on fire. Nothing, but nothing, has ever cranked the weirdometer to eleven like the time Father Christmas inadvertently sent us after Mother Hubbard's Dragon.

I'm getting ahead of myself here, which you'll have to forgive seeing as how my ADHD has gone untreated since the world came down. First I have to tell you about Wall Street. No, not the one buried under the fifty-million tons of rubble that constitutes the Big Rotten Apple these days, smartass. The Wall Street I'm talking about is the name of a trading post just off I-70, west of the interchange with Route 54 near what's left of Columbia, Missouri. If you've never been, think of it as a giant, open-air flea market on equal parts steroids and crack. I mean, you want it, Wall Street's got it, from pilfered chemical weapons and assault rifles to old party favors and salt packets, and probably more commerce in the new barter economy occurs there than any place between Neo-Texas and the Greater Chicagoland Empire. You run into all walks of life at Wall Street, too: businessmen and con-men, thugs and thieves, bikers, rednecks, rent-boys, dope dealers, the off-their-rocker types, and like anywhere else, after a while you get to know who's who.

Father Christmas was a middle-man of sorts, a big, heavy-set black dude with a gnarly white beard, gold rings on every finger and a deep, booming laugh. He conducted his business out of a salvaged carnival tent decked out with holiday lights, right next to a bicycle repair shop and across from Buddy's Beagle Barbeque. I never even knew his real name, but what I did know was that if you brought your goods to him, Father Christmas would barter you a better deal than fifty other fuckbags who'd just as soon slit your throat than give you anything.

John and I had just plundered an old CVS Pharmacy in some blink-and-you-miss-it town and loaded up our ten-speeds. When we went to fence our loot John gave me that self-assured, goofy grin of his right before entering.

"Let me do all the talking," he said. All I could do was laugh. John's got a lot going for him, but wheeling-dealing ain't one of his strong suits; once he traded an entire case of motor oil—solid gold around these parts—for an iPhone, an item which is about as useful as a hockey puck nowadays.

A pair of guards in battered tactical police riot gear and armed with sport crossbows frisked us before allowing us entrance to the tent. Inside was a warehouse's worth of goods of every imaginable kind, from dehydrated food to sleeping bags and old camping equipment to a junkyard's amount of car parts and more bottles of booze than even *I* could possibly drink. It was like the world's biggest, most fucked-up pawn shop, and in the rear of the place, sitting in a recliner behind an office desk was the man himself, dressed in a threadbare pinstriped suit with holes in the elbows, surrounded by even more guards and a harem's allotment of women, all of them far chubbier and healthier-looking than ninety-nine percent of the rest of Wall Street's patrons, which was solid testament to Father Christmas's ability to secure basic necessities.

As soon as he spotted us, Father Christmas's face cracked a wide smile, bearing a grill of gold teeth. "Well, well," he said, walking over to us. "If it isn't Chia Pet Hepburn and her trusty sidekick John the Boy Blunder. Last I heard, you two were on the catering list for that cannibal enclave over in Kansas City. Guess you made it through without becoming someone's baby back ribs, huh?"

"Grill marks clash with my tattoos," I said, unloading my duffel bag on his desk. "We've got some stuff for you."

"Let me see," Father Christmas sorted through the items, his smile slipping away. "Maxi-pads? Expired iodine? What's this, an earwax cleaning kit?" He looked at me. "This is the most pathetic offering you've ever tried to sell me on."

"It's getting scarce out there. Stores aren't as easy to scrounge from as they used to be," John said, pulling out an unopened case of body spray from his backpack. "What about this?"

Father Christmas shrugged his massive shoulders. "It won't go very far in helping the stink around here, but they'll go fast anyway," he pointed to our bicycles. "Still rocking the Huffys, I see. Now *those* would go for some good trade. Had a lot of complaints lately from the motorcycle crowd about gasoline sources drying up. Those damn Texas honkies are strangling the market. There's gonna be war over that, you watch." Father Christmas sized up our meager lot. "I'll give you a couple cartons of Pall Mallss and a few jars of peanut butter I just got in, but that's the most I can offer this time."

"You trying to kill me or what?" I asked, ripping into the cigarettes, lighting one up. "I'm *so* allergic to peanuts."

John tried to press for a better bargain, but Father Christmas held firm. As we were about to leave, though, he held up a ringed finger and smiled again. "There is *one* thing that could fetch a sweet deal for you, Chia Pet, if you're willing."

I groaned, flicking some ashes on the ground. "I've told you before, I'm not going to let you pimp me out to that warlord chick who runs Las Vegas. I don't care how much of a fetish she has for girls with spiky Skittles-colored hair, pussycat's not on my restaurant's tasting menu, you follow me?"

Father Christmas chuckled. "It's not *that,* although the offer still stands if you change your mind," he sighed. "There's a commune down in Fulton, and their leader's contacted me about procuring some antibiotics, which wasn't too difficult, but actually getting the order there has been challenging," Father Christmas's face grew serious then. "I've sent two shipments down that way, but neither group of mine returned. That's six of my guards either missing or dead, and I've heard rumors from traders that others have disappeared in that area, too. Someone with your Wile E. Coyote ingenuity, though, might just have a shot at getting the shipment to Fulton and finding out what the hell's going on."

"Wait a minute," I said. "Your own guys, fully armed and armored, can't get through, but you'd be perfectly willing to send us to the slaughter?" I cringed. "Doesn't sound like a very kosher kabob in my book."

Father Christmas cocked an eye and walked back to his desk, opening one of the drawers. "See these?" He jangled a set of keys. "There's a place out near the old University that I keep stocked with enough food and provisions for an army. A safe house of sorts, you might say. I've even had it rigged up on solar panels, so there's refrigeration, electricity, everything. You do this for me and it's yours. All of it. Heck, you two could retire there like a couple of blue-haired bitties in Florida."

"I don't get it," John asked. "I mean, I know antibiotics aren't the easiest thing to get your hands on, but can't you have another trader handle the delivery? Why risk your time or your people's lives, or our lives for that matter, trying to get them there?"

Father Christmas shook his head. "Look, I'd like to say it's because I believe in the need to rebuild some semblance of society and all that idealistic crap, but the real reason is that I've got a reputation to uphold here, okay? I've got a contract with that group in Fulton, and if I fail in my capacity to fulfill that contract, I lose face around here and then I've got to start watching my back." He jiggled the keys again, like an angler baiting a hook. "Do we have a deal, Chia Pet?"

I wanted to say no. I really did. But every fucking decision I've made since the late, great planet Earth went belly-up has been made by my stomach, and Father Christmas, damn him, knew it. Just the thought of relaxing on a porch with a big bowl of Coco Puffs made me salivate.

"We'll do it," I agreed. Father Christmas smiled again, returning the keys to his desk.

"Good," he said. "I'll try to have one of my couriers gather up another shipment of antibiotics and whatever else you and your stud-muffin will need for the trip. How about a gun? I just got a nice .357 in a few days ago. You could pretend you're Dirty Harriet."

I pointed to the machete strapped to my leg. "This pig-sticker's always done me well, and John's got lousy aim, besides."

"As you wish," Father Christmas said. Then, as we were about to leave, he called out to me again. "And just so you know, Chia Pet, if you two attempt to screw me in any way on this, or try to renege on the deal and find the safe house without delivering the goods, or anything like that, I'll have you killed."

"Many have tried, Santa Claus, but none have succeeded thus far." I stamped out the cigarette. "Just make sure you've got the welcome mat laid out for us, because I'm already hungry."

People always ask why John and I ride bicycles instead of, you know, tearing mad shit up with a Harley or sitting tall in Mr. Ed's saddle. It's simple logic, really. Bicycling is safe, it's quiet, it doesn't require gas or hay, you can go on- or off-road, navigate narrow areas better, and plus it tones your calves like a motherfucker. The only real drawbacks are that it can be difficult to haul everything you pillage and it takes forever to get anywhere, mainly because you have to avoid the major highways unless you want to end up a hog-tied sex monkey for some backwoods survivalist encampment.

It was that latter problem that reared its ugly head after the two of us set out from Wall Street the next morning with as many supplies as we could carry and a canvas satchel filled with rattling bottles of medication. According to the raggy road atlas I keep it's only about thirty miles from Columbia to Fulton. In the old days that would've been a half-hour's drive; now it takes the better part of three days, longer if you run into obstacles like the washed out bridge that forced John and I to detour through a town ten miles and a full day out of our way, or that little rain shower that made the ground too swampy to pedal through.

On the second evening we set up camp in a half-collapsed post office and decided to binge on the rations Father Christmas gave us. To anyone who hasn't known starvation, Spam and Vienna sausages washed down with a fifth of Smirnoff doesn't sound like Thanksgiving, but it was fucking amazing.

Maybe it was the vodka, or the post-feast friskiness John and I indulged in afterwards, but I ended up sleeping deeper than I usually like and woke up with a bitch of a hangover. The rain had stopped, but it was still sloppy on the back roads, and with the headache I had I was in no mood for a Tour de France. Things went from bad to worse less than a mile from the post office when we came upon the rusted remains of a FedEx truck tipped on its side and sprawled across the road like a beached whale. John, always on the hunt for schwag, smirked when he spotted the wreckage.

"Look at *that*," he said, dismounting from his bicycle and walking to the pile-up. "I wonder how many goodies we can strip off this baby?"

At first I just ignored him, wishing that Aspirin, like cockroaches and Twinkies, had been able to survive the apocalypse unscathed, but as I watched John poke around the overturned cab of the truck, I felt my spider-sense tingling like something wasn't quite right. When I told him so, he glanced back to me, making a face. "Come on, Chia, don't tell me you think this is some sort of trick."

I wanted to rattle off the endless number of times we'd encountered booby-trapped houses and vehicles, but all I said was, "Let's just go, huh?"

John walked around the front of the cab, disappointed. "There's nothing here, anyway. Maybe we should—"

He never finished his sentence; two steps away from the truck John's sneaker snagged on a wire neither of us had seen, and a second later he was on his back, sliding across the pavement and up into a tree along the roadside, screaming all the way. Swinging upside down from a branch, one ankle bound in a loop of rope, John's frantic cries as he flailed were almost funny.

"Chia! Chia get me down!" He shouted, ponytail flopping in his round face. "I'll never doubt your woman's intuition again, honest!"

"*Sure* you won't," I grumbled, hopping off my bike and heading towards the weed-clogged ditch. "Not until the next time, right?"

I pulled out my machete, stomping through the grass to where John was strung up; right before I reached him, though, I tripped on something, fell, and soon found myself dangling in the tree right beside him.

Clever, I thought, the blood-rush to my head worsening my headache. *Very clever. Whoever set these traps knew that if one person were to get snared, a companion might try to free them and get snagged themselves. And I walked into it like a big, dumb dog.*

Hanging upside down with little conception of time fucks with your head; when you've got ADHD, it's like a mental gangbang. I don't know how long we swayed there in the breeze, but it was enough to clear my hangover and for me to sing the entirety of Bowie's *Aladdin Sane* album. *Twice.*

Around sunset I heard the crunch of leaves in the woods behind us, and hoped to hell it was just Bambi coming out for a snack at dusk. Then I heard the voices and knew we were screwed.

"Why are we always the ones that have to check the traps?" one voice asked.

Another answered, more gruffly, "You'd think you'd like to get out for a little bit."

There was a pause before the first voice unsteadily spoke again. "What if we run into The Dragon?"

"The Dragon only comes out at night, Molly. If we hurry we'll be back by then. Now pay attention. We're almost there."

Two figures, blobby in the gathering gloom, emerged from the brush and made their way over to us. Upside-down it was hard to get a lock on them, but one was heavier than the other, though neither were really very big. As they neared I realized why. Despite all the crap John and I had been through, all the precautions and rules-of-thumb we'd learned about navigating the smoldering shitheap that passes for civilization, we'd apparently fallen into a trap laid by a couple of mangy-looking *Lord of the Flies* rejects. One was a girl, maybe sixteen, with short, bobbed blonde hair and wearing an oversized, dirt-stained black jacket and cargo shorts eaten out at the knees; the other, older than her, was black, his hair corn-rowed, dressed in a torn hoodie and jeans.

"Are they alive?" The girl asked. Until that point John and I were mouse-quiet, but nerves got the better of me and I laughed.

"That answer your question, Molly?" The boy said, retrieving the machete from where I'd dropped it, waving the blade in my face. "What's so funny, lady? I were you, I wouldn't be laughin' at nothin'."

"Oh, it's silly," I said. "I just can't get over the fact that I'm going to be killed by refugees from *Sesame Street*."

The girl went to our bicycles, smiling when she uncovered our stash. "They have medicine, Wolfie, and food, too. Can we eat some? I won't tell if you don't," she asked hopefully. The boy—Wolfie—sighed.

"Not now. We need to head back before it gets too dark," he pulled zip-ties from his back pocket, binding John's hands before doing the same to me and cutting us down with the machete. We crashed to the ground and before I could orient myself properly Wolfie yanked me up, motioning to the brush. "Get walking, both of you."

"I can't," I sneered. "My leg's cramped. Tends to happen when you spend all day as a human piñata."

Any further glibness in me dissolved when I looked down and saw a small revolver clasped in the youth's free hand, and I silently chastised myself for so casually refusing Father Christmas's gun. Wolfie glanced to Molly. "Carry what you can from their bikes. Just make sure to bring the medicine. Mother will appreciate that," he gestured to John and I again. "You two. March."

So march we did, as best we could, anyway, given the tangled terrain and the fact that it was getting darker by the minute. When we came to a wrecked trailer park, a loud, dull roar echoed in the distance that caused all of us to stop dead.

"What the hell was that?" John asked. Molly looked back to Wolfie, saucer-eyed.

"It's the Dragon," she said nervously.

Wolfie, suddenly skittish, hurried us along. "Keep going."

A short hike from the trailer park was a dilapidated county jail, a razor-wire chain-link fence surrounding its perimeter, the parking lot a graveyard of rusty, burned-out cars. At the main gate Wolfie tucked the revolver into his pants and rang a small brass bell mounted atop the fence. Dogs began barking, the gate clattered open, and another pair of dirty, malnourished children carrying crude torches came into view with two snapping mutts at their side.

"Go get Miguel," Wolfie told them, forcing us beyond the gate. One of the kids ran off, returning a few minutes later accompanied by a paunchy, middle-aged Hispanic man with a pitted face, in patched-together mechanics' overalls.

"Who're they?" The man asked, looking John and I over like we were lepers.

"We found 'em in the traps near the junk-wreck," Wolfie handed him my duffel bag. "There's some antibiotics in here that may be good for Mother's hand."

As the man riffled through the satchel, Molly politely cleared her throat and said, "We heard The Dragon, Miguel."

The man looked at Wolfie. "Is that true?"

Wolfie shrugged. "We heard *some*thing."

Miguel's expression turned fearful. "Get that gate closed," he commanded before glancing from John and I to Wolfie and saying, "Take them inside."

Remember that bit about I mentioned about John being handy in a fight? Yeah, forget that. As Wolfie forced us across the overgrown yard towards the main building I could clearly see John wasn't going to do squat to improve our captive status, so that's when I made my move. Looking back with 20/20 goggles, trying to Chuck Norris my way out of a hostage situation with my hands still bound probably wasn't the sharpest course of action, but suddenly I was a woman transformed, a blur of kicks, my worn-out Doc Martens connecting with Wolfie's mid-section, crumpling him to the ground.

I pivoted, shouted for John to follow and started for the gate, laughing with every step, not believing I had been so daring, so bold, so brutal. Halfway there, though, my lungs heaved for breath--*too many cigarettes, bitch*--and I initially didn't hear the barking dogs or that brass bell ringing again, didn't see the dozen other children rush from the building carrying old police nightsticks—all I cared about was Chia's impending freedom.

If I'd been smarter, I would've stopped to ask myself how a scraggily group of kids could overpower the fully-armed guards Father Christmas sent to begin with.

You ever see ants swarming over a picnic basket?

Yeah, it was kinda like that.

Bam. Lights. Out.

Fuck.

You know, the best part of being unconscious is getting another opportunity to have my favorite recurring dream, the one where I'm working my way through the all-you-can-eat breakfast buffet at Golden Corral.

I was on my sixteenth plate of syrup-slathered short stacks when I came to, and as my eyes adjusted to the dim light, the phantom taste of Aunt Jemima still on my lips, I realized I was on the lower bunk in a cramped, mildew-covered jail cell. Sitting up my head pounded, dwarfing the hangover I'd suffered earlier. My hands were still zip-tied, but I reached back, feeling the egg-shaped lump on my skull, my fingertips coming away sticky with blood.

Great escape, Chia, I thought. *Steve McQueen would've been proud.*

"I'm glad to see you're finally awake." An unfamiliar voice said, startling me. Opposite the cell's bars a beautifully tan-skinned woman stood smiling at me. She was dressed in dirty military fatigues and combat boots with an old, soiled serape draped from her shoulders, long, black hair streaked with gray trailing down her back in a braided ponytail. Despite her pleasant demeanor I could tell this lady had seen some serious shit in her day—a vicious scar wiggled its way from the left temple down her cheek and across the bridge of the nose, and her left arm hung in a sling, a blood-stained, bandaged stump where the hand should've been.

"I'm not," I replied sarcastically. "You interrupted my breakfast fantasy."

"Are you hungry?" She paused, correcting herself. "Where are my manners? Of *course* you are. We *all* are anymore. There's plenty of food here. This jail's not as well-stocked as that National Guard depot my babies and I squatted in near Memphis, but there's a pretty good supply of canned goods, and a good mother can stretch anything to make it last."

My stomach growled as I studied her. "I take it you're the Mother I heard the kids talking about?"

Her smile widened. "It's what they call me, but my name's actually Janice. Janice Hubbard."

"*Hubbard?*" I smirked. "You mean like Old Mother Hubbard? Well, bang-up job you've done with your little Cobra Kai death cult," I jeered. "A better group of burgeoning sociopathic brats I've never seen."

Janice's smile disappeared. "You've no idea the horrors we've endured and no right to ridicule us, any of us. The children may be a bit rough around the edges at times, but they mean you no harm."

"Not everyone here's a kid, though."

"Most, but no, not all. I used to be a kindergarten teacher and was determined to keep as many of my students alive as I could after the end. It hasn't always been an easy task, but others have helped me build a little community despite everything. We've only been settled here a few months. It was just too dangerous in Tennessee anymore. Militia marauders. *Nasty* fellows. I hope they don't make it this far north," she smiled again. "But rest assured, you're not a prisoner here."

"Really? My current accommodations would argue otherwise."

Janice sighed. "And where were we supposed to put you after last night? As it is you injured four of my babies during your outburst. Nothing more than cuts and bruises, but still, we didn't know if you were dangerous, and if you want to know the truth I'm *still* not sure," she leaned in closer to the cell bars. "You *talk* in your sleep. Caviar spread on Oreos and a front-row seat at the Oscars with Lee Harvey Oswald? The inside of your head must be a *terrifying* place. No offense."

"You don't know the half of it," I said. "So your people didn't kill the other traders who came this way?"

"The ones in SWAT gear? No. But we found what was left of them readily enough. And the traps you and your companion unfortunately stumbled into weren't set for ambushing innocent travelers, either. They're for the Dragon."

"There's *that* again." I said, remembering Wolfie and Molly's fearful conversation. "What *is* it with this Dungeons and Dragons baloney?"

Janice's face grew serious. "The children named it that, and the rest of us followed suit, but in reality we don't know *what* it is."

"So, wait, you're telling me there really *is* some kind of King Ghidorah running around out there?"

"Funny girl," Janice sniped. "But it's no joke. Every night something tries to break through the fences, and whatever it is, it's *hungry*. We've lost half our dogs in the last few weeks, and when that wasn't enough it decided to snack on something a bit more substantial." She held up her handless arm. "One night about a month ago there were screams in the woods—one of the traders you mentioned, presumably—and Miguel and I went out to investigate when we were attacked. The Dragon killed our dog and then got hold of me," Janice's voice faltered. "I fought with it, stabbed it even, but it took my hand and then took off when Miguel shot at it."

"And you still don't know what it was?"

Janice shook her head. "Look, I barely survived after losing my hand. It was dark, a surprise attack, and with the shock from blood loss I didn't get too good a look, but it was big, strong, and like nothing I've ever seen before.

Ever since then the situation around here has just gotten worse. That's why Wolfie zip-tied you—he gets overzealous sometimes, and I guess he thought you and your man were responsible for the attacks. But we're all on edge. The assaults are constant. Every night."

"Why don't you just bug out of here?"

"We *can't*," Janice said, exasperated. "The old school bus we drove here broke down and we're not familiar enough with the area to scavenge any replacement parts. So it's hike through unfamiliar, hostile territory or hunker down and weather the storm."

I've had a lifelong aversion to authority figures and, being the one in charge, Janice represented The Man, but I couldn't help but feel for the girl. Trying to raise all those kids in a world gone mad, it was admirable in a, you know, fucked-up kinda way, but it didn't mean *I* had to hang around for the rousing finale if I didn't have to.

"Look, Janice, I'd love to stay and help with the dragon-slaying, but if you don't mind giving back my duffel bag, me and my buddy John will be on our merry way," I held up my wrists, hoping she'd get the hint and cut me loose. By the way she hesitated, though, I knew something wasn't keen, and I asked, "Where *is* John?"

Janice pursed her lips. "He's, well... There's something you should know. After your little one-woman-army show last night, the front gates were accidentally left open and the Dragon managed to slip through and drag a girl, Molly—you met her—off into the woods. Your man, he must be a regular superhero in disguise, because he went charging after the thing, right into the dark. Problem is, neither one came back."

Ha! See, what did I tell you? John *is* handy to have around. Of course, that's not what I was thinking as I lunged at the bars, spitting a slew at Janice.

"What the fuck do you mean, 'Neither one came back'? Where the fuck is he?"

"I *told* you," she reiterated. "He's *gone*."

In case it hasn't been made clear by now, I've got some anger management issues, so when I asked, nay, *demanded,* to be let out of the cell, I was surprised that Janice bypassed my rabid, mouth-frothing threats of bodily harm and did just that, cutting the zip-ties to boot. Rubbing my sore wrists, I glared at her.

"Call your people to a meeting," I said with a stony-balled resolve that surprised even me. "We're going on a hunting trip."

The adults around Janice's encampment were such a motley crew that, when assembled, I swear I heard the opening guitar lick from *Shout At The Devil* whistling on the breeze. Along with Miguel the mechanic was Tom, an old Haight-Ashbury holdover who'd been so fried by 'shrooms he still thought he was at Woodstock half the time, and a supermodel-skinny former lounge pianist drag queen named Liberace Hudson Jones who tended to the dogs and made me jealous by looking better cleaning out the kennel in full Frederick's of Hollywood regalia than I ever could.

The closest thing Janice had to a militarily trained individual was Doug, a Grade-A dweeb who'd been some kind of online video game champion back in the day and had somehow managed to survive the apocalypse without being skinned alive. I swear, if it wasn't for all that first-person-shooter experience giving him enough working knowledge to help run weapons ordinance I would've saved everyone the trouble and strangled him myself.

If Old Mother Hubbard's cupboard wasn't bare at the jail, the same couldn't be said of its armory. Besides the .38 that Wolfie had pulled on me, the only firearm in the camp was a pump-action shotgun with nine shells to go with it; everything else had been vulture-picked clean through the years. Yet some interesting items remained in the arsenal nonetheless; there was an ample supply of batons, Tasers, pepper spray, and I easily recognized the sport crossbows toted by Father Christmas's guards that Janice's kids had pilfered from them post-mortem.

Janice appeared in the doorway with Wolfie, who looked no worse the wear from our tussle the evening before. In his hand was my machete, and when Janice nudged him the teen held it out to me handle-first. "I believe this is yours."

I snatched the machete from Wolfie, feeling reunited with a long-lost friend, but when Janice took Tom's crossbow and slung it over a shoulder I gave her a puzzled look. "You're coming with us?"

"Absolutely," Janice scowled. "Whatever that thing is out there, it *ate* my hand. So, yeah, count me in."

I slapped her on the back. "Well, welcome aboard the *Hispaniola*, Captain Hook. You'll get that white whale."

Janice sighed. "Classic literature *weeps*."

"I'm sure," I shoved a can of pepper spray in my pocket. "Now let's kickstart this shit."

Which we did. Leaving Tom and Liberace behind to watch over the younger children, Janice, Doug, Miguel and Wolfie followed while I hacked a path through the wilderness beyond the jail, and it wasn't long before I remembered why I'd never been one of those trail-mix-snacking, vista-basking, take-a-dump-behind-a-tree types Before, because really, I hate hiking. I mean, I was kicked out of Girls Scouts 'cause I pretty much loathed everything about The Great Outdoors. Well, that and I stabbed our Den Mother with a plastic fast-food spork, but that's another story.

We'd been out about an hour when Doug spotted Molly's dirty, fleece-lined leather jacket in the underbrush, one sleeve shredded, the fly-smothered remains of a disemboweled Rottweiler not far away.

"It's Zeke," Janice told me, crinkling her nose at the smell. "He chased after the Dragon last night with Molly and your man."

As I wondered what could be capable of turning Fido into finger-food, Wolfie called out from the opposite side of a clearing and we found him staring up the trunk of a large oak tree where Molly sat stranded on a high limb like a frightened blonde kitten, eyes red from crying, right shoulder streaked with blood, but when Janice told her to climb down, the girl stubbornly shook her head.

"I'll get her," Wolfie assured us, ascending the tree and carefully leading Molly to the ground, where she was a scattershot ball of nerves, her story encrypted jibber-jabber: "TheDragontookmetothewoodsbutMr.Manfoughtit-offandthenIclimbedthetreebutTheDragongotMr.Manandtookhimtoitslair..."

"Mr. Man?" I plucked the name from the girl's babble. "You mean John?"

Molly nodded, pointing to a rocky outcropping on the opposite side of another clearing near a dry creek bed, and immediately I started marching towards it, ignoring the girl's hysteric pleas of opposition. I was half-way across the field before Janice and Doug caught up to me.

"Wait, will you?" Janice said, grabbing my arm.

"Don't touch," I snarled, suppressing every urge to deck her. "It messes up the wardrobe."

The two of us started squabbling like hens, and it was only when Doug's frantic cries echoed Molly's lunatic screaming that we stopped; I turned just in time to see movement in the foliage and catch the goofy, terror-stricken look on Doug's face right before something heaved up from the shrubbery, ten feet long with a tail to match and quick as a sprinter, tackling him with linebacker force, and suddenly all the loopy, Looney-Tune tales I'd heard were validated, because there, not ten yards away, tearing the poor dork apart with its forelimbs like a kid pulling the wings off a fly really *was* a dragon.

A *Komodo* Dragon.

"A *what?!*" Janice shouted after I screamed the creature's name.

"A fucking Komodo Dragon," I yanked her to the edge of the field. "*Varanus komodoensis.* Native to Indonesia. The largest carnivorous lizard on earth. Their scales are practically chain-mail, and the damn thing's bite is loaded with poisonous anti-coagulating venom. They're known to eat wild pigs, deer, livestock, even other Komodo Dragons. And oh, yeah, people."

"I'm not even going to ask how you know all that."

"I used to watch a lot of Discovery Channel when I'd trip out on cough syrup. I guess some of it sank in."

From our hiding spot we couldn't see Doug in the tall grass, but his cries were still wild in the air until with an abrupt, sickening crunch of bone they ceased altogether. Janice, horrified, looked at me.

"How the hell did a Komodo Dragon get *here?*"

"Who knows? They probably escaped from a zoo after the end, and lucky girl, you set up a snack bar smack dab in their territory."

"*They?*" Janice's voice cracked. "As in *plural?*"

There was a low, guttural hiss from behind us then, and the leathery snout of a second Komodo Dragon emerged from the brush, its long, yellow, forked tongue flicking from a razor-tooth mouth. "Yeah, I forgot to mention," I said, backing up. "They're group hunters."

There wasn't time to run; the creature launched from its camouflaged position, a single swipe from its huge tail taking me down so fast the machete flew from my hand and I was pinned under the dragon's girth, viscous globs of pinkish snot-slime dripping from its jaws onto my face.

You know, wrestling with a two-hundred-pound Jurassic relic might sound fun if you're a hillbilly or some Norman Bates-level psycho, but really, its not. Wedging my right arm underneath the Komodo Dragon's neck I attempted to shove it back, but it was too strong, and I felt the tear of claws at my belly. Just then I remembered the pepper spray I'd stuffed in my pocket; looking back now it's a miracle I managed to grab it, much less aim a clear shot in the struggle, but I did, Macing the fucker like a late-night mugger in the park.

The Dragon let out a wicked, shrieking hiss, but its attack barely slowed; only a quick arrow piercing its neck accomplished that. I looked up to see Janice gripping the crossbow, the weapon's shaft balanced on her handless forearm, a vengeful expression on her face.

"Come to Mother," she said, fumbling to reload. The dragon did, too, abandoning me and charging at her with full-on locomotive speed.

Freedom from the assault was almost as disorienting as being attacked to begin with, but seeing the dragon rampaging towards Janice laser-trained my focus and I rolled, snatching up my machete before grabbing hold of the creature's tail, hoping to stop its advance. Instead I became a rodeo-rider, sidewinder-sliding through the dirt, hanging on for dear life as the Dragon plowed into Janice, knocking her off her feet and causing the second crossbow shot to go astray. Janice screamed, kicked and flailed, but still it came, an angered jabberwocky of claws and teeth.

In desperation I jabbed the machete into the lizard's hind legs as hard as I could; at first it ignored the slices, but I kept on hacking until the Dragon's thick skin split and I saw blood. It bellowed again, slimy jaws snapping, tail thrashing fiercer than ever, succeeding with one last powerhouse slap in tossing me aside.

I hit the ground hard, but scampered upright just as Janice's screams renewed. This time I was a Whirling Dervish of frenzied female fury—I was Kali, I was Joan of Arc, I was Buffy—and with the shrillest war cry I could muster I leapt onto the beast's back in a red-hot rage, machete grasped with both hands, cracking it down on the Komodo Dragon's head like I was playing Whac-A-Mole, slashing and smashing and bashing until at long last it stopped moving.

Janice, trembling, her face and right arm a mess of bleeding cuts, leaned against a tree. "Please tell me it's dead this time."

"Well it's not pining for the fjords," I said before giving an extra machete-smack to the Dragon's splintered skull, spattering Komodo brains all over Janice's torn serape. "But that's just in case."

Another scream punctured the quiet as Miguel, Wolfie and Molly came upon the spot where the first Komodo Dragon had attacked Doug, the trio staring in open-mouthed shock at the aftermath. Like an enormous snake the creature was attempting to swallow Doug's corpse whole, its jaw distended and oozing copious amounts of red-tinged saliva to lubricate the proceedings, the entirety of Doug's head up to his shoulders disappearing down its toothy gullet. I glanced at Janice.

"Well *there's* something you don't see every day."

Miguel stood closest to the gruesome tableau, pump-action shotgun in his hands, but appeared too mind-fucked to use it. I sheathed my machete, took the gun from him, and slowly walked over to where the Dragon dined; so engrossed with digesting its meal the thing didn't even notice my approach, much less feel the barrel against its skull.

Yeah, you can pretty much fill in the blank here, can't you?

"Are there any more of them?" Janice asked after I handed the shotgun back to Miguel.

"I don't know," I answered, distractedly looking to the rocky area Molly had pointed out earlier; before I knew it I was tramping across the field again, the rest of the group struggling to keep up with my frantic pace.

The dry creek bed was permeated with an overwhelming road kill stench, clogged with a thick cloud of flies and I soon found out why--the crags all around were a barf-inducing butcher's-shop of rotting, half-eaten carcasses; raccoons and opossums, dogs, deer, even the upper torso from one of Father Christmas's guards.

In the midst of it all John lay curled in a fetal ball looking like he'd been tossed in a meat grinder. I rushed over to him, not sure at first if he was even alive; slowly his head raised, a small smile spreading across his battered face.

"Hey, babe. What's up?"

I didn't say anything. I couldn't. All I did was kiss him hard on the lips. John breathlessly let a weak laugh escape after I pulled back.

"See, Chia," he said. "I always knew you loved me."

I groaned. "Don't flatter yourself. I'm just glad you're not Dragon chow. Can you walk?"

"We won't be doing the Jitterbug any time soon, but yeah," John replied, proving it by taking a few wobbly steps back to where everyone waited for us.

As we left the Dragon's den Wolfie pointed to a huge hole dug deep into the earth; inside was a half-exposed nest of twenty or so oblong eggs. One of them quivered even as we watched, the Dragon within primed to hatch.

"Not so fast, Norberta," I said, grinding the eggs beneath my heel like squashed bugs before following Janice and the others out into the woods.

And then I woke up and realized it was all a dream.

No, I'm fucking with you. Couldn't resist.

Anyway, once at the jail Janice doctored everyone up as best she could. Except for Doug, of course. For him it was Game Over, and it took an additional expedition and half an hour of dissecting to remove enough of him from the Dragon's digestive tract to bury.

When John recuperated enough we pedaled around a few nearby towns for the replacement parts Miguel needed to repair the school bus, and with their transportation fixed, Janice surprised me by announcing she was packing up the entire camp to look for some new digs. When I asked her why she'd want to abandon such a secure place, she looked first at the jail and then to her bandaged stump, telling me, "It's like a piece of cake that you've dropped on the floor after taking two bites. No matter how sweet it is, you just don't want it anymore."

She agreed to give John and I a ride to Fulton so we could deliver Father Christmas's shipment. The commune there was based at an old dinosaur-themed amusement park and when the bus arrived, a bunch of black beret wearing beatniks-with-Uzis met us at the gate, but once we explained who we were and why we were there, a celebratory feast of teriyaki MREs and pickled pigs feet was thrown in our honor.

The commune's head honcho was some self-help-guru-turned-cult-leader who called himself Emperor Hirohito Studpuff, and afterwards he actually invited Janice and her group to settle in at his camp. Surprise *numero dos* was that she accepted, and even though Janice asked John and I to stay on with her, I'd had enough of reptiles. So with visions of Fruit Roll-Ups dancing in my head we set out on our bicycles with a confirmation message from Hirohito addressed to Father Christmas saying that we'd accomplished our mission.

Like I said earlier, I'm a glass-half-full thinker, but the problem with life is it has a tendency to spill that glass when you aren't looking. Unbeknownst to either of us and true to Father Christmas's prediction, two days after John and I left Fulton, war broke out between Neo-Texas and the Southern Militia Confederation over the oil supply down that way, and not unexpectedly Wall Street was one of the first places hit by the Confederation's raiders. The entire place was sacked, and what happened to Father Christmas is anybody's guess. Maybe he slippery-eeled his way out before the battle, or maybe he became a giant human tetherball. I don't know. All I *did* know was there was no way for John and I to claim our prize for the work we'd done.

So. Here we are again. Open road ahead of us, the past behind. I try to focus on that freedom, the opportunity and possibilities each day brings, and not, you know, the gnawing black hole that is my stomach, and if I get too down I think about that new feather in my cap, that billion-year title I never thought I'd have.

Chia Pet Hepburn: Dragon-Slayer.

Cool.

Hey, you think Disneyland's still there?

Damascus Mincemeyer *was exposed to the weird worlds of horror, comics and sci-fi as a boy and has been ruined ever since. He's now an artist and writer of various strangeness and has had stories published (or set-to-be published) in the anthologies* Fire: Demons, Dragons and Djinn, Earth: Giants, Golems and Gargoyles, Air: Slyphs, Spirits and Swan Maidens *(Tyche Books),* Bikers Vs The Undead, Psycho Holiday, Monsters Vs Nazis, Mr. Deadman Made Me Do It, Satan Is Your Friend, Monster Party, Wolfwinter *(all from Deadman's Tome publishing, and books for which he also provided cover art),* Crash Code *(Blood Bound Books),* Hell's Empire *(Ulthar Press),* Appalachian Horror *(Aphotic Realm),* A Tree Lighting In Deathlehem *(Grinning Skull Press),* On Time *(Transmundane Press), the* Sirens Call *ezine, and the magazines* Aphotic Realm, Gallows Hill *and* StoryHack. *He lives near St. Louis, Missouri and can usually be found lurking about on Twitter @DamascusUndead.*

AMANDA KESPOHL

THE NAGA'S MIRROR

The heat against my back is not the sun. It is far less friendly, licking at my heels like the tongue of some venomous beast. It occurs to me that man was not meant to outrun dragon fire.

Good thing I'm a woman.

The muscles in my body tighten. As they uncoil, I spring over a rocky lip, plummeting through the air and into the lake below.

No need to wonder how I came to this pass, frog-kicking through silver-green weeds to avoid the flames piercing the subterranean darkness above me. The Caverns of Reflection are a great place to meditate on your past. These mystical waters reflect the history of any person who touches them. At the moment, I am quite literally drowning in my own memories.

I swim through the image of a gawky teenage me as she strolls along the bank of a different lake, taking a break from her chores. A gleam in the shallows catches her eye. A sword protrudes from the silt left bare by the lake's retreat from the heat-drenched shores. It is brilliantly silver, so bright and pure that it seems to glow in the afternoon sun. The hilt is tilted invitingly in her direction. The girl—all knees and elbows and ratty red-gold hair—reaches out to touch it. A spectral wind blows her wavy hair pin-straight as light flares from the hilt and passes through her body.

One cannot live between an enchanted forest and mystical mountains without knowing what it means when a humble village girl finds a magical weapon—a heroic destiny. Teenage Magda hefts the blade, scowling at her reflection in its surface, and heaves it back into the lake. It whistles as it slices through the air, revolving end over end before it plunges beneath the surface. She walks back toward the squat, thatch-roofed cottages clustered together in the middle of the fields like a mushroom ring, dead set on marrying her childhood sweetheart, raising horses, and producing fat babies.

I can't breathe.

I kick to the surface, alert for the flash of orange and gold to warn me that I'm more likely to fill my face with fire than my lungs with air. No choice about it, either way. I can't stay down here.

I gasp in deep breaths as I tread water in the middle of my wedding day. Out of the corner of my eye, I can see myself, bonny blue forget-me-nots woven into my hair. His favorite flower.

A serpentine head churns through the water in my direction. I knew better than to think I'd escape her in the lake. Nagas are excellent swimmers. She glides along like a crocodile with her golden eyes slitted, her snub nose protruding above water.

My sword hangs heavy in the sheath on my back, but I have no faith in my ability to hack and slash and swim at the same time. Instead, I meet her with my fists as she hurtles toward me like a thrown spear. I land a solid blow to her nose. Her momentum propels me backwards through the water to slam into a rocky outcropping. For a moment, I see two long, sinuous serpents, rising from the water to spread iridescent gold and brown hoods. Then I blink and there is only one. One is enough.

Fangs flash, wicked white arcs seeking to bury themselves in my bones. I dive down, getting lost among the tickling grasses.

I've swum farther back into the past. Child Magda sits on a bench, sipping cider from a cracked mug. A girl glides past her through the streets, about the same age, but bearing herself as regally as any queen. Her black hair is long enough to sit on, and her dark brown eyes are flecked with hints of gold. Though she looks respectable enough in her scarlet robe and gold satin sash, the people in the streets shrink from her. As always, she speaks to no one, passing among them like a ghost as she visits the shops, buying strong teas and soft cloth in shades of red and blue and green. Then she departs, walking back down the winding road that leads into the Mystic Mountains.

Or, at least, she tries to. Child Magda, already a head taller than most of the village boys, gets up to follow her.

"Don't, Magda," someone hisses. "Nothing normal comes out of those mountains. You don't know what she is."

She shrugs. "No way to find out unless I ask." In a flurry of long legs, she jogs through the crowd to catch up with the slight figure in scarlet and gold. When Child Magda stops her, those strange eyes are filled with surprise. Beneath that, gleaming among those star-like flecks of gold, is gratitude.

The naga has no patience for my reminiscences. She barrels through the image of the two girls, her mouth open wide. I kick my legs out, catching the top of her mouth with my left foot and the bottom of her mouth with my right. As I ride through the waves in this precarious position, she shoves me through the surface, flipping me off her nose the way a dog might toss a treat in the air. I tuck into a ball, plant my feet against the ceiling as it comes within reach, and propel myself downward at an angle, away from those gaping jaws.

The rocky floor rises to meet me. This may have been a mistake.

The cavern is not tall, and the fall is not far. Still, the pain that jangles through my limbs reminds me that no fall is a good fall.

I roll onto my side, groaning, and see the naga coursing through the water. As she draws near, she sways in the air above me, and her beauty is hypnotic. I am distracted by the images in the water behind her. Two girls dangle their bare feet into a lake. One girl is slim and brown, with black hair down to her butt. The other is tall and raw-boned, her red-gold hair a frizzy bird's nest above her sharply angled face.

I left my memories in the lake. I don't recall that being a part of the legend.

Glittering fangs descend, scraping the ground as they close around me. The world darkens as I'm scooped into the naga's jaws. It does not smell good inside the giant snake's mouth. Sadly, it's still not the worst place I've ever been.

I grab her forked tongue, wrapping my legs around it as the naga tries to swallow. With my knees bent, my dagger is within reach. Struggling to hold my breath as I involuntarily bathe in stinging saliva, I slip my right hand down into my boot to free the blade, then plunge it into the rubbery slickness of the naga's tongue. She opens her mouth to roar. I take this opportunity to dive past her sharp teeth and back into the water.

Child Magda waits for me, and for her friend, in the shadows of the enchanted forest. Dainty slippered feet patter up and her friend sinks down to sit in the grass beside her.

"You're not afraid of this place?" Nalini asks.

Child Magda shrugs. "Why should I be? If you pay attention to the stories, then you know how to handle yourself."

Nalini smiles cautiously, always cautiously, as if the expression makes her nervous. "You're very brave. I guess that explains why you weren't afraid of me."

"I wasn't afraid of you because you didn't give me a reason to be." Child Magda shoots her a sidelong glance. "You're not gonna, are you?"

"No. I thought I'd give you this, instead." Nalini passes her a red, blue, and green star, cleverly sewn together from bits of fabric.

"Wow." Child Magda turns it over in her hand. "This is beautiful. Where did you get it?"

"I made it. I can show you how, if you like."

"Oh, there's no point in that. I'm clumsy with my hands. May as well have hooves at the ends of my wrists."

Nalini smiles. "Well, maybe you just haven't found what they're good for yet."

I drop my dagger as I hit the lake's rocky bottom. Again, pain jolts through my body, ripping up and down my limbs like claws. Something broke that time. Hopefully not something important. I kick awkwardly through the grasses, past girls playing dice games by the river and petting horses in the stable yard by the inn. I dart beyond Nalini coming down the mountain, her eyes brightening as her only friend barrels up to hug her. Then the naga's thrashing tail catches me and whips me across the lake.

I enter a dark part of the water. It's deep here, seemingly bottomless. A young woman returns after taking her horses to market in the city. The village is nothing but rubble and ash. After a search, she finds a man buried in the wreckage. Eyes as blue as forget-me-nots stare without seeing her. Without seeing anything ever again.

A few strokes carry me through the next few days, to the shores of the drought-stricken lake. In a place where fish once swam and weeds once swayed, a silver sword protrudes from the cracked earth. A young woman pulls it free, then turns her back on the ruins of her village, never to return again.

Until recently. Until the day that someone sent me word of a rampaging naga who had killed enough men to make the waters in her cavern run red. So here I am, beaten, bleeding, and half-drowned once again as I try to do what no one else could.

I'm tired. Not from this fight, but from the dozens that came before it. With each one, the fatigue makes me a little slower, bringing me closer to the fight that will be my last.

This is how I die. Heroes do not get to retire, fading out like the sun sinking gently into the horizon. They flare, bright as dragon fire, and are extinguished. But not today. Not if I can help it.

The currents stir behind me, and once again the beast is coming, jaws parted, teeth bared. I dive down, though my lungs are squeezing painfully in my chest, and tangle my fingers in the grasses to yank myself against the lake's bottom. Her passage ripples my clothing over my back. Triumph flickers momentarily in my breast.

Then her tail wraps around my torso, pulling me after.

My arms are pinned to my sides. I kick and thrash, trying to squirm free of those thick coils, but she squeezes so tightly that my joints pop, my muscles twang like broken bowstrings, and above all, gods, I can't breathe. I can't breathe.

She lifts me and the top half of her body above the water. Above the water, below the water, it makes no difference. My ribs grind into my internal organs, my lungs crushed into uselessness. It suits her, I suppose, to watch me drown on dry land, my mouth gaping like a beached fish.

There are still worse ways to die. When she bares her fangs again, I am reminded that one of them would be to disintegrate in the naga's stomach after being swallowed alive.

The whole world seems tinged by fire. Her head rears back. I close my eyes in anticipation of the strike.

It never comes. To the contrary, her coils loosen. My lungs inflate just enough to make me see stars as I open my eyes. She is staring at me. After a while, I feel stupidly self-conscious. Dropping my gaze after hers, I spy the discolored red, blue, and green star peeking out from the neck of my tunic. When I raise my head, I notice flecks of brown in the gold of her eyes. We recognize each other in nearly the same moment.

"Well," I say, "I guess you gave me a reason to be afraid of you after all."

"And now you know what your hands are good for." Her voice has a sibilant quality, but I recognize it, all the same. I've heard that voice sing and shout and laugh. It used to belong to my friend.

"So how long have you been a monster?"

"As long as you've been a hero, I'd imagine. Such creatures cannot be made, only born."

"You never said."

"You never asked."

The pale golden coils are loose enough now that I can wriggle my hands free. When I bring them out, I have a pipe carved into the shape of a pelican cupped in my palm. The leaves in the bowl are wet. I tip it toward Nalini. "You mind?"

She wafts a gentle stream of flame across the bowl. I set the stem to my lips, puffing thoughtfully. "Heard there was a naga rampaging through these parts, killing folks. It's the reason I came."

"I'm the guardian of this lake. I only kill those that offer me harm or try to take the water with them when they leave."

"That's what all the dragons say."

"Well, then maybe you should listen to them. Men can only tolerate the presence of a beast nearby for so long before they feel compelled to slay it, whether it means them ill or no. Besides, why would you believe strangers who happen to have human faces over a friend who doesn't?"

Smoke simmers out between my lips. "I suppose you're right."

"Of course I am. Haven't I always been?" At my look, she smiles. Seeing a snake smile ranks high on my list of the weirdest things I've seen. "You've been gone a long time."

"Yeah. Sorry about that. I didn't think about you when I left. Couldn't think about much of anything at all."

"I know. I understood. Still, I missed you."

"I missed you, too." I frown down at the burning embers in my pipe. "What happens now?"

"Mm, well, I believe one of us kills the other. Perhaps I drown you in my coils, or you cut me open and take my head."

My free hand rests on a scar, a long half-healed furrow where her scales are chipped and mottled. Up close, I can see similar scars running all over her body. "Who says?"

"Hmm?"

I make an impatient noise. "Well, let's start with who says you have to guard this damn lake?"

If she had eyebrows, she'd have raised them. "I was born with the markings of a guardian, so it was my destiny, I suppose. My parents would not have sent me away so young for anything less."

The idea that my friend spent most of her childhood alone in a dark cavern had never occurred to me. I find the notion no more pleasant than my earlier vision of being digested by a snake.

"Fuck destiny." My fingers fumble over my shoulder until they find my sword hilt. Yanking it free, I send the silver blade spinning out over the lake. It hits the water with a splash that sounds like laughter. "Do you want to get out of here? Maybe find an inn, have an ale?"

"You really think it will be that easy to walk away? To thwart destiny?"

"Oh, no. I assume it'll be a pain in the ass. But do I strike you as someone who shrinks away from a fight?"

Again, she smiles. The smile is still cautious, and still indescribably creepy stretched across the face of a snake. "Not in all the years that I've known you." Still, she hesitates.

"What?"

"Well... It's a long way to the nearest inn."

"And?"

"And a sword might come in handy."

"You're a giant fucking snake."

"Still..."

Muttering under my breath, I set down the pipe and pull myself out of her coils. Standing, I raise my arms over my head and dive into the water.

When I resurface, huffing and puffing and dragging the sword behind me, she's waiting on the shore, holding my pipe cupped in her small hands like a captive bird. Her gown is emerald silk edged in gold. Her mouth is a bit pinched, her eyes lined, but her hair is still long enough to sit on. Only the glints of gold in her brown eyes give her away.

As I approach, she nods to the sword. "It was never really about the sword, you know. It's all in how you choose to use it."

"If I had a gold coin for every time a man's said that to me..."

Her laughter is bright and brief, like her fire. She puts an arm around my shoulders. "Come on, let's get out of here."

"Yeah, I'm tired of this place anyway." I lean on her, and together, we limp out of the caverns.

Amanda Kespohl is a fantasy writer, attorney, folklore enthusiast, and beagle mom from Jacksonville Beach, Florida. Her short stories have been featured in anthologies such as Sirens *(World Weaver Press 2016) and* The Death of All Things *(Zombies Need Brains, LLC 2017). Check out her website at https://amandakespohl.wordpress.com/ or find her on Twitter at @amandakespohl.*

M.L.D. CURELAS

MADAM LIBRARIAN

Miriam smiled as she took the neon-colored board book from the toddler, ignoring the sticky patches on the cover. The child's mother bleated a nervous apology.

"Nothing a little soap won't fix," Miriam assured her, and the mother's face relaxed as she tugged her child towards the library's main entrance.

Miriam chuckled as she followed them. Maybe she'd tell the next nervous parent that jam didn't bother her at all—not like the acrid odor of the potty-training books. She wore rubber gloves handling those, until they'd been disinfected.

She waved to the child as she locked the entrance. There. Another day at the Erebville Library completed. Her smile faded as she turned away from the door. Time for the library board meeting. The first item on tonight's agenda was a challenge to one of the Young Adult novels in the collection, *Flowers' Waltz* by Delia Strike. The board director, Kenneth, wanted the book removed, and Miriam was anticipating a heated discussion.

Miriam sniffed. She hadn't banned a book in all her years as librarian.

She paused at the kitchenette tucked into one corner of the staff workroom, and her mouth puckered with annoyance. None of the board members had bothered to put on the kettle when they'd brewed coffee. Mindful that she was now tardy, Miriam poured a cup of coffee and stirred several sugars into it. The bitter odor irritated her nostrils, despite the added sugar.

No one looked up at her as she entered the meeting room. Amy, her longtime friend and president of the Library Friends fundraising group, shuffled papers and stared at the table. Petra, the student member of the board, was focused on her phone, her face blank and stony. Miriam's gaze swept the table, but everyone avoided her glare... except Kenneth, who smirked at her, his small, piggy eyes gleaming.

"So glad you could *finally* join us, Miriam," he said. "We were just about to vote on our first agenda item."

"Vote?" she repeated. The library board rarely surprised her, but now she was stunned. Her eyes flicked to the clock. "I'm only three minutes late, and you're voting on *Flowers' Waltz* already?"

Kenneth shrugged. "It's not a difficult debate, Miriam. We can't have filth like this"—he pointed to the glitter bedecked book on the table— "in our library."

"*My* library," she said sharply.

"*Our* library," he said again. "The board's library. You're just an employee."

Miriam took a hasty gulp of coffee. The scalding drink seared its way down her gullet, burning away any rash words she might have spat at Kenneth. After all, silence nourished wisdom, according to Francis Bacon.

At least the horrid drink was good for something, she thought as she stalked to her seat by Amy. Her friend, as usual, smelled faintly of dried grass, which always reminded Miriam of her youth, and the sheep in the nearby meadow.

"Very well," Miriam said, calmly, "as your employee, I'd like to point out that *Flowers' Waltz* depicts loving, healthy relationships between teenagers, providing reassura—"

"We've already discussed the book," Kenneth interrupted. "It's time to vote. All in favor of removing *Flowers' Waltz* from our shelves?"

Miriam kept her hands flat on the table. Amy did likewise.

"Petra?" prompted Kenneth impatiently.

The teenager set down her phone. "Miss Thorn, isn't there anything you can do?" she asked, looking at Miriam directly. "They decided about the book before they even got here."

"Miss Thorn can't do anything. She was late, and it's now time to vote," Kenneth said sternly. "How are you voting, Petra?"

"Nay," she said, stuffing her hands in her pockets.

The resolution passed five to three. All eyes flew to Miriam as Kenneth announced the outcome for the minutes, but Miriam didn't crumple under their stares. She raised her coffee cup, obscuring her face, and forced down another swallow of the bitter drink.

An anger like nothing she'd felt in decades burned in her belly. The nerve of these people, making decisions about *her* books.

She felt her cheeks tighten and her smile become more brittle as the meeting progressed. Amy passed her a miniature chocolate bar, murmuring about blood sugar.

Miriam popped the entire sweet into her mouth, hoping the chocolate would dampen her anger. She needed to get a hold of herself, or else there'd be another Incident. Nobody on this board was old enough to remember, but Miriam had found the process of building a new library stressful and exhausting. She couldn't do that again.

The painful memories doused her anger, and she was able to finish the meeting without biting anyone's head off.

"Can I give you a ride home, Miriam?" Amy asked as they meandered with the other board members to the staff entrance.

"I still have to close up the library, but thank you, Amy." Miriam leaned closer to her friend and whispered, "The chocolate worked wonders."

Amy smiled and patted her purse. "I never leave home without a stash."

"Quite sensible of you, my dear," Miriam said. They hugged, and Amy ambled out to her car.

A few more board members left, and Miriam managed to politely bid them farewell. Soon it was Petra's turn through the exit.

"I thought you'd be able to do something," Petra said as she pulled on a denim jacket.

"I am sorry, Petra," Miriam said. "Kenneth outmaneuvered me this time. I'll put together a counter-proposal for the next meeting."

"Really?" Petra asked.

Miriam nodded. "Really."

Some of the stoniness melted from the girl's face, and she smiled. "Thanks, Miss Thorn."

And with her departure, Kenneth was the last board member left. Miriam held the door for him.

"Petra sure has a lot of confidence in you," he said.

"I *am* the librarian," she said, brows arching.

He nodded. "Yeah, but there's something more, isn't there, Miriam? You're not just a librarian."

Her face froze; she could feel the muscles stiffening. "I don't know what you're talking about, Kenneth," she said softly. "I've been the Erebville librarian since before you were born." She pulled the door open another few inches. "Now, I have to finish closing the building for the night."

Kenneth stepped forward, but paused in the doorway. "This isn't over, Miriam. That filthy book doesn't belong on our shelves, so don't try any tricks."

Then he faded into the darkness of the parking lot, and she was alone, finally.

She proceeded with her usual closing tasks: shutting down the computers and copier machine, emptying the recycling bins, straightening the circulation desk. She wiped clean the jam-splotched book the toddler had enjoyed so much. Then she trudged to the meeting room.

There were half a dozen copies of *Flowers' Waltz*—it was insanely popular with the teenaged girls. And, she knew, the tween girls as well, although she'd kept that tidbit of information from the library board. The official reason for removing the book was its depiction of lesbian relationships. But what she suspected really stuck in their craw was that the book showed girls and women having full and happy lives without men.

It was an important book, especially in a small, stodgy town like Erebville, where gender roles were rigid.

Sighing, Miriam gathered up the books and carried them to her desk. With the automated system, it took just a couple of minutes to have the books formally withdrawn from the collection. She didn't stamp them, though. She stared thoughtfully into space for several minutes, and then she shut down her computer.

Tucking the books under her arm, she turned off the lights to the library. The dark didn't bother her, and she easily made her way to the supply closet. Her fingers hooked the latch under the shelf struts, and the rear wall opened with a click.

A dim, orange glow illuminated a staircase. Miriam trotted down the familiar, narrow stairs. At the bottom, she inhaled deeply, with pleasure. She loved the smell of books. She especially loved the smell of books in her true workspace.

Books were everywhere. On the bookcases that lined the walls. Stacked haphazardly on the floor. In piles on her large, wooden desk. They covered every available surface, except for a narrow path that weaved from the stairs to a large circular patch directly in front of her desk. In the low light provided by strategically placed floor lamps, the books shone warmly. Miriam adored all the books in her library, but these—these were special. These were *hers*.

Over the years, books had to be withdrawn from the collection. Broken; missing pages; old editions. She brought them all down here, to her workspace, where they were given new bindings, pages were repaired or replaced, and they were read and loved. While her library had several book repair tools, it was this space, her lair, that had specialized equipment for extensive repairs and preservation.

She cleared a space on her desk, pushing aside an inkwell and quill, her old-fashioned nameplate, and a shriveled apple. She set the short stack of books down and drummed her fingers on the desk, thinking. Finally, she nodded. Not only had she promised Petra, but *Flowers' Waltz* was important. *Knowledge* was important.

Miriam extended her right pointer finger at the books. The finger elongated, her skin peeling to reveal copper scales, her nail splitting to release a long, sickle-shaped claw.

She opened the first book and, using her claw, sliced along the crease of the inner hinges, separating the manuscript—the text block—from the front and back covers. From there, it was relatively simple to separate the text block from the spine. She tossed the used cover to the floor and repeated the process on the next book.

When she had six sets of bound text blocks, Miriam knelt on the floor to rummage through a trunk that abutted her desk. What sort of material to cover the books? Buckram, perhaps? Yes… a wonderfully dull, tan buckram. It would repel adults' gazes, dismissed as stuffy literature. Old books.

It took some time, even for someone as skilled as she, to measure and cut the boards and buckram to fit her text blocks. Fortunately, Miriam didn't need much sleep.

She had just decided on a new title—*Botany: Wild Roses*—and was preparing her stamping machine to emboss the covers, when she heard footsteps.

Her breath caught. Someone dared to enter her sanctuary? Scowling, her belly broiling with anger again, she set down the new cover and called, "Hello?"

The footsteps paused, then clattered down the stairs. It was Kenneth. His eyes were wide and his cheeks flushed.

Miriam stood up. "What are you doing here?"

"What is this place?" He gawked at the towers of books. "This isn't in the library blueprints!"

"This is my workshop," she growled. "What are you doing here?"

"I wanted to talk about that filthy book," Kenneth said. "But you weren't home. So, I came back here." He took a few steps toward her, parting his lips in an oily smile. "You see, I know your secret."

Miriam kept very still, not daring to even twitch. This again. She'd been careful—not toasting her own marshmallows during breaks at work and taking only the occasional flights during nights of the new moon. No, she reasoned, he didn't know about her true self. She relaxed, tilting her head. "Oh?"

"Yeah." He stepped closer. "I know that you're really Delia Strike, the author of *Flowers' Waltz*! That's why Petra thought you could keep it in circulation!"

Miriam laughed. She howled, bent over and clutching her stomach, as the laughter bubbled out of her. When it subsided, she straightened, wiping a tear from the corner of her eye. "Oh, I needed that. Thank you, Kenneth."

Kenneth blinked. "I don't understand."

"Of course not." Miriam gave him one of the patient smiles she used on unruly children. "I'm not secretly an author, Kenneth. I don't know where you got such an outlandish idea. But we do need to talk about you finding my lair."

"Your—what?" He shuffled closer and peered at the nameplate on her desk. "Your name is spelled wrong."

"Is it?" Miriam spun it around.

WYRM, it read.

Miriam turned it to face Kenneth again. "I think my current name is a clever take on it, don't you? I'll miss it. I'll have to create a new one when 'Miriam' retires."

Kenneth was starting to look less confused and more afraid. She liked that look on him.

She stepped around the desk. "You silly human. I've been librarian of Erebville since 1754. First, you try to take my treasure, and now you've defiled my lair. What *am* I going to do with you?"

She grinned, showing off too-large and too many teeth. Kenneth squealed and stumbled backwards, landing on his rump. The pungent odor of urine bit the air. One of the book towers teetered and fell, scattering books.

"Don't eat me!" he cried.

"Eat you?" Miriam laughed again, smoke curling from her mouth. "Oh no, I'm not going to eat you. Humans taste terrible."

Her nose and jaw stretched into something resembling a crocodile's snout. A jet of flame streamed from her maw.

"However, I can't let you live, either," she said, leaning forward to inspect the pile of ash on her floor. She sighed, more smoke seeping from her mouth. She had important book binding to do, and now she had to cover up Kenneth's late-night visit as well.

Worst case scenario, there would be a repeat of the Incident of 1902, when she'd burned the library to the ground. That had been traumatic, for both her and the town, and she didn't think it would come to that. The library didn't have any alarmed doors or security cameras, thanks to Kenneth's penny-pinching ways, so all she had to do was return his car to his home, maybe start a little rumor about Kenneth's out-of-state girlfriend at the Seniors' Tea tomorrow, and let the police investigation run its course.

Humming, she turned to her desk and stroked the pile of buckram-covered boards and text blocks. "Soon you'll be on the shelves," she crooned. A few quiet recommendations would see *Botany: Wild Roses* in the hands of every girl in town. She'd personally give a copy to Petra.

Bacon seemed appropriate again. "*Ipsa scientia potestas est*," she murmured as she swept the ashes into a tidy pile. "Knowledge is power, Kenneth, and my humans will be properly equipped."

Ribbons of smoke trickled from her maw as she chuckled, disposing of the ashes.

M.L.D. Curelas lives in Calgary, Canada, with two humans and a varying number of guinea pigs. Raised on a diet of Victorian literature and Stephen King novels, it's unsurprising that she now writes and edits fantasy and science fiction. Her most recent short fiction appears in Brave New Girls: Tales of Heroines Who Hack. *She's very excited to be in the same anthology as* Shortcake.

JENNIFER LEE ROSSMAN

OF DRAGON GENES AND PRETTY GIRLS

The first eleven were easy enough to collect. Okay, that's a lie. The tiger was a bitch to track down and the boys in the cryo zoo almost refused to part with the embryo, but I've never met someone who can't be bribed for the right price. Theirs ended up being unlimited access to the ship's information core. A little hacking, one artificial womb missing from a gene splicing lab, and three months later, and I had a white tiger cub sucking on my finger.

Now Bái Hǔ is big enough that she's getting dangerous to share a bed with, and I'm still no closer to finding myself a dragon.

I knew what to expect when I volunteered for the task. Dragons were rare enough on Earth that people called them myths—folkloric monsters that evolved from our collective fear of snakes and the unknown. But finding one on a spaceship?

Just this side of impossible.

I pace my quarters, Bái Hǔ matching my strides, occasionally rubbing her cheek against my knee like a housecat. A housecat the size of a large dog, but a housecat nonetheless. Her massive paws make no sound on the steel floor and it occurs to me how silent she'd be sneaking up on somebody if she ever got out, and how I should really put a bell on her, but I have more pressing issues at the moment.

We're scheduled to enter New Earth airspace in less than a month. The twelve animals are supposed to precede us into our new home, racing out of the ship and determining the new order of the zodiac that will rule our lives for generations to come.

We're a beautifully superstitious culture, and being in space for the last hundred years has messed us up something awful. Time dilation and all that Einstein crap means a year spent traveling close to the speed of light isn't the same as a year on Earth, making it hard to know how to mark the calendar.

I think I was born in the year of the snake, making me intuitive and enigmatic like the ball python tracking us from his terrarium above my bed, but some calendars say I'm a horse. Energetic and humorous, irritable but overly sentimental.

Might not make a whole lot of difference to me, but there are sects within the community that say it determines everything from your lucky numbers to the people you're compatible with. My girl's part of one of those sects, and she won't make a commitment until we know our signs. Typical goat.

So we need to hold a race, just like Buddha's way back when, to decide the order of a new zodiac for a new planet.

So I need a dragon.

I find Ah Fen in the stables tending the livestock that supplement our mostly-synthetic protein diets. She works there as well as in the fields. We have all sorts of droids to do that stuff, but some people like tradition and it does make the ship feel alive when you walk the decks and hear a distant whinny or bellow.

Her face lights up when she sees me. "There's my little cinnamon roll."

I raise an eyebrow.

"No?"

I laugh and kiss her. She smells like straw and animals and honey. "No."

"My lucky cricket," she tries instead, cooing it in my ear.

"Or you could try 'Min,'" I suggest. "That being my name, and all."

She rejects this with a wrinkle of her tiny nose and goes back to raking the stall we commandeered for our ox. Her parents have cutesy pet names for each other, and she's determined to carry on the ridiculous tradition.

"No friends today?" she asks, peering at my hands and shoulders as if I might be hiding a rat or rabbit somewhere.

"This isn't a social visit."

"So that was a business kiss, then?" she teases.

I lean heavily on the stall door. "I don't know where I'm going to find a dragon." It's not an easy thing to admit. Back on Earth, my family were dragon tamers. We're genetically predisposed to seek out the impossible, to go into the mountains with nothing more than the clothes on our backs and come out a month later riding a feathered serpent.

They would have gone extinct when the Industrial Revolution chugged its way into China if not for us relocating them and teaching them not to make nuisances by challenging zeppelins. My baba used to say we could talk to them because we were descended from the Dragon Emperor, a great dragon in human form, and thus we shared the same blood.

I don't know about all that. I only know they all got left behind, and I'm a dragon tamer without a dragon.

Ah Fen leans her rake against the wall and puts her elbows on the door beside mine, mirroring my pose. She nods at the horse across the way, a short and stocky dun stallion with a black mohawk. My boy Chevy, who we've had pegged as our racehorse for months now.

"Przewalski's horses were extinct by the time we left Earth," Ah Fen says softly. "We bred them back. DNA is just code, and most of an organism's DNA is backups of old versions. Modern horses only needed a few tweaks to revert to a common ancestor they shared with Przewalski's horses, and from there it was easy enough to breed for the qualities we wanted."

"I like how you say 'we' like you were part of it."

Ah Fen's cheeks turn a shade rosier. "'We' being us humans. My point is that Chevrolet looks identical to the extinct species he was modeled after, even at the molecular level. He may have been manmade, but he's a Przewalski as sure as I'm a human."

She says "human" with a pointed glance in my direction that turns my blood cold. Not because it's ludicrous, but because it's *not* actually ludicrous. Here in the stables, surrounded by sawdust and horse crap, it's hard to forget we're hurtling through space in a ship filled with the most advanced machinery humanity has ever seen.

"You're serious."

She shrugs, tracing the wood grain of the stall door. "You told me what your father said about the emperor. Do you know if it's true?"

"No," I whisper. "You want me to..." I can't even say it.

"My little snowpea—" She pauses, brows raised in query, and I shake my head at this latest attempt at a nickname. "—I think you should genetically engineer a dragon."

The people at the genetics lab balk at my request. They can't let just anyone mess around with gene splicing, and I'm hardly trained for this kind of work. Or any work, really; I'm more a Jill of all trades on this ship, doing odd jobs and taking on impossible tasks no one else wants to tackle.

I can hem a silk robe and fix the couplings on a G20-X droid. I can bake a mean gāo diǎn and hack the code in the lighting systems to give us a few extra hours of sunlight a day.

But go inside the DNA of a living embryo and splice wings on a snake to make a dragon? Yeah, that might be a little out of my wheelhouse. Which is why I'm not going to do that, but I can't tell them why I *really* want access to the lab.

My plan is so absurd and farfetched, I don't think it's even possible. But on the off chance it isn't... I just need a minute with one of their badass microscopes to check.

"All right," I say, putting my hands up in surrender. I start to leave but turn back, pretending to remember something. "Did I ever mention I have a coydog?"

This grabs their attention. The lead researcher sits up straighter in her wheelchair, and her assistant's eyebrows disappear in their hairline.

"Coydog," they repeat in disbelief, sharing a look with their boss.

"As in a hybrid of coyote and dog?"

I nod innocently. "Yeah, seems her mother—purebred Chow from the upper decks—snuck down and slummed it with a coyote from the American Southwest biodome. Now, I know hybrids aren't allowed on the ship because they're less fertile and we need all the biodiversity we can, right?"

They nod like they're starving and I'm offering them a continental breakfast.

"But from a genetic standpoint, it's got to be pretty fascinating, yeah? I mean, you were born on this ship. You've literally never seen something like Bo's DNA." I surreptitiously slip a plastic baggie of hair from my pocket, placing it on a nearby desk.

The researchers kindly turn their backs, leaving the door to their lab unguarded. I waste no time sneaking through and sitting down in front of one of the large microscopes connected to a computer.

I don't know enough about these machines to use them to their fullest capacity, but I spent enough time dicking around with the one in my high school bio class to run a simple analysis.

I prick my finger, and a dark gem of blood bubbles to the surface. I wipe it gently on the glass slide and wait as the little blue progress bar inches across the screen.

This is ridiculous. What result am I seriously wishing for? The one that leaves us as hopeless as we already are, or the one that turns my world upside down because my baba's old myths aren't myths at all?

The one that gives us a dragon, I guess, because that's the one that gets Ah Fen and I the greatest chance at a happy life together.

The computer gives a cheery little ding, and I can't look at it right away. I just need everything to stay the way it is for another minute.

When I finally summon the courage to look, there's no denying the results flashing on the screen.

My DNA closely resembles human DNA, but only closely. There's a lot in there that doesn't match anything in the computer's database.

I bury my face in my hands and breathe deeply. I'm a dragon. Or descended from a hybrid, or... or something. I don't even know anymore.

"Hey guys?" I call out weakly to the researchers. "You got a sec to take a look at something?"

Bái Hǔ notices the changes first, and curls her lips up in a snarl. I must not smell right anymore, or maybe it's the way I move. Am I moving different? More like a predator? I only know that I see every little movement my animals make, and that I feel the cold more than ever before.

I think Ah Fen has noticed that. Hard not to notice your girlfriend suddenly wearing oversized sweaters and always wanting to cuddle, but she hasn't said anything about it.

The sweaters are nice. They hide the scales on my arms far better than my tank tops would have.

They're ugly, my scales. They don't have any real color or shimmer, so they just look like hard patches of skin. But I love them. They feel... right, somehow. My soft human skin is a beautiful tan and I love having it—I would never want to go full dragon and lose it—but it feels so good to have a few scales, even if I have to hide them.

We're less than a week out from our new home. An electric excitement goes through the people aboard the ship at the announcement, spirits soaring.

It seems like my doorbell never stops ringing. By now, everyone knows Ah Fen and I are the ones planning the race, and they all have questions. Where should they stand to get the best view? Where is the finish line? How long after will the new zodiac be issued?

Do we have a dragon?

Ah Fen patiently answers every one. The big viewing windows on the aft decks should provide the best vantage, the finish line is the river a few hundred yards from our prospective landing site, and Ah Fen's cousins will be working as hard as they can to calculate the new zodiac and get charts drawn up within the day.

"And of course we have a dragon," she says for the hundredth time today, already starting to close the door. "My girlfriend comes from a long line of dragon tamers. We'll see you when we land, thank you, zàijiàn." The door shuts with a click and she leans against it, weariness threatening to encroach on her perpetually sunny demeanor. "*Do* we have a dragon, lotus blossom?"

She knows. She might not know exactly what I did, but she knows I did something.

I idly doodle on the margins of my paper, where I've been trying to figure out all the configurations of zodiac signs that will make us compatible. I figure Bái Hǔ will win the race with the monkey close behind, but I haven't had as much time as I'd like to watch the others run. Their placements are anybody's guess.

Ah Fen is a year younger than me, so our signs will be next to each other. And because my age is a multiple of twelve... I do the math in my head. I'll have been born in the year of the winning sign, and she'll be in the second place. Dragons and tigers are very compatible, but tigers and monkeys? Not so much.

So I'll have to make sure I win.

In a footrace against a tiger.

"Min," Ah Fen says softly.

I look up. "What?"

She sits on the edge of my desk, taking my hand in hers. The warmth radiates off her skin and I soak it up like she's the sun. "What's going on? You never told me what you found out at the lab. Even if they couldn't make a dragon from your DNA, if you are descended from dragons, *you* can run the race and—"

"But I won't win."

Her brow furrows in confusion. "You don't have to win. Just having a dragon in the race is enough."

I bite my lip and gesture to the paper. "Not if I want you to marry me. I need to win, or at least place second, and my old body couldn't do that."

That was the wrong thing to say. Her eyes go wide and she backs away, afraid of me and what I've done.

"You were supposed to use your genes to make a dragon, not—" She looks at my eyes, her head tilting as she notices their yellow tinge. "Not *change* yourself."

"A baby dragon wouldn't have won, and there was no guarantee we'd end up compatible." I can feel my leg muscles as I flex them, like coiled springs ready to propel me straight to the finish line.

"But we're already compatible," she says quietly. "Do you really think I wouldn't marry you because of our zodiac signs?"

Yes. No. I don't know what to say. "Then why didn't you say yes?"

She's quiet, staring at her hands for a moment. "Everything is changing. This ship and its people are the only home I've ever known, and we're about to leave it and meet all the people from the other ships, and..."

I can hear her heart beating faster, even from a few feet away, just like I can hear the location of every animal in the tanks behind me.

"I don't know," she admits. "Maybe I thought you'd find someone better, maybe I thought I would. I was afraid."

And she still is. She smells like fear, that tangy scent of a mouse staring into the jaws of a snake.

"Everything is changing," Ah Fen says again, and looks at the scales that have crept onto my hands.

I've never seen a blue sky before, never felt a wind that smells of grass and soil instead of industrial fan oil, yet something in my soul, the part that remembers we didn't always live in space, recognizes this planet as home. The animals do, too. They whine and chatter and scratch at their cages, eager to get out and taste that fresh water burbling just on the edge of sight.

If people thought my inclusion in the race, or my scales and eyes and my claim of draconian heritage, was odd, they haven't let it overshadow their excitement. A palpable buzz fills the air.

I tense at my own gate. Maybe it doesn't mean anything anymore—I haven't seen Ah Fen in days—but I still intend to win, if only to prove to myself that I can. This body may not be the one she fell in love with, but I love it.

The bell sounds, our cages open, the other eleven rush out.

But among all the cheers behind us, one voice stands out like a flashing light in the dark.

I turn to see Ah Fen standing in the middle of the viewing windows, waving and screaming and carrying a sign with my name on it. She's here for me. I run back inside, weaving through the crowd, and take her in my arms.

"Marry me?"

She nods vigorously and kisses me. Chinese dragons supposedly don't breathe fire, but the heat inside me is hot enough that I'm not so sure about that.

Ah Fen finally breaks away, smiling, and pushes me towards the door. "Go race, my gorgeous dragon."

Now that's a nickname I love.

Jennifer Lee Rossman *is a queer and disabled nerd born in the year of the horse. She lives in a group home in Binghamton, New York, with her fish Mazie, Rey, and Dr. Sarah Harding. She tweets @JenLRossman and, along with Brian McNett, is the editor of* Space Opera Libretti.

JB RILEY

BLACKOUT

You never go into the caves alone.

Lynne knew as soon as she set foot into the dim recess she was violating policy, but the survey was already behind schedule and now Buster had texted her he needed a sick day.

Probably hung over again, Lynne thought. He'd been closing down Hurley's Bar and Grille every night since they had arrived at Sluice Narrows. Brendan "Buster" MacAndrews had a wife and baby back home, but you'd never know it from the way he hound-dogged his way through the coffee shop, the grocery store and the mercantile. At night he trawled the barstools at the town's only tavern, and the more he drank the more obnoxious he became.

So far Buster had shown sense enough to leave her alone, at least. Lynne wasn't sure how long it would take him to work his way through the local talent and try to make a move on her, but she planned to finish her contract before that happened.

Of course, the way he was drinking, his liver might give out first. Last night had been epic, even for him: as Lynne waited at the counter for her carry-out, Buster had been tossing back tequila like water and bellowing along to jukebox Bon Jovi.

Stacey had rolled her eyes at the racket as she rang Lynne up. Young, blonde and pretty, the tavern's sole waitress was Buster's primary target.

"How long is your project supposed to take? We're going to run out of Cuervo."

Lynne shrugged. "That may not be a bad thing."

"That's because you're an early bird. Jimmy cut him and his new drinking buddies off last night and things almost got real nasty." Stacey curled her lip. "Horny *and* mean, how can any girl resist?"

As an independent contractor Lynne didn't have oversight for Buster's actions, and the survey would not require his input. Delays could cost her money, as more days on site meant rushing to complete her report for the survey's deadline. Policy or not, Lynne was not going to lose another day to Buster's bad habits.

Besides, she thought, as she hammered a 3-foot section of rebar into the gravel floor at the entry and attached a loop of neon pink mason's line, it would be nice to get some work done without knowing Buster stared at her ass every time she bent over.

She checked the spool where it attached to her belt. Buster had laughed at her "little pink string" but Lynne had insisted on the spool-and-string failsafe. Software could fail, compasses could break or be lost, but her string would guide her out no matter what.

Thus far, getting lost had not been a real danger. The caves they were mapping had remained uncomplicated, with few branches and only a handful of switchbacks. Carved millennia ago by an underground river, the ground was reasonably level, the ceiling stable and high, walls almost smooth. Still, this next turn might reveal more of the same, or it might become a maze of splits and fissures, all needing to be measured and logged. In her career, Lynne had learned each cave held its own dangerous secrets. If something happened to her—an injury, or she became trapped—her string could lead others right to her.

Lynne checked her gear bag to confirm she had ample mason's line. The spool carried enough string for one-third of a kilometer, and she had ten of them tucked away in her pack. More than enough to cover a day's work, and well worth the extra weight. Her 12-kilo pack would grow lighter as she drank her water and ate her protein bars and apple slices.

Also packed was the 3-D mapping system which would create digital, rotational images of the caves as she moved through them. The system's laptop, battery pack and hand-held laser scanner were heavier than the manual tools and sketch pad she had first learned to survey with, but the results were admittedly more accurate and much faster than she could draw and mark by hand. Besides, this way she didn't need Buster to hold the other end of the tape measure.

Settling her helmet and turning on her headlamp, she switched her prescription sunglasses for her clear-lensed pair, checked her camera in a pocket of her cargo pants and her flashlight clipped to her belt, then slung her tripod over her shoulder and entered the first bend.

The temperature dropped almost immediately, wind and bird sounds cut off, and Lynne felt her shoulders loosen. She loved caves, loved how the dark soothed—

Hiding under the porch, hands over her ears

She set her jaw and pushed the memory fragment away, sweeping the laser scanner around her so it could take its readings. If she focused she could get a significant amount of work done without the need to jolly Buster through his hangover.

Maybe he was just afraid of the dark, she mused, setting up her camera at the junction where they had left off the day before. Satisfied it was level on its tripod, she stood behind the camera and picked up the remote shutter release. Using her headlamp and the camera flash, she'd add serviceable photos to the computer's 3-D map, giving the civil engineers another set of data from which they would plan the new tunnel.

Lynne closed her eyes against the flash and hummed to herself. There was a rhythm to the work that pleased her. Swing the laser scanner as she walked so it could take its readings. Take a dozen steps and then stop, sweep her headlamp to look for hazards. At each branch, switchback or new opening stop, set the tripod, take a few photos. Pack the camera, pick up the tripod. Repeat.

Most importantly, keep watch on her neon string as it unspooled smoothly from her belt clip. At each tunnel branch she sought out a crack in the rocks, hammering a piton in where she could and tying her string so it would angle smoothly down the branch she chose. When the branch dead-ended she gathered her string as she doubled back then chose the next branch, unspooling as she went.

Buster had mocked this, too. "What are you trying to do, knit a scarf?" he had asked, leaning against the wall and slurping Gatorade. "You're just going to have to come through and untangle that mess when we're done."

Lynne had shrugged and set her piton then moved down the next branch of the tunnel, not waiting for him to heave himself off the wall and follow. He did so, but not before whipping the empty bottle down the tunnel branch they had just come from. It hit the wall and ricocheted with a loud plastic *tock!* that echoed as Lynne winced. "You're going to have to come through and collect *that* when we're done," she said.

Buster snorted. "I don't think one little bottle is going to matter. It's going to get blown up then ground out in the construction, anyway."

Lynne opened her mouth to point out if that was true then her string certainly wasn't going to do any harm, but gave it up as a battle she wouldn't win. This job didn't pay her by the hour, which meant arguing wasn't worth her effort.

She worked her way along to the end of a third spool, which meant she had mapped a kilometer, plus retracing steps. That was a good day's work, mapping more by herself than she had managed working with Buster.

She ran her fingers lightly along the rough wall as she retraced her steps to the entrance, instinctively cataloguing the different layers beneath her touch. Her light caught a particularly lovely bloom of pegmatite crystals in the rockface and she stopped to admire it. It was thrilling to know she was the very first person to walk here. The Salmon Arm Earthquake had sheared off chunks of the mountain range with its fierce buckling of the earth, burying large swaths of the main highway near the center of the quake. However, the devastation had revealed a tantalizing option even as it destroyed sections of the Trans-Canada Highway between British Columbia and the rest of the country—engineers assessing how to remove countless tons of rubble had found a newly-revealed opening to what appeared to be a long series of caves running through the range that made up the Northern end of Sluice Lake.

If the caves continued, the engineers declared, the best way to reconnect the highway might be to bore them out clean and run the Trans-Canada through. It might take years, sure. But the alternative was being talked about in decades.

"It's all about calculating statics and equilibrium against the makeup of the rock and volume displacement," Buster had explained over lunch their first day at Sluice Narrows. "We will have to review potential tension, compression, shear and torsion against the loads." He took a hefty bite of his club sandwich, continued with his mouth full. "My team will calculate the weight of the structure itself plus the weight and vibration of the vehicles moving through the tunnel." He swallowed, then drained half his glass of beer with one gulp. "But don't worry about doing math. You just need to make pictures of all the caves so we know what we're working with."

Lynne's degrees had included classes in physics, calculus, extrapolating fluid and motion dynamics but Buster didn't need to know that. She was being very well compensated to consult on the caves survey so decided to avoid any comments outside her area of expertise. Comments drew attention. Attention drew—

Back of the closet under a pile of clothes, fist stuffed into her mouth to keep silent

She nodded and sipped her iced tea. He was just a blowhard, and she'd dealt with far worse.

That evening Lynne downloaded the photos onto her laptop, reviewing caverns and colors only glimpsed earlier in the light of her headlamp. Thus far the chambers lacked stalactites and other natural structures like in other caves she'd explored, but there were some lovely crystalline fractures running through the granite walls. She studied the photos for cracks and potential weaknesses in the rock, noting jpeg tags for a "best of" folder she'd transfer to a flash drive for the engineers.

The last few photos included odd shadows in a section she had not explored in depth. Lynne squinted and leaned closer to the laptop screen. The one shadow looked like a side branch off the main tunnel she would need to map tomorrow. The other... she clicked the final photo.

It looked like a long-snouted and heavily-toothed skull. Lynne blinked, trying to reset her brain. The tripod flash threw stark shadows that could make mundane objects look odd, but this was odder than usual. Lynne rubbed her eyes, then checked her watch. It was full dark but she knew the drive well by now, and it wasn't like time of day mattered where she was going. She studied the image on her laptop screen again, then clicked "delete" and grabbed her car keys.

Lynne's flashlight fell from nerveless fingers and hit the cave floor.

She knelt and picked it up, then slowly approached the skull—the big, long-snouted and heavily-toothed skull—that seemed to jut out from the deep shadows of the cave notch behind it like a dog poking its head out of a dog house. She had found lots of bones over her years exploring, of course. But they were usually small prey of the creatures who made the caves their home. This was bigger than a bathtub.

"What could you be?" She had a smattering of paleontology as part of her Geology studies, but most of what she knew about fossils came from a school trip to Chicago in 9th grade; the one trip her foster family had let her attend when Lynne's teacher had offered to cover some of the expenses so his best student could go.

Was the rest of the skeleton attached? She leaned to look, one hand holding her flashlight ahead of her, the other reaching out to rest on the broad forehead.

A voice so deep her fillings vibrated spoke.

You have come

Lynne jumped back and ducked, throwing her arms over her head and waiting for the low rumbling frequency to pull debris from the ceiling. Not even dirt sifted down.

How long the years, Jackie?

The voice was in her head, but it was the words that pushed Lynne onto her knees, heedless of the gravel. "How do you know my name?"

She felt confusion. *You are my Jackie*

"I'm—I'm sorry, I'm not your Jackie." Lynne hesitated, rolled off her knees so she could sit. "My name is Jacklynne Carta. I'm not—what are you?"

I am your dragon, Jackie. I knew you would come to this place and would need me. Oh look, you brought me strings

"I am very, very sorry but I am not who you think I am." Lynne swallowed, then stepped closer and shone her flashlight past the jaws' hinge and thick ridges around the ear holes, along vertebrae that stretched like a fallen redwood back into the darkness. A reflection of light caught her attention and she took a cautious step closer.

"Please don't move," she whispered as she bent over and picked up a glittering sharp-edged disc the size of her hand. She blew it free of dust and held it up to the light of her flash, watching the play of iridescent green.

"Oh my God," she breathed. "Puff?"

A wash of joy. *I knew you would remember*

Four-year-old Jackie had cradled the music box close to her face as its little green-enameled dragon turned a pirouette.

"I'm sick of that damn song," the man on the couch snarled.

"She won't go to sleep without it," Jackie's Mom snapped back and then flopped down beside him and grabbed for the glass pipe. She inhaled and held the smoke in her lungs.

Five-year-old Jackie tucked the music box with its little green-enameled dragon under the porch after Mom had thrown it across the room, cracking the wood and warping the spindle so the song slurred in places. Mom said she'd done it to teach her a lesson: Jackie had eaten the last gob of peanut butter for dinner. At night she crept outside and—with her head under an old quilt to muffle sound—played it, away from the acrid haze and strange people that filled the house.

Six-year-old Jackie cupped the green-enameled dragon in her hands as she hid under her bed. She had picked Puff out of the trash where her stepfather had thrown her music box, along with all of her toys and books. This and his fists were to teach her a lesson; she had spilled watercolor paint on the kitchen table.

Seven-year-old Jackie hid the dragon in her book bag, and her book bag in the shed out back. She washed up every morning at the McDonald's bathroom near school, until the new manager told her to not come back.

Eight-year-old Jackie had long talks with Puff late at night, planning to fly away. "If you were bigger you could carry me," she whispered as they hid. "Please, Puff. Please grow big."

Ten-year-old Jackie stayed away from home as much as possible, avoiding the cold-eyed man who watched her too closely when he came by to give her stepfather little packets and pick up money.

Twelve-year-old Jackie ran out of the house away from the cold-eyed man while her stepfather yelled get back here, dammit, and be useful for once.

Twelve-year-old Jackie took Mom's cigarette lighter then denied it despite the beating. She waited until night, and then touched the lighter to turpentine-soaked rags she had brought in from the shed out back.

Twelve-year-old Jackie clutched her little green-enameled dragon in her hands, laid down on her bed, and sang their song until the smoke overwhelmed her.

Twelve-year-old Jackie woke up blinded, first in the hospital, then the foster system.

Fourteen-year-old Jackie's eyes healed enough for her to read again.

Eighteen-year-old Jackie worked three jobs to afford school, burying herself in books and hard effort.

Twenty-four-year-old Jackie took up rock climbing and spelunking, reveled in the need for total concentration on the task at hand, graduated with PhDs in Geology and Land Surveys, and refused to remember.

Forty-two-year-old Jackie sat weeping on the floor of the cave, remembering.

Finally she shuddered, wiped her eyes, and wrapped her arms around herself. "I am hallucinating," Lynne said aloud. "Some sort of long-term hidden PTSD, I suppose."

Sing the song, Jackie

Lynne stood up, dusted the seat of her jeans off. "Visual *and* auditory." She took her glasses off and rubbed at her eyes.

I could make of myself bone from the bones of the earth, but I need you to make flesh. I got big for you. Sing the song for me. I will carry you to the sea and we will travel by boat like we are supposed to.

Lynne carefully put her glasses back on. "'Supposed to'? There is no 'supposed to' Puff, except I wasn't supposed to survive the fire." She stepped closer to the skull. "The blind kid of a junkie? I was always supposed to be a failure, but here I am."

She wrapped her arms around herself shivering at her memories. "There's no song. There's no noble kings, no pirate ships—"

"What's all this?" Lynne spun around and squinted into a blinding beam of light. When her eyes cleared she saw Buster standing there, one hand cupped lightly around her pink mason's string, the other holding a massive Maglite.

He ran his light over Puff's skull and gave a piercing, appreciative whistle. "Ho-lee *cow* would you look at this?" He released the string and sauntered closer, stumbling a bit on the uneven surface. "Some kinda dinosaur, all the way down here."

"You can see it?" Lynne took a step to the side, squinting, to try and cut the angle to give her eyes a break from his light.

"Don't know how I could miss it." Buster reached out and patted Puff's forehead, then ran his flashlight along his jawline. "Look at those teeth! Bet this was one of those Indominus Rex guys."

"That was a movie, Buster." Lynne winced as he spun and shone his lightly direct into her eyes again. She was going to see spots for days at this rate.

"Maybe." He pulled a fifth of tequila out of his barn coat's cargo pocket and tipped it up, muscles in his throat working beneath three days' scruff of beard then wiped his mouth. "But maybe not. Either way there's a decision to make." He returned the bottle to his pocket with a belch. "Who do we tell about this?"

Taking Lynne's stunned silence as an invitation, Buster smiled slyly. "I know guys who would pay serious money."

Lynne shook her head. "Still a movie," she replied, then jumped as he slapped his hand on Puff's orbital bone with a loud smack.

"*Not* a movie," he insisted loudly. "We either ignore it and let the tunnel bore grind it right up, we alert the," he made finger quotes with his right hand, "authorities and they take it from us and the job stops, or I make some phone calls for serious money." He pulled out his phone.

Lynne tried to think fast. Waves of alcohol were rolling off Buster, and as he held up his phone to take a photo he swayed like a palm tree in a storm. Maybe he would pass out and forget? She couldn't easily drag him out of here. Maybe she could coax him outside and then he could pass out and forget? She pulled her own phone out of her pocket and held it up.

"Hey, I already have a bunch of really good photos, but I have no bars. Why don't we go outside where we can get a signal so I can text them to you?"

Buster swayed for a moment, one eye closed as he tried to focus on picture-taking, then hiccupped and nodded. "Good idea. Let's go." He fumbled his phone toward his coat pocket, oblivious as it fell in the grit at his feet, then turned and reached out with careful attention to grab onto the pink string with his right hand, holding his Maglite in his left. "Your stupid schtring came in handy for once."

Lynne suddenly regretted her safety line. "That's how you found me," she agreed. She watched him stumble a few steps, wondering how he'd managed to avoid driving off one of the switchbacks along the roadway.

"Hey!" Buster turned around so suddenly he nearly fell into her. "What're you whistling about? Are you whistling at me, girl?" He smirked, expression satanic in the flashlight beam.

"I, uh—" Lynne hadn't realized she was whistling the old song. "Just, um, checking the harmonance." At his confused look she kept talking, trying to crowd into him and make him move in the correct direction. "You know, harmonance. Vibration theory. It's a geological concept of how sound waves travel through different density rocks. It will help me work out my final recommendations."

Buster's eyes had glazed over (more) at "theory" so Lynne didn't think he would call her bluff so long as she kept him moving and distracted. Time to pile it on thick. "I know you will work out all the math but any help I can give, well, I'm just thrilled to do so."

Buster stood and swayed for a moment, then turned toward the way out. "Don't need math," he replied. "Not with that big boy in there. Only math I'm going to need is how to spend the money." He stopped again and Lynne had to take a quick step back to avoid running into him. He fumbled in his pocket for the bottle, took a healthy gulp, then mumbled "where my manners" and offered it to her. Lynne shook her head but Buster waved the bottle at her.

"We got to toast," he insisted, then scowled. "You too good to drink with me? You never drink with me. You got a problem with me?" He took a step toward her and held out the bottle. "We are going to toast our good forsh-forsh— luck and then we're going to go somewhere and really celebrate." He leered, his eyes cold. "And after I'll make some phone calls."

Forty-two-year-old Lynne reminded herself she knew how to handle cold-eyed men, even if Buster was between her and safe exit. "Sure, big guy," she agreed, taking the bottle to upend it against closed lips before handling it back. "Now let's get out of here so we can go celebrate."

Buster put the bottle in his pocket, then lurched forward, knocking her hard hat off and pulling her against his chest before she could move out of his way. "Here works," he said and bent down to kiss her.

His grab had trapped Lynne's arms between them, which made it easy for her to position her flashlight under his chin and shove. Hard. His teeth snapped together like a shot and he bellowed, let go and stumbled back, then tripped on the uneven ground and fell hard on his side with a crunch of glass, his bellow turning into a scream.

"*You bitch!*" he dropped the Maglite as he staggered to his feet, blood dripping down his chin and tequila staining his front. Buster shook his head and spat a red stream, then wiped his face and focused on Lynne. "You're gonna be sorry for that!" he snarled, stumbling in her direction.

Lynne dodged his first rush then tripped herself. She turned her fall into a roll and scooped up his Maglite as she tumbled toward a side channel. As Buster tried to stop his momentum she clicked both flashlights off and scooted back into the channel further, trying to control her gasping breaths.

There was clattering, cursing, and then Buster spoke in the darkness from somewhere to her left.

"I have my hand on your stupid string. You want out of this cave, you have to go past me. I'll just wait outside at my truck, where there's light to see and more to drink. We're not done here, not by a long shot."

Lynne lay on her belly in the darkness, darkened flashlights in both hands, and listened to the scrapes and staggers of his footsteps recede.

He was walking in the wrong direction.

She lay quietly and counted to 300, then 300 again: ten minutes with no sound of Buster coming back. Between the tequila and his adrenaline subsiding he had probably passed out. She felt a little like passing out herself, but Lynne knew she had to find her string and follow it to the right. She clipped her flashlight to her belt, hefted Buster's Maglite, then pulled out her phone and carefully peeped its small flash from between her fingers, letting just enough light out to see her hard hat where it had rolled some feet away, and then a faint pink line a few feet off the ground along the far wall.

String for safety. String for rescue.

Lynne sighed.

String to find a drunken idiot who had a young family in Vancouver and who—if he hadn't passed out—might trip and break his neck, leaving them behind.

Twelve-year-old Jackie would have left without a second thought.

Forty-two-year-old Jackie told herself she was better than that.

She picked up her hard hat and settled it onto her head, then wrapped her right hand loosely around the pink string and turned left.

The old ways of moving came back to Lynne as she walked through the darkness. Months of blindness and years of partial sight had taught her to point her toes like a dancer and skim her feet along the surface, seeking out impediments to her path. She shuffled quietly, steel-toed boots locating the few rocks in her way. Every dozen or so steps she stopped and listened for a count of sixty as her pulse slowed enough that she could hear beyond the blood pounding in her ears. The left side of her face caught a slight movement of air that meant she was passing the tunnel branch at the entry to Puff's space, and her nostrils flared to catch any changes in the scents around her.

No sound from Buster. If he had blacked out she might walk right past him in the dark, but if she turned on her light and he was still conscious she would be an easy target.

Maybe there was a better way.

"Puff?" She thought. "Can you hear me?"

Jackie? Did the ogre hurt you?

Ogre? Well, she could see Puff's point. "I'm fine," Jackie thought. "And the Ogre isn't really bad, he's just, um, he's not feeling well, and that makes him mean. I need to find him. Can you help me? Can you see?"

He tried to harm you. I will protect you. Sing so I can save you.

"I can save myself," Jackie thought back. "And I need to stay quiet right now."

Like when we were small. But I am not small this time. This time I am large. This time I can save you

"Save me how?" The hair on the back of Jackie's neck stood up. No response. "Puff?" she said aloud.

She felt air move, and had a moment to start to turn before a heavy body slammed into her, banging her skull onto the rock wall as a burst of red flashes lit in front of her eyes. Her hard hat took some of the impact before it was knocked off her head. Buster clutched at her, ripping her shirt sleeve as she bent underneath his grasp and twisted away, swinging the mag-lite like a baseball bat. It connected somewhere with a meaty thwack.

"*Ow fuck me* that hurt!" he yelled, and Lynne could almost taste his anger as he thrashed around nearby in the pitch black. She staggered forward then froze, one hand pressed against the wall to stay steady. The red flashes had become dull orange that strobed with each throb of her head and the darkness spun; she wondered if this sudden stomach-churning roller coaster feeling meant concussion.

A blast of tequila reached her nostrils and she almost vomited, clenching her teeth around a mouthful of salty saliva. Her breath whistled but Buster was making far too much noise to hear her. A scuffling and then he yelled again, almost in her ear. She jumped before she could stop herself and the cave floor seemed to tilt. Lynne staggered, arms flung out in the darkness to protect herself and ran right into Buster.

A big hand closed over her wrist and the mag-lite was yanked from her grasp. A pause and then six D-cell batteries' worth of painfully bright light shone right in her face. The pain in her head spiked and the roller coaster took another swerve; her stomach could not keep up. Buster released her and stepped back as Lynne bent over at the waist and vomited, then fell to her knees, hands flat against the cave floor and helpless against the heaving of her gut that continued long after her stomach had emptied.

She finally stopped and looked up, squinting against the beam of theMaglite.

"What's wrong with you?" Buster actually sounded concerned.

"You gave me a concussion, you jerk." Lynne spat foul bits out of her mouth. "Quit shining the light in my eyes." She reached out toward the cave wall and slowly clambered to her feet, feeling like she'd pulled every muscle in her abdomen.

"Well, I think you broke my arm. Look!" Buster moved the light to shine on a massive purpling knot on his right forearm. "Look what you did."

Lynne couldn't tell if she was swaying or the cave was, but at least Buster sounded marginally more sober. She tried closing her eyes but that made the swaying worse. She fumbled at her belt, surprised to find her own flash still clipped to it, then turned it on and shone the light around, spotting her hard hat. Bending over wasn't an option so she knelt to pick it up and settled it on her head, hissing in pain as the fitting strap touched her left temple. Her ribs ached from Buster's tackle, her left shoulder was going to have a heck of a bruise from hitting the wall, and she'd twisted her right ankle.

Lynne set her jaw and told herself she wasn't seriously injured. Then another wave of nausea hit and she suddenly had to sit down and lean back against the smooth rock wall, taking slow deep breaths.

Buster, surprisingly, sat as well, settling a few feet to her right and stretching long legs out, crossed neatly at the ankles. He fumbled chunks of tequila-soaked glass out of his coat pocket and threw them into the darkness, hissing as the alcohol entered cuts in his fingers. "Jesus, you made a mess."

Lynne closed her eyes and gingerly sett the back of her hard hat against the wall. "I made a mess? You drink way too much, Dude. Plus you're a total asshat."

Buster grunted. "Maybe I whoop it up a little too much. So what? It's not a crime that I'm aware of."

"No, but banging my head against the wall is. Not to mention selling dinosaur bones."

A brief pause. "Well, I didn't mean to. Besides you really hurt my arm." He sounded like a sulky schoolboy.

They sat for long enough that Lynne found herself humming the old song as her thoughts wandered sluggishly. She drifted, knowledge that she shouldn't fall asleep struggling against the cotton batting in which her mind wanted to wrap itself. Buster said something about money but her thoughts were sluggish—by the time she thought to listen he had gone quiet.

Her attention perked up only slightly when Buster stood up with a grunt and shone his Maglite at her again.

"So now what am I going to do with you?" His voice was slow and musing.

She knew she should feel alarmed, but found herself giggling. "I'll just frolic in some autumn mists. Don't mind me." Her hands and feet felt like ice. She raised her flashlight to illuminate his face.

His eyes were cold. "It's a shame that you came in by yourself. You tripped and hit your head. Got a nice concussion, maybe even fractured your skull." He crouched on one knee next to her, mag-lite shining on the puddle of vomit. "You suffocate on your own puke and even though I don't find you in time, I'm a hero for trying." He twisted the lens on his Maglite and placed it on the ground so it cast a pool of light around them, then reached out and slid one hand behind her neck, squeezing the palm of the other over her nose and mouth.

Lynne let out a muffled squeak and tried to jerk away but her head exploded with fresh waves of pain as Buster squeezed harder, forcing his hand harder over her mouth and pinching her nose firmly shut.

There was a deep rumbling sound to their right. Buster looked over his shoulder as Lynne grabbed at his arm to try to force his hand away. Without aim or intent, her hands grabbed and locked down on the still-swelling knot where she'd hit him with the Maglite.

Buster shrieked and let go, spinning around on his knees to shake her off but Lynne—as disoriented as a sparrow in a hurricane—held on. Eighteen years of rock climbing gave her one ferocious grip, and she felt the fractured edges of the bones in his forearm shift and grind as her hold tightened.

"Ohgodohgod *let go!*" he screamed and slapped at her. There was a sudden basso growl and beyond the very edge of the pool of light Lynne saw something large and terrible... move.

Buster saw it too, and his scream filled up with terror. He jerked frantically; with an unsettling pop something in his arm gave way under Lynne's hands and she released her grip and fell backwards. Buster staggered away, then tripped and fell out of the light. There was a wet crack, a few thuds, and then silence.

Grimly ignoring a head that felt like it was about to split in two, Lynne rolled onto her hands and knees. Her own flashlight was dark and lost somewhere, but if she could crawl to the mag-lite she could gain a weapon. After what seemed to be a mile her hand closed on the big flashlight and she clicked it off, then held her breath and listened.

No noise from Buster. Only the sound of huge lungs moving air—inhale, exhale, inhale again.

Lynne got a knee underneath her then staggered two steps, almost falling, before being caught gently in an immense, soft-furred wing. She ran her hands along velvety skin to the warm, scaly shoulder, then across a broad chest and up until she rubbed the jawline, triggering a deep rumbling purr as if from a monumental cat.

"Puff," Lynne whispered, leaning her head carefully against the dragon's shoulder. Then darkness spun her away.

42-year-old Jackie woke up blinded, in the hospital in Kamloops.

She was just a consultant on the project, but the company still covered all of Lynne's out-of-pocket costs for care. They had even offered to pay for a driver and part-time domestic aide when they found out Lynne didn't have any family to help, but she turned them down. She would find her own way, she firmly told the insurance adjuster who had visited her in the hospital. She'd been through the drill before.

She didn't turn down full payout of her contract, of course. There was independence and then there was stupidity. She had briefly debated asking for a bonus, but decided that might be pushing it. As she left the train station and turned right toward the warmth that meant she was walking west, Lynne fingered the little green-enameled dragon figurine in her pocket. The searchers had found it next to her outstretched hand when they followed the pink mason's string to where she lay at the edge of the drop-off. She had been airlifted to Kamloops and was already in surgery by the time Buster's body was recovered from the crevasse beyond.

Lynne pointed her toes like a dancer and skimmed her feet along the surface, white cane tapping the path ahead. Her case worker had warned her it might be years before a guide dog became available, and that she needed to learn to be self-sufficient. She had assured the case worker she would be just fine.

There is something across your path, five steps ahead the voice whispered in her mind. In four steps Lynne reached her cane out, tapped and discovered a fallen bicycle, and with Puff's voice guiding her passed it safely. She reached into her pocket again and rubbed the tip of a finger across the miniature jaw of the little green-enameled dragon figurine, triggering a tiny rumbling purr like that from a miniscule cat.

JB Riley writes and edits technical healthcare proposals for a major US-based corporation, but has loved reading and writing speculative fiction ever since discovering The Chronicles of Narnia *at Age 8. When not trawling the shelves at the local bookstore, she enjoys travel, hockey, beer and cooking. JB lives in Chicago with her family; which currently includes a 90-pound dog, a 15-pound cat, and a 5-pound cat that scares the hell out of everyone.*

STEPHANIE LORÉE

GINNY AND THE OUROBOROS

The cop eyes her photo I.D. "Virginia Washington. That an alias?"

Ginny shoves her hands in her coat pockets and doesn't mention her nickname. "My mama's got a sense of humor."

"She know you're wandering the streets this time of night?" he asks, drumming the fingers of one hand on his holster.

"No," she says. "She's dead."

The cop frowns and mumbles something into his walkie-talkie that sounds like the make-believe language she and her little sister invented when they were young. All jargon and slang and official-sounding TV-type talk. Ginny's mama called it Pig Latin, but Ginny learned later it wasn't nothing like Ig-pay Atin-lay. Though now she thinks the term is appropriate for cop-speak.

A dispatcher on the end of the line says some Pig Latin back that makes the cop inspecting Ginny scowl.

"You got any weapons or drugs on you? Anything I should know about?" he asks.

"I don't smoke," she says. "Don't do none of that."

He nods like he believes her, but she can see the fake painted in his eyes. They're blue as storybook skies and touristy pictures of the Mississippi River and that baby she found last year in an alley and never told no one about but God. She has nightmares of a blue like that.

"Turn around and put your hands on the wall," he says.

She shrugs and places her palms against the cracked brick building, spreads her legs shoulder-width apart without him asking. She keeps her face forward and watches her breath fog and disappear into the dark, trying hard not to think how this cop will be the first person who wasn't her sister to touch her in a long time. How she hopes he doesn't remove her thin gardening gloves.

He runs his hands over her arms and sides, down her legs to squeeze her ankles. He dips inside her coat pocket and grunts. "The hell," he says. He rummages inside the pocket and scoops out the clump of dirt Ginny'd dug up not an hour earlier. Holding it out for her, he says, "What's this?"

The lump of soil is still damp, and it drips a bit through his white fingers and muddies his palm. Inside it, a worm has wrapped itself around an acorn like a dragon guarding the last known world. She sees this even if the cop can't.

"It's for school," she lies, then tacks on some truth. "I study at Jackson State."

He sniffs the soil, frowns, and shoves it back in her pocket. "You got class in the morning?"

"Yeah, bio lab."

He lifts her hands from the wall and positions them behind her back. The cuffs click closed around her wrists. "I'm sorry," he says.

"What'm I charged with?"

He hesitates. "Loitering."

She rolls the bullshit around her mind for a moment, sliding into the backseat of the cop car. When the cop settles up front, she says, "What'd Dakota do this time?"

Startled, the cop glances back at her, and she notices how pretty his face is. No lines around the pale eyes or between brown brows. He hasn't been a cop long enough for the city to sink into his skin, but it would happen soon.

"A detective wants you to answer some questions," he says.

He drives cautious as an old lady, weaving around potholes and buckled macadam and trash tossed aside like trivial memories. A lonely shoe, a sofa cushion gone moldy, bags with shiny logos, and cups with golden arches, a tire, a broken doll, a hobo. Ginny slouches, studying the images flashing by her window. She draws comfort from the soil in her pocket, tries to reassure the worm of her presence as the radio chirps more Pig Latin.

"Hey," she says when it's silent, "thanks for giving me back my dirt."

The cop shifts uncomfortably in his seat. "Sure."

"And for not being a jerk. Nicest arrest I ever had."

He glances in the rear-view, and she catches his soft smile. "Sure," he says again.

Ginny thinks maybe his blue eyes don't look nothing like that baby. Maybe they're just eyes like skies she's never seen and that's why they scare her.

"Get whatever you like, Ginny baby," Mama says.

Ginny looks around, sees the dresses hanging like flower petals. Her hand glides over the fabrics, soft cottons and scratchy sheer laces. She's never seen so many beautiful things in one place. As if God took all the pretty from the world and strung it up on racks.

"Anything?" Ginny asks, unsure.

Her mama nods.

She's never gotten new clothes before, only hand-me-downs from neighbor kids and the Salvation Army. Now, the unfaded colors and sharply creased materials threaten to overwhelm her. She considers running down the aisles, grabbing everything within reach, and stuffing it into the cart. But she restrains herself and straightens her spine. At six years old, Virginia Washington knows this is a moment to savor.

She chooses a green dress. Plain fabric, smooth as spring-soaked grass, with daisies blooming along the waistline. Later, she chooses to forget how her mama hides the dress in her purse and carries it past the cashier, or how the sewed-on daisies fall off the first time Mama does the wash. Ginny does not want to remember the way green fabric turns brown when stained with blood.

The cop shop is old, broken. A square building that squats on the corner of two streets with busted pavement and decorative orange barrels. Moss creeps over the barrels, and roots push between cracked concrete. The cop shop stares at the intrusion defiantly, but the ivy still climbs graffiti-covered walls.

Inside, Ginny is escorted to an interrogation room. She recognizes it from the one-way mirror, glaring fluorescent lights, and the stick-thin table and chair that would shatter if she bashed it over a detective's head.

The blue-eyed cop eases her into the chair and leaves with a little nod. She learned his name is Stephens from the desk cop out front who'd greeted him and gave Ginny a nasty, puckered expression. Stephens had frowned and whispered, "Ignore him, he's always ugly," once they were out of earshot. Replaying it now in her mind, she smiles and decides she likes Stephens.

They let her sit in the room for some time, arms still secure behind her back, dirt humming in her pocket. The worm grows weaker; its grip around the acorn slackens and sickens her stomach. She watches the mirror with a bored, blank gaze but says, "Please don't waste my time."

They make her wait anyway.

When the detective finally enters, it's with a puff of perfume that makes Ginny want to puke. It reeks of dead flowers, of lies that make a person sweat.

"Do you know why you're here?" The detective crosses her arms and looks down her pointed nose at Ginny. She's an older lady with steel roots in her bottle-black hair and a long, line-riddled face that reminds Ginny of wrinkled bedsheets.

"Kinda philosophical question, but I guess you mean my sister," Ginny says.

The detective lays a mugshot on the table. A man stares out like he's devouring the world with his eyes. The markings on the wall behind him say he's over six feet tall, and Ginny thinks his loam-like skin would be beautiful in sunlight.

"Recognize him?" the detective asks.

Ginny shakes her head.

"Robert Jamison, goes by Bobby James. Twenty-two years old and already wanted for burglary, assault with a deadly, and a slew of misdemeanors. But for the most part, our Bobby prefers arson. He's burned six homes in the past week, one of which nearly cost the lives of two squatters inside."

"What's this have to do with me?"

"He's been seeing your sister," she says.

Ginny furrows her brow. "Dakota don't have any boyfriends."

The detective shrugs. "Right now, she's wanted as accessory to Bobby's most recent burn-job. When's the last time you saw your sister?"

The chair below Ginny squeaks as she adjusts herself. She slides her tennis shoes along the linoleum, feeling the cool push of wooden floorboards through her soles, of poured cement and copper piping and the deep, dark press of earth. Fat roots slink through the ground and stab toward her position above them. The worm inside her pocket whimpers. She hears the soil sing.

The last time she saw Dakota, Ginny came home to her sister passed out in front of her door. Bruises and malnourishment had turned Dakota's brown skin yellow, and meth had rotted her teeth. Ginny carried her inside, made the sofa into a bed, and removed Dakota's worn sandals. She whispered lullabies and stroked her baby sister's hair until she fell unconscious beside her.

In the morning, Ginny discovered only emptiness: couch, purse, and refrigerator. The only things Dakota left were shadows under Ginny's eyes, hollows in her cheeks, and dead leaves in her garden.

"Don't know," she tells the detective. "Couple weeks."

The detective paces around the table, circling Ginny like a vulture. "Your sheet stretches back to juvie. Been in the system, never leaving. You and your sister've made trouble since you crawled out of your mother's belly."

"Guess you know all about us then."

"I know your type." She narrows her eyes and rests a hand on Ginny's shoulder. "Dakota's in a lot of trouble, and the best thing you can do is help me find her. She's still a minor. She can make a break of it, get clean."

The detective's acrylic nails bite into Ginny's collarbone in a way that is part comfort, part threat. They carry the smell of beauty parlors and Swisher Sweet cigarillos and remind Ginny of her mama.

A cold finger snakes down her spine. In her pocket, the worm hisses.

"Look," Ginny says, "I got nothing to tell you. Dakota comes and goes. I'd like to see her as much as you, but unless you're gonna hold me on trumped-up loitering shit, I got a class to wake up for in five hours."

Without warning, the detective slams Ginny's face against the table. Stars burst in her eyes and her ears ring. She grunts, mouth half-smashed to the tabletop. Spittle dribbles between her lips.

The detective holds her there by the collar, leans in and whispers, "Don't get smart. You've been arrested enough I don't need a reason to throw you in the tank overnight. You find your sister and you march her ass in here. You do not want me to find her and Bobby James first."

Ginny can't nod, can't speak until the detective releases her grip and storms out of the room. When the fuzz clears, she notices a business card on the table for Detective Rosa Henneman.

Underneath Ginny, the linoleum floor has spider-webbed with cracks.

"Make it go." A two-year-old Dakota points her sister toward an acorn. It's nearly rotten and wedged between an uneven sidewalk. "Make it go, make it go," Dakota says, bouncing on wobbly legs.

Ginny–nine years old and already slouching from the press of the city–crouches next to her sister. She wraps one arm securely around Dakota, hugging her, and cups the acorn in her free hand. It pulses against her palm, tickling a greeting and smelling of sunshine and freedom and warm, wet grass. Ginny tickles back and invites it inside her. Slowly, like sucking a milkshake up a straw, the acorn pulls on her. It starts under her rib cage, lower like a stomach ache, and tugs at things inside her that were never meant to be tugged.

The seed opens, a green shoot budding before their eyes.

"We can plant it here," Ginny says, leading her sister toward a vacant lot filled with overgrown weeds and car tires. "It'll grow big, like you, and make acorns of its own. It'll be part of us. Our secret."

She digs a hole with her hands. The dry earth darkens, and the soil becomes strong. She sets the acorn inside. Roots take hold, caressing her skin before sliding into the earth. Dirt streaks Ginny's arms and stains her knees; the touch of it makes her sigh.

But Dakota giggles and dives into the ground, pushing her fingers deep. She digs with fervor until dirt peppers her face, her body. She laughs until the weeds around her wither. Laughs until tears roll down her cheeks and splash the soil like acid rain. Fissures form around her fingertips, like veins leading toward the sapling protected at its heart.

"Make it go," she says and reaches for the budding oak tree.

Ginny grabs her sister's hands and pulls her into a careful embrace.

"It's done," she whispers and stares at her lonely island of green surrounded by Dakota's destruction. She inhales the ashen remains of weeds fluttering in the breeze. She stops herself from crying.

"You make everything better," Dakota says.

But Ginny knows she can't fix what her sister has wrought.

Stephens offers her a ride home when he sees the bruise along her cheek, the blackening around her eye. He's pulled a hoodie over his uniform and stuffed his gun and cuffs and police paraphernalia into a backpack slung over his shoulder. Off-duty like this, he looks good, human.

Ginny hesitates, but he insists, and who is she to argue with a cop who's already arrested her once tonight?

He walks her around back to the fenced-in cop lot. Only a handful of vehicles remain at three AM, but she knows the bike is his the moment she sees it. All shiny chrome and blue paint job like his eyes. He holds a helmet out to her, and she slips it on.

"Little cold for motorcycles, isn't it?" she asks.

"I like the outdoors," he says, mounting the bike and gunning the engine.

She wraps her arms around his waist. "Me, too."

They arrive at her apartment building and idle awkwardly at the curb. She almost expects to see Dakota passed out against the door again, but it's as empty as it will be in her basement studio. Only her garden and the sough of crawlers through her bedroom walls to welcome her home.

"You want to come in?" she asks, still clinging to his back.

He tenses. "That would be inappropriate."

"Yeah," she says and hops off the bike. She hands him the helmet and meets his gaze. She's never thought of herself as pretty, but she knows her eyes are dark and deep and sometimes people get lost in them. "You want to come in anyway?"

Stephens stares at her a long moment, then he kills the engine.

She leads him inside, down the narrow stairs to her apartment. It's one room plus a shower-only bath. The windows are set high, near the ceiling, so it's always darker and damper and smelling of rain. She doesn't have a TV or microwave or a real bed, but she does have walls lined with bookshelves and potted plants, a drop-ceiling threaded with hanging vines, and a hydroponic garden that would put a pothead to shame.

"I'm a biologist," she tells Stephens, more apology than explanation. "Or I want to be." She frowns. "I'm supposed to graduate in May."

She rinses a bowl in the kitchen sink, sets it on the counter. From her pocket she removes the clump of dirt—the worm and acorn hiding inside—and puts it in the dish. She takes a scoop of soil from a nearby plant and packs it on top, sprinkling it with water. The worm whispers its pleasure.

Then she turns to Stephens, watches him survey the room with round eyes. He inhales several times, breathing in the thick, heady scent of life. The tension between his shoulders seems to dissolve; his posture relaxes. With a hesitant hand, he traces the bruise on her cheekbone.

"Who are you?" he asks.

Ginny doesn't answer, just molds her mouth to his and listens to the leaves breathe around them.

The green dress doesn't fit anymore, so she holds it up to Dakota's shoulders. The hem kisses the stained carpet.

"It's beautiful." Dakota's black eyes are big and bottomless. She glances at Ginny in the mirror. "Can I keep it?"

Ginny nods. "It's yours now."

Dakota squeals and spins. She lifts the dress over her head and shimmies into it. The daisies are long gone, but the fabric remains petal-soft. In love with her own reflection, she doesn't notice the man stepping out of their mama's bedroom, but Ginny does. He's tall and too thin, sunken cheeks and a jaw sharp enough to cut. He reeks of old tobacco and brine.

"Pretty," the man says, his eyes locked on Ginny.

She's seen this before, a clarity passing over some grown-up faces when they look at her, as if they're waking up from a long sleep. They want to touch her then, stroke her hair and kiss her forehead, hold her until they pull on her like the acorn. But she won't welcome them.

The man approaches the girls. He lays a hand on both their shoulders, but jerks away from Dakota as if burned. Instead, he leans into Ginny, rubbing her back. She tries to move but he fists her hair. She cries out. Dakota growls. The man nuzzles Ginny's neck, swatting Dakota with the back of his hand. The younger sister flies, smacking the wall with a sickening crunch. When she rises, her shoulder is cocked at an impossible angle and she lurches toward the man with hands outstretched.

Then there are only the man's screams deafening Ginny's ears and charred meat filling her nostrils and a brilliant red soaking Dakota's dress.

In the morning, Ginny leaves Stephens lying on the pillows of her pull-out couch. His nude back glows under a shaft of sunlight spilling in from the uncovered windows. She wants to thank him for making the vines dance and the flowers blossom—for taking only what she gave—but she doesn't know how to explain the fading of his old football injury or where the silvery scar on his shoulder went or how his tongue tastes like honeysuckle and promises.

She lifts the bowl with her secret buried inside. Overnight the acorn has sprouted. A shoot of green peeks from the soil, and the worm waltzes around its roots. Today everything will change, she knows, and she carries it to the curb.

The bike remains on the street. Crabgrass and morning glories have wrapped between its spoke wheels and tied tight to its handlebars. With a whisper, Ginny draws them back to sprawl across the sidewalk like a blanket cushioning the concrete. More greenery grows to join it, and the blanket spreads into the street. Underneath the pavement, roots contort around pipelines and sewer systems; they squeeze and push and punch the surface. They call to her.

She slips Stephens's keys from her pocket, secures her grip on the bowl with the acorn, and heads toward the Coliseum. Behind her, the exhaust plumes and the blacktop breaks.

The husks of Dakota's handiwork grow thicker as Ginny approaches the eastside. Blackened buildings dot the landscape, and the January air is ripe with rot and smoke. Plywood-covered windows watch as she parks the motorcycle. The Mississippi Coliseum stands untouched by the decay, a domed structure surrounded by cement. But below it, far down in the depths of the world, she senses the seam between mantle rocks, hears it sigh like a slumbering dragon.

Ginny nestles the plant and bowl in the crook of her elbow. Everything is empty in the dawn, and no one stops her as she touches the main doors. For the first time, she pulls back on the earth, draws the dragon into her, feeds on it as it comes alive under her feet. Wood and iron buckle, bowing inward enough to allow her passage. Her steps shake the walls, rumble supports and braces, shatter glass. It cannot be helped.

The ground trembles.

Inside is all stadium seating and a floor shined in preparation for the next basketball game. The lacquered wood twists and snaps. The noise enfolds her. Her teeth vibrate.

"Figures you'd find me here," Dakota calls over the chaos. She's standing opposite the broken entrance, half-obscured by shadow. Her hair has fallen out almost completely, a few strands of black curling over her forehead. Her skin is sallow, one giant green bruise, and peppered with open sores. She limps and coughs and smells of gangrene.

The Coliseum shudders.

"Looks like you're finally ready." Dakota says.

"I'll help you." Ginny nods. "Please, God, let me help you."

Dakota comes closer. Wooden bleachers wither in her wake. Her footsteps singe the floor in the shape of her toes. She smiles, revealing ruddy gums. "Bobby said the same thing. You two would've liked each other."

"Where is he?"

Dakota shrugs. "Can't stand the heat..." She staggers to half-court, kneels and splays her hands on the ground. Her fingers sink in as the flooring disintegrates. Tiny sparks ignite along the edges, and the sick scent of burning plastic fills the air. "I can only get so far," she says. "You'll need to open it the rest of the way."

"And when it's over?"

Her little sister looks up at her, and for a moment Ginny sees the sixteen-year-old girl inside Dakota. Not the addict or the anarchist or the death goddess, just a scared kid in a green dress.

"We'll start again." Hope shines in Dakota's endless eyes. "We can build whatever we want, be whoever we want."

Holding the potted plant close to her side, Ginny nods. "All right."

Sirens sound over the cacophony of splitting timbers and shredding steel. Distantly, a voice she recognizes shouts through a megaphone, but she ignores whatever it's saying.

Ginny reaches down and wakes the dragon.

"That's fucking stupid." Dakota's small breasts push against the tabletop as she bends to snort the white line. "Why would you build something on a fucking volcano?"

"It's extinct," Ginny says, pointing at the textbook propped over her thighs. "Has been forever."

Dakota squints and leans her head back. "But one time?"

"Long ago, I guess it was active."

Her sister smiles, a sly, lop-sided thing that is part childish, part devil. Her eyes glaze over and blood from her nose fills the indent of her upper lip. "Bet you could make it work."

"Dunno. And if I could, I wouldn't. The whole city might burn."

Dakota takes her hand, squeezes it. "Nothing but steel and sinners. The city did this to us, Ginny. Imagine what you could grow if you started fresh?"

The pull is an easy, lazy tug on her heart. Ginny's fingers start to ache; her knuckles flake and crack. But in her grasp, Dakota's wrinkled skin turns rich and dark and lovely.

Tectonic plates shift and shudder. The hot, slow flow of magma begins to bubble and writhe. Ginny delves into the earth, feels its rhythmic rumble. She opens herself to its pull, feels it snake inside her stomach, coil around her lungs. She gasps.

"Like that." Dakota clasps Ginny's hand. Energy rushes like wildfire from the earth's core, between them, through them. Uncontrolled and unfathomable. Dakota's hair grows in first, then her teeth. Her skin glows with health, and her eyes sparkle with unshed tears.

Ginny ages a dozen years.

Chunks of debris rain around them, crashing like waves against mountains. The ground opens where Ginny wills, a pit descending into shadow and fire. Her muscles burn and the bones in her legs snap. She cries out from the force of it, the swirl of life and pain and power.

Then Stephens appears beyond a collapsed wall. He's calling her name and he's still in his hoodie and does he have to look at her like that? Beside him, Detective Rosa Henneman raises her gun.

"No," is all Ginny can mumble as the bullet flies. She doesn't even hear the gunshot over the storm, but she sees it pierce Dakota's back and exit her breast. It nicks Ginny's bicep, and her secret—the tiny pot of dirt and worm and acorn—tumbles to the shattered floor.

For a moment, Dakota seems surprised, unaware that she's injured, then her smile droops and she slumps unmoving to Ginny's lap.

The scream that tears from Ginny's mouth is all fury and thunder, rippling the earth for miles. She clutches Dakota to her chest and buries her face in her sister's hair.

"I know it's not how you wanted," she murmurs, "but we're gonna start fresh."

Cradling Dakota against her, Ginny gathers her acorn. The worm says it's ready. She tosses it slow, like rolling dice, into the hole she's created. Then she welcomes the dragon's pull, feeds it everything that is left for her to give.

It begins quietly. The dust settles; the fire dies. Roots take hold and a tree grows. It springs from the earth and pushes toward the sun. A thick web of grass and bluebells and morning glories spreads outward, cloaking the city in a green gown. The verdure knits itself across concrete and over cars. It scales skyscrapers and fills factories. It cannot be stopped.

In the center of it is an oak tree that towers above all. Two trunks twine together at the base, but only one reaches toward a blue, blue sky.

Born and still based in Ohio, **Stephanie Lorée** *writes fantasy fiction and occasionally moonlights as a rock star. Her stories have appeared in such places as Abyss & Apex and as tie-in fiction for the Pathfinder RPG. With her editor hat on, Stephanie freelances for indie authors and small presses. She loves gaming, good sushi, and bad kung fu flicks. Stay up to date at her website: stephanieloree.com.*

"Ginny and the Ouroboros" was originally published in Urban Fantasy Magazine in 2014.

LAURA VANARENDONK BAUGH

RED IN TOOTH AND MAW

The footage was grainy and muted; they had cheaped out on the trail cams. Dr. Jessi Kemuel thought that was a mistake, as spectacular footage would be a real boost to capital, but the argument was they didn't have the funds to buy cameras to raise funds.

Dragon conservation should have been a shoo-in for public support, but it seemed information overload and queasy politics had rendered everyone jaded these days.

Regardless, the imperfect scene on the conference room screen showed clearly enough the enormous beast pausing from dissecting a moose to shake its head repeatedly, as if dislodging something from its ear, and pawing at its snout. It was difficult to tell on the pixelated image, but Jessi thought the scales on the side of the jaw showed wear.

"It's not going away." Jackson didn't sound happy about it.

Beside Jessi, Dr. Lackland sat back in his chair and scowled. "We can't dope another dragon. If it goes wrong again—the population can't afford it, the Foundation can't afford it."

"We all know the stakes," Dr. Freeman said, waving her hand. "But we can't afford to lose another specimen, and especially not through neglect, which it will certainly be called. You think funding is a problem if an animal dies during treatment? Try having one die for lack of treatment—again."

"And kiss that future accreditation goodbye," Lackland added. "The world's only dragon reserve fails to meet minimum standard care? There'll be 'Free the Dragons!' protests everywhere and we'll be scraping change off the metro floor."

"There are no published standards of care for a barely recognized species," Jackson muttered. "And the dragons are already free, just protected."

"You want to explain that to the public? Because I've tried, and the nuances just don't get through."

Jessi didn't enter the grumbling debate. It was an old argument over old territory; they returned to it only because it was familiar and therefore safer than the looming threat of losing another dragon.

Three months ago, their fledgling reserve had made headlines when one of their five known residents dropped dead. Now they had a second showing similar symptoms, a bad situation for both a critically endangered species and their mission.

Jessi's stomach sank as three pairs of eyes turned on her. "You're awfully quiet," Jackson observed. "What do you suggest?"

Jessi drew a slow breath, as if delay would help. "We could try cooperative care."

Lackland's eye roll was audible. "Not this again."

"There are so many reasons it won't work," Pamela Freeman said, lifting an explanatory finger. "Time, for one. If that dragon's in danger, we don't have time to teach it to open wide while someone crams a thermometer into the opposite end."

Which is why we should have started training before it was critical, Jessi thought, but she did not say it aloud.

It didn't matter, because Freeman rolled to the next objection anyway. "And training is unnatural, invasive, the opposition of preservation. We are a reserve, not a circus, and we're trying to save this species, not debase them and turn them into public playthings."

"They wouldn't be playthings, they would be participants in their own healthcare," Jessi said despite herself. "It could save their lives."

"What about the lives of the people trying it? Who's going to wrestle a dragon down and stick it with a needle?"

"There wouldn't be any wrestling. All kinds of species have been trained for cooperative care, even big ones, elephants and bison—"

"Elephants have thousands of years of history with humans."

"Tigers don't, and they give voluntary blood draws."

"Tigers don't breathe fire when they get irritated. And you don't know how to train a tiger, much less a dragon."

"I feel like I've heard this before," Jackson interrupted. "Possibly a dozen times."

Jessi didn't answer. There was no point.

Jackson sighed. "Look, Pamela's right; we're trying to preserve a species, not run a dog and pony show, and there's no protocol for teaching a dragon to submit to invasive procedures." He hesitated. "But we are probably under a deadline, and we don't have another solution. If you can get this started, get it working before it gets critical and we have to dart—I'll give you a chance."

Jessi's heart leapt. A chance! This could mean real checks, not just guesses from scat and trail cam footage. This could enable care before it became critical. But how could they establish a program so quickly? "I'll get started right away."

"We can't afford to lose time on this." Jackson looked at the screen, where the dragon was scraping a talon across its jaw, scoring the scales. "If we don't see progress in two weeks, you'll have to dart."

"Two weeks? Do you—that's not possible. We don't have even the minimum—there's not the equipment—do you know how long this takes in an established facility with specialized trainers?"

Jackson pointed at the distressed dragon. "Do you know what will happen if that dragon drops dead?"

Jessi bit down her protests. It wasn't possible. Not in two weeks.

"This isn't my field," she said, not as an excuse but as a plea for help. "I don't know how to start, much less how to make progress so fast."

"You just said all that about elephants and tigers."

"I've seen video at conferences! I know it's done, but that's not what I do. You want to diagnose a skin infection or set a bone or something, I'm your woman. You want a whale to give you flukes for a blood draw instead of flipping you the flipper and swimming away, you need a trainer."

"Fine, we'll get you help. Pamela, you find an expert, so you can feel comfortable about the goals and make sure this isn't going to be a circus when we're done."

Jessi gave Freeman a sidelong glance. Would she sabotage this? No; she wasn't so petty, and the stakes were too high. Sabotaging the training meant risking the dragon's life as well as the reserve. No matter how they bickered, they were united in their goal to preserve a near-mythical species, and that goal came before any individual ego.

Freeman looked at Jessi and nodded. "I'll email some of the safari parks and big zoos tonight."

Jessi slammed the microwave door, punched the start button, and slid into the chair in front of her laptop. She had several tabs open, showing various designs of protected contact walls for use with elephants.

Though Hollywood liked to depict herbivores as complacent and tolerant, in fact any creature could be startled, could be in pain, could have a bad day. When it weighed six tons or more, it didn't take much of a reaction to maim or kill a human even unintentionally. The Association of Zoos and Aquariums required protected contact for elephants—and elephants didn't have predatory instincts, six-inch teeth, or fire breath.

Jessi watched video of an elephant sidling sideways toward a high opening in a steel-barred wall, working its ear through the gap in response to the cues of its handler, who spread the ear for thermal imaging and then a blood draw. The handler reached through the bars to scratch the elephant as her partner drew blood.

Jessi closed the tab.

Jessi was a veterinarian. Pamela Freeman was a herpetologist, Sam Lackland an ornithologist, and Neil Jackson had worked his way up through decades of zookeeping to administration, one hand on animal programs and the other on public relations, fund-raising, community integration, and the delicate web of facilitation. Each was expert in their field, which was why they were here. None were trained to do this.

The microwave dinged, and she retrieved her cardboard-tray lasagna. She should contact some people from the conferences, ask for help with the training, even help with the tranquilizers. Maybe someone would have some new ideas.

No moss grew on Dr. Pamela Freeman, Jessi had to give her that. Forty-eight hours after the meeting, she had a trainer to introduce in the conference room. "This is Milo Firenze. He's been a master trainer for thirty years, and he's come to help us with our dragon."

"Excellent! We're glad to have you," Jackson said, extending a grin and a hand. "What's your background?"

"I've been all around Europe and North America," Milo answered. "I've done some work in Asia too."

"Zoos?"

"Yes, lots of zoos."

"Good, good. Our ultimate goal is AZA accreditation."

"Sorry?"

"The Association of Zoos and Aquariums?" Jackson's welcoming grin held steady.

Milo's smile faltered and then resurged. "Oh, right. Well, not so much with AZA zoos, but after all they're only a few."

Jackson had not become the chair of a cutting-edge conservation effort by letting his reactions show. "Well, Pamela and Jessi can take you around, let you get the lay of the land and start planning. I look forward to hearing your thoughts."

A few minutes later, when Milo had excused himself to the restroom, Jackson turned on Freeman with a whisper of rage. "What did you bring us? Is he some second-rate animal show trainer who is going to get us into hot water? I thought you were going to bring in someone with a reputation that would help us, make it obvious we're doing the best we can do for these animals."

"Do you have any idea how hard it is to get someone here on zero notice?" snapped Freeman.

"What about that guy who trained the butterflies?"

"He's in Africa, retraining a thousand-year-old migration to avoid poachers. They spent years prepping their ten-day window, so he's not just going to drop it on a phone call. All the people with the credentials and reputations are booked, so we had to take the guy who could fly out the next day. But at least he's a trainer, which puts him ahead of anyone else in the room."

Jackson looked at Jessi. "What do you think?"

Jessi shrugged. "I think he's here, and we don't have a lot of options. Besides, he's going to try his best; this will make his reputation. First dragon trainer? He's going to bust everything for this."

Jackson nodded. "All right. Take him out and show him what he has to work with."

Chavah saw the Land Rover bouncing along the track toward the trail cams and observation points, and she ran to wave it down, her other hand supporting her camera backpack. "Hey! Mind giving me a lift out toward Window Rock area?"

"We can do that." Dr. Freeman gestured, and Chavah climbed in the back seat beside Dr. Kemuel, tucking her camera bag between her feet.

A stranger was in the front. He turned with a flash of teeth. "Hi, I'm Milo."

She shook his hand. "Chavah Abeles. I'm the photographer."

Her photos allowed for more detailed observation of dragon physiology and boosted their social media into enviable engagement rates, and the framed prints provided additional income. Spending days in the field taking photos of dragons was the kind of work that didn't have to pay well, and Chavah was an intern, having completed a previous internship at a more traditional aquarium but not yet leveled up to full conservation employment.

"Milo's here to help us with Kiba," Freeman said.

"Oh?"

"Jackson has said we'll try training, so Jessi doesn't have to dart anyone again."

Chavah's heart jumped. "Training?"

"What's wrong with darting?" Milo asked. "Seems pretty straightforward."

"It's not," Kemuel snapped.

"Shoot it with a needle, shoop!" He mimed using a long gun. "I guess you have to be a pretty good shot."

"Watch a lot of movies, do you?" Kemuel challenged.

Milo's grin wobbled.

"Most drugs cause disorientation before the animal finally goes down. I've seen animals freak out hard—I had a gazelle with a broken leg try to run on its stump, lower leg just flopping behind. You remember when that kid climbed in with the rhino last year and everyone was angry because staff didn't just dart the rhino? You want that kid to face ten or thirty minutes of panicky defensive rhino? That would have been a death sentence."

"I—"

"And sedatives work by suppressing the central nervous system, which is important for things like heartbeat and breathing. Dose too little, and the impaired animal runs away, maybe hurting itself, or maybe he runs to water before he drops and he drowns. Dose too much, and he drops dead."

"I didn't know," Milo said apologetically.

"And," Kemuel continued, looking as if she knew she should stop but not stopping, "there's the stress. Sedatives reduce exhibited stress—but all the physiological effects are there, and sometimes that can kill on its own. And all this is assuming you even started with the right drug. We've had fifty years to figure out you can't dose a rhinoceros like a buffalo, even though they're both African mammals of similar size. This is a whole new species with no data and crazy physiology we didn't even believe in ten years ago, and we don't know if we should be using haloperidol or carfentanyl, or how much, and experimenting on a population of a dozen known specimens is wildly irresponsible at best."

Milo raised his hands in surrender. Kemuel sat back against the jolting seat and crossed her arms, looking out the window. Chavah wanted to put a hand on her arm but didn't know if she should.

"But this species is in crisis," Freeman interjected, "and the animals we know about are under immense pressure, and there's not enough of a population to risk a completely hands-off approach. We let the last situation go, because we didn't want to risk chemical capture again, and the animal died."

"Ludwig's angina," Kemuel supplied, still looking outside. "Treatable, but we weren't treating. Probably died of either sepsis or asphyxiation when it swelled into the airway."

Milo tried to paste on his charming smile once more. "But then you had one to examine for science, yes?"

"It was on fire," Chavah offered, trying to shift the focus.

"We left the body for a day," Freeman said. "Dragons are a social species, not so tight as elephants but definitely social, and we wanted the others to be aware of the death so they wouldn't go searching or something. We don't know yet if they mourn like elephants or chimps or crows, but they did come by the remains. Then about twenty hours after death, best estimate, it spontaneously combusted."

"So I guess we know why there wasn't much in the fossil record," Chavah volunteered. No one laughed.

"Ooh, there's one!" Freeman slowed the car.

Chavah pulled her camera.

"Where?" Milo leaned forward, scanning, but clearly saw nothing.

Freeman pointed to a rocky jumble about seventy feet away, but it took even Chavah's practiced eyes a moment to pick out the dragon camouflaged against the boulders.

"I don't see it," Milo admitted.

Freeman tried to trace the dragon for him. "See that big boulder with the orange streak? Just below that is the hip. Go forward—left—and you'll see a shoulder. See the sweep of the wing?"

Chavah had her telephoto lens up. "It's Sombra."

"That's the youngest female," Freeman added. "See her now?"

But Sombra decided to help by stepping away from her concealing rocks. She moved gracefully, more like a cougar than a crocodile, to endless taxonomic debate. She was lithe, her head and neck possibly mistakable for a large serpent on their own, with just a fringe of horny frill to mar the impression. As she gave up her predatory concealment, she spread her wings wide to catch the sun, and her drab coloring vanished in the brilliant display of her under-wings. She was enormous, a man's height at the shoulder and with a wingspan of fifty feet.

Milo swore under his breath, and Chavah smiled. It didn't matter how many photos you saw, the actual animal was always stunning, and dragons were still hardly more than a myth to those who had seen them only online, just as before their discovery. She slid onto the Land Rover's door and began snapping rapid photos.

"That's the *female*?" gasped Milo.

Sombra swung her head toward them, her tail rising behind her.

"Not happy to see us," Chavah observed, still taking photos. "Might want to back off."

"We're not moving," Freeman said. "We're no threat. She'll be fine."

"Looks kind of rigid for fine," Chavah said.

Sombra made a sound like the purr of a twelve-hundred-pound cat, and Chavah noted the apparent flare of the horny fan as she arched her neck.

Kemuel said, "I think Chavah's right. Maybe we should back off a bit. We don't want her feeling defensive."

And then Sombra convulsed her torso, like a cat bringing up a hairball, and spat fire at them. The flames roared out about fifteen feet, much too short to be dangerous, but there was always an involuntary flinch and Chavah hunched toward the car. Milo yelped.

"Right," Freeman agreed, and she put the Land Rover in reverse.

Sombra watched them go, wings extended, and then lost interest as they moved away.

"Should have backed up sooner," Chavah said. "Now she knows her mild threat didn't work but an escalated threat did. She'll be more likely to throw fire the next time." Should she have said that? She tried to distract. "But I got some sweet shots out of it. Look at this one!"

She proffered the view screen with a close shot of the orange fire, licking and curling and dramatic, with Sombra's open mouth and eyes just visible at one side, all six-inch teeth and dark pupils. Kemuel nodded appreciatively. "That's fantastic."

Chavah tried to hand the camera up front, but Milo was still staring forward. "Tell me what equipment you have for the dragons."

"What?" Freeman asked.

"How do you tether them? Are there big and small cages? Do you use prods or bullhooks?"

Chavah caught her breath.

Freeman didn't like it either. "We don't have cages or bullhooks. We're a preserve."

"Oh, hell, no. You want me to just walk out to that in an open field? No tether, no hooks, no nothing? No way, man. You build me a proper facility to hold it, I'll get there, but with nothing? No way."

Freeman put the Land Rover in park and turned to him. "I bought you a day-of plane ticket because you said you were a trainer. You knew what you were coming to work with."

"I work with all kinds of animals, but on my terms! I have equipment to keep me safe! It works because they don't have a choice; you can't just hope it all works out."

"So that's it? You're quitting before you start?"

"If you're asking me to take an animal that threatens a car at seventy-five feet and hold it down for a root canal without any proper tools, hell yes I'm quitting."

Freeman's lips compressed, but she didn't speak. She just put the car in gear, spun it on the road, and headed back to the Quonset hut that served as their center.

Chavah cradled her camera as they jounced faster than usual. Kemuel asked her, "Anything new?"

"Not much. I do have new photos of Kiba's jaw. I'll send them when we get back to internet."

Freeman and Milo did not speak on the way home. They did not speak as they entered the hut. They did not speak as they entered Freeman's office and closed the door.

Chavah turned to Jessi. For a moment, her secret clogged her throat, climbing, wanting to escape—but she thought of facing the others, of losing this dream position, and she swallowed it down.

She forced a smile. "So, can I get a ride out again?"

Jessi slouched in her chair, ate her frozen dinner, and glared at her computer.

Onscreen, a cheetah pressed its neck against a chain link fence, chin upward, with all the space of its enclosure behind it. A man squatted opposite the cheetah, sliding a syringe through the fence and up into the animal's jugular, drawing out blood. "Gooooood," he praised in a long, low tone. "Look how relaxed you are. Super chill. Good girl." He finished the draw, pressed a cotton pad to the site, and gently scratched the throat. Then he clicked with his tongue and the cheetah pulled back, eyes bright as he picked up a bucket of meat cubes and began sliding them into the feeding chute.

In the next tab, a grizzly extended its massive paw through an opening so that a keeper could grind its nails. In the next, a shark floated on its side, rostrum lightly touching a small buoy on a stick while the trainer watched a vet examine an ugly contusion on its side. In the next, a sea lion inserted its head into a device so an ophthalmologist could check for retinal damage.

Two weeks. Jessi banged her head against the back of her chair. It was like knowing there was a road out of town, but having no gas and no map. It was *possible*, it was obviously possible. It just wasn't what she knew how to do.

With a savage, unsatisfying click of the mouse, she closed the videos. Her email inbox was next, topped by a message from Chavah with the new photos. Jessi doubted it would be enough to diagnose, but telephoto was better than anything else they had.

The first two were profile shots, showing clearly a swelling along the mouth and the irritation where Kiba had been rubbing it. Chavah had caught one with the mouth open, and Jessi zoomed in to try to see details of the tongue and gums. Nothing conclusive. Kiba had been photographed among trees, and the dappled light made it difficult to determine discoloration. Jessi sighed.

The next photo was in bright sun, Kiba's head resting on a rock. The photo was tight, the sunlit colors clear. The dragon's eyes were on the viewer; he'd been aware of Chavah photographing him at a distance.

It was possible to go from trees to rocks in a few dozen feet, or he could be traveling across the park. Activity was an important health indicator. Chavah hadn't included photo locations. But that was simple enough; Jessi clicked open the EXIF data on each image.

She copied the GPS coordinates of the first photo in the trees and pasted them into the reserve map. Then she copied the location of the rocky photo—and froze, leaving the data unpasted. There in the EXIF details was *Camera maker: Samsung. Focal length: 4mm.*

She switched back to the photo in the trees. *Camera maker: Pentax. Focal length: 400 mm.*

She looked at the rocky photo again. *Camera maker: Samsung. Focal length: 4mm.*

This photo had been taken with a cell phone. Up close. With the dragon looking directly at Chavah.

Jessi reached for her phone, started to text, decided to call instead. Chavah answered with her mouth full. "Hello?"

"I just got your photos of Kiba. They're really helpful."

"Oh, good! I was hoping you'd be able to tell—"

"We need to talk. Tonight."

There was a pause. "Is this bad?"

"I don't know."

Chavah was already sitting in the conference room. She'd pulled a chair out for Jessi on the opposite side of the table.

Jessi opened without preamble. "I saw the photos. They're good. But they're not all distance photos."

Her shoulders dropped. "How'd you know?"

"EXIF data."

She dropped her forehead into the heel of her hand. "Stupid mistake."

"You want to tell me why you were within touching distance of a dragon? A wild dragon? A wild dragon we believe is in pain?"

Chavah took a breath. "I was trying to decide whether to tell you. If I'd known Jackson had okayed a trainer… After we lost two dragons… Look, either we are totally hands-off or we take responsibility for them, we can't go back and forth, and this is a critically endangered species, and wouldn't it make more sense if we did everything we could to save them?"

"That's a lot of justification, no explanation."

"I started right after Freya died. That's another reason I didn't want to tell you; it would sound accusatory. But we obviously needed another way. And then when Gonzo died because we didn't want to risk treating him, I blamed myself, because I hadn't said anything. So I got more serious, put more time into it. And I knew if the board found out, I'd be gone, but they keep talking about eventually becoming an accredited facility, and so we've got to have some way to show we can care for these animals…"

"You're still justifying."

Chavah set her jaw. "I set up a training station, and I've been training the dragons, working toward cooperative care goals."

Jessi knew, but hearing it so plainly was still shocking. "What have you done so far?"

"Felix and Kiba will recall to a signal, will station, will present with a chin rest for brief tactile examination. Sombra will recall and station, nothing else yet. Kiba will target his rostrum to a paper plate." She smiled weakly. "I didn't have a lot in the way of gear."

Jessi was boggled. "What? You—translate all that."

"Three dragons will come to the training station when called. Felix and Kiba will prop their heads on the rock—that's how I took that photo—and let me touch them just for a second. And I can put Kiba's target in different places and he'll follow it to touch it."

Jessi needed a moment to find words. "I have been in this room just begging for some way to treat these dragons, and you…"

"Do you think the other three would have let me?"

"Not a chance," Jessi agreed. "But now we have a two week window and a head start, and I'm not giving either back. How close to killed have you been, and how many times?"

"Only once. Twice. The first time I tried touching Felix, he jumped and I jumped and that spooked him worse, and it took a long while for either of us to come back to station. But the big mistake was trying to touch Sombra. She flamed at me, and thank God the rock took the brunt of it and I just got singed."

Realization hit Jessi. "Window Rock. You're using Window Rock as a contact wall."

"Well, I wasn't going to just walk up to a dragon in the open and try to grab it, was I?"

Jessi grabbed a notepad. "What do you need to make this work? That I can have by tomorrow?"

Chavah's expression melted into relief. "Really? It would save a lot of time if I didn't have to catch and cut up my own rabbits."

Window Rock was a large slab of rock coming off one of the ridges with a water-worn hole approximately an arm's-length wide. The rocky outcropping itself was only a couple dozen feet wide. "You know," Jessi said, "any dragon could just walk around the end."

"Protected contact is not just to keep the trainer safe from the animal." Chavah opened her bag. "It's also to make the animal feel safe from the trainer—dragon gets unsure, she just pulls her head back, instant distance and barrier from the offending human. It helps the team trust each other. I got the idea to use Window Rock when I remembered a guy setting up a wall for some elephants in the middle of a field." Chavah drew out a red and white circle of hot-glued craft foam from her camera backpack and taped it to the rock. "Now we go to the other side and wait."

"What's that?"

"That's Felix's recall. He's probably the best, so I figured we'd start with him so you could see—"

"They have their own signs? Like, the bat-signal or something?"

Chavah grinned. "We don't want them all coming and fighting over the training station, right? They each have their own sign. Oh, look!"

Jessi followed her gaze and saw Sombra near the top of the slope. Her neck curved as she looked down, and then with an irritated snort she moved off over the ridge.

"Not her sign," Chavah said. "Now we wait for Felix to notice. It won't be too long; they probably heard us coming."

It was about fifteen minutes before Felix appeared. But he didn't approach the wall.

"Back off," Chavah told Jessi. "You're the variation here."

She moved back fifty feet, and after a moment the dragon descended to the rock wall. Chavah pressed the button on her training clicker and began praising as she reached into the cooler of chunked rabbit. "Look at you, what a fine dragon. Don't mind her, you just have an audience today. You ready to show off?"

Felix hesitated, looking between Chavah and Jessi. Jessi didn't know if it would be worse to remain where she was or move unexpectedly.

But even so—there was a dragon, standing ten feet in front of Chavah, eating chunks of rabbit off the ledge of the rock window, looking unsure but not flaming or mauling or devouring. It was amazing.

He dipped his head slightly, and Chavah clicked and then reached for a piece of rabbit. Felix ate it off the ledge, lifted his head to swallow, hesitated, dipped his head again. Chavah clicked and fed again. Their routine assured, Felix lowered his head to the ledge, touching his chin to the stone.

Jessi stopped breathing.

Chavah fed Felix, who swallowed and returned to the ledge each time. And then Chavah spoke, lifted her hand so the dragon could see, and slowly lowered it to touch the side of his snout. She clicked and fed.

For a moment Jessi could see not just the woman and dragon, but detailed examinations, questions settled, research, publications, conferences and lectures, books, all centering on this dragon's choice to place his head within reach of her grasp.

She took a step forward, and Felix jerked his head back. Chavah stayed still, confused, but Felix snorted and retreated, glancing back as he left the station.

Chavah turned and saw Jessi, who held up her hands in apology. "I'm sorry. It was only one step."

"That's enough." Chavah gestured. "But what do you think?"

Bloodwork. X-rays. Anatomy studies. Reproduction and conservation. "I think we're going to save dragons."

Jessi sighed. "I wish we didn't have to talk by radio."

The dragons were used to Chavah talking to them as she worked, and they didn't seem to care about Jessi's faint voice in a headset. If Jackson or the others had noticed Jessi and Chavah were more consistent with their radio checkouts, they hadn't said anything. But then, Jessi and Chavah didn't want to be noticed.

"I've been out here nearly every day for well over a year. I've been nothing but boring, until I opened the training station bar, and then that's been nothing but predictable and within their control. Other humans, not so much. They don't see you nearly so often, and when they do…"

"I was chasing Freya in a Jeep, and then she collapsed, and then she died." Jessi nodded. "No one is going to trust me for a while. But while you're a freakin' brilliant trainer, you aren't a vet."

"We're not going to get Kiba to let you handle his sore face in a week."

"We've got one and a half."

"The half is to teach him to work with treatment."

"Oh."

"Let me try again with the turkey baster. We can talk more on the next break."

Chavah had a bucket of blood and meat juices, a turkey baster, and rain pants that would never be the same. When Kiba approached the window this morning, she'd started with simple nose touches to the paper plate, and then she started delaying her click; as he waited with snout touching the plate, she brought up the turkey baster and squirted blood into his teeth, well away from his swelling.

The first time had startled him, but not badly, and after a moment he'd decided he liked the blood baster and had returned for another repetition. Chavah explained she hoped he would, in anticipation of the baster, start opening his mouth as he pressed his rostrum to the plate, allowing her to peer inside.

During the break Kiba might have considered how to speed the delivery of his treat, for this time as soon as Chavah raised the plate overhead he touched it and opened his mouth a few inches. Jessi thought her heart might stop, seeing those gaping jaws with hand-width teeth at the level of Chavah's face, but Chavah was so focused on trying to see through the teeth as she praised the dragon and brought up the baster that she seemed to forget to be afraid. "Good boy, that's a very good boy, I can almost see, not quite, but that's okay, you did your part, here you go!"

Jessi didn't speak, not wanting to distract her.

Chavah reset, took a breath, held up the paper plate. Kiba put his snout to it and opened his mouth a few inches. Chavah waited, and Jessi wanted to click her own tongue, wondered why she delayed. But after a second Kiba gave a little sniff and opened his mouth wider. "Yes! Good boy! Oh, that's so good, I'm gonna give you all the blood and here's some rabbit and oh my gosh I see it Jessi I see it!"

Chavah lay out chunked rabbit for the dragon, ended the session, and sprinted to the shady tree to join Jessi. "Right inside the teeth on the lower jaw there's something stuck in the gum, next to the tooth. Like wedged in the tooth-hole. All infected and nasty."

"That's a periodontal abscess," Jessi said. "That's fantastic. I mean, obviously not fantastic, but it's treatable, more treatable than a periapical abscess or cancer."

"We just have to get you into Kiba's mouth."

Jessi's stomach lurched. "I stopped breathing, seeing that mouth open in front of your face. I can't even imagine."

"Oh, man, you should see it. It's a heart-stopping view. I need a video camera mounted on—oh, that's it! That's how we'll do it!"

Chavah had practiced again and again, giving so many saline injections to a pair of peaches that they were likely more salt than fruit now. She'd made a target stick that would stand on its own and practiced mouth clicks, freeing up her hands so she could treat medically with one and treat with blood with the other. She had accustomed Kiba to nitrile gloves and built up to a full forty seconds of open mouth while she basted his tongue with blood, edged her hand hesitantly into his mouth, and spritzed his tongue and gums with a misting bottle full of more blood.

Twice Kiba had decided he'd had enough, and she'd stood absolutely still as he huffed backward. But without any constraint to panic against, he'd stood a moment, considering, and then come back to the station. She'd taken it very slowly, and he'd not recoiled again, and then she'd gone home to practice sticking her peach a few dozen times more.

It was absolutely not what was standard. What they should have was a padded metal frame for Kiba to grip on cue, with a gap for her hand. What they should have had was a proper wall. What they should have had was more time so that they didn't have to risk so much; if this went wrong, Kiba wouldn't volunteer for training again, even if Chavah was still around to train.

If this worked, she would be ashamed to describe it to anyone who knew better.

All the great scientists experimented on themselves, Chavah told herself. *Salk, Bier, Jekyll. It just shows confidence in your work.*

"Are we ready?" Jessi asked. "And by that I mean, are you ready?"

"I don't know, but I'll never be more ready, so I guess this is it."

They checked radios and cameras, she hung Kiba's sign and drew on her gloves, and Jessi retreated to her distant tree.

Kiba arrived in a display of bright wings, pausing to rub uselessly at his mouth. The skin was wearing under repeated chafing, but that was only a symptom, they knew now. If she could clear the abscess, he'd stop rubbing, and his jaw would heal on its own.

She set up the target. "Okay, boy, let's do this."

Kiba approached and placed his nose directly on the paper plate. She made it worth his while, with plentiful squirts of blood. She looked through her safety glasses with the mounted camera. "Okay, I'm going in," she said in a sing-song voice that sounded like praise. "First to numb the surface."

She switched from the turkey baster to the misting bottle, today spraying both blood and lidocaine. "You're a good boy, Kiba," she said, clicking and setting chunks of rabbit on the ledge. "And now we count down two minutes."

"Three minutes," Jessi said in her ear. "Let's be really sure he's numb."

Chavah tossed rabbit through the window, letting Kiba kill some time browsing for it, returning, browsing for another.

"Okay, phase two," Jessi prompted.

Phase two scared her. "Phase two," she repeated.

She replaced the high target, waited for Kiba to open his mouth, basted him once for luck, and then slid the first long syringe into the base of the inflamed mound. Did he flinch? Or was that her?

"Don't forget to treat him!"

She fumbled for the baster and squeezed several rounds of blood in. Kiba pulled back to swallow. Chavah's heart was pounding, and she tried to take slow breaths; her agitation would only agitate the dragon.

"All good?"

"All good," she tried to say, and she realized her mouth was dry. She hadn't been praising Kiba, either; no wonder he was standing a few paces away, giving her side-eye. She licked her lips. "Halfway there, boy. Sort of. If we're counting generously. Come on, we've got more targets here."

Kiba came back, looked dubiously at her, touched the target, opened his mouth. She basted blood. Basted more blood. Basted more blood.

"You going to do this?"

"Right." She reached one hand over the enormous teeth to the object protruding from the gum—a bone shard, she could see now. She braced her thumb against it and tried to slide it, but it did not move.

"If it could wiggle out, it wouldn't be stuck in a mass of infection," Jessi observed.

Chavah nodded before remembering it would bounce Jessi's vision and basted more blood onto Kiba's tongue. She was going to drown him in her procrastination.

She drew the scalpel from its clean sheath on her belt, sucked her breath, and cut into the reddened flesh alongside the bone shard. Kiba did not move. Chavah slit the abscess and forced herself to speak to the dragon. "Oh, you good boy, I'm doing it, dear God, oh this feels hideous, good boy."

She threw the scalpel behind her, seized the bone, and drew it free with a sucking noise. Blood and pus began to ooze.

"Nice work. How's the patient?"

Kiba had noticed something, but he seemed more perplexed than pained. It might be due as much to her worry as to any sensations coming through. "We're taking a short break." She ended the target, set rabbit on the ledge.

"You're on a countdown with that lidocaine. You do *not* want him to start feeling it when you push on that."

"I know." She took a few breaths and pretended her pulse slowed. "Okay, next step, let's go."

In some ways, the sheer size of his jaws—once she stopped imagining them snapping her in half—was an advantage. Kiba could taste the blood for his targeting behavior on the feeling half of his mouth, and he could swallow with little risk of choking from impairment. On the numbed side, she could use her whole hand to squeeze the abscess from the base upward, letting warm pus gush over her gloved hand.

"Get that last bit—right there, in the back," Jessi said in her ear. "That's good enough. Almost done. Got your next syringe?"

After pressing the abscess, another injection no longer felt a challenge. Chavah squirted blood into Kiba's mouth, shot him with a mega-dose of antibiotics, pulled back. "Good boy, Kiba, almost done. Hold on, boy. Have some rabbit."

The last part was the trickiest, or at least the squickiest. They had opened the blister pack ahead of time, and now she removed the cotton towels weighting it so she could reach the row of tiny chips.

"Last time, Kiba. Let's do this."

He opened his mouth, and she treated with blood. Then she took a pair of forceps and, glancing down, picked up the first chip.

"Curved side down," Jessi reminded her.

"I know. Good boy." She placed the slow-release chip against the affected tooth and slid it down into the periodontal pocket. Then the second. Then the third.

They were guessing as to the antibiotics doses, of course. They didn't know how this species handled drugs. She had been prepared to abort if Kiba had seemed unaffected by the lidocaine.

"Done." She squirted more blood into his mouth and pulled back, then clicked and removed the target stand. She laid out chunked rabbit, and then, as Kiba finished it, upended the cooler through the window. "Here you go, boy, you earned it."

Her legs felt weak, and she suddenly wanted to reach Jessi before she collapsed with the adrenaline crash. She pulled the gloves from her shaking hands, dropped them beside the abandoned scalpel and syringes, and staggered toward the trees. Behind her Kiba hooted, a sound she didn't remember hearing before.

Jessi ran to meet her, caught her under the elbows, hugged her. "You were fantastic. Great work. All those injections, just like a peach."

"Like a peach."

"But I didn't get the video, so you have to do it again."

She blinked. "What? No!"

Jessi laughed, and Chavah tried weakly to punch her arm, but her fingers felt numb as if the lidocaine had worked on them. It hadn't, it was just the rush of stress and success.

"Sit down," Jessi said. "I'll clean up. Then we've got a report to prepare."

"You all remember I said I would pursue the training angle on Kiba, after our other trainer didn't work out," Jessi began. "Then Chavah brought some new photos of Kiba's condition, and those really jump-started our process." She gestured to Chavah. "Video, please?"

They played it cold, no preamble. They'd intercut the footage from Chavah's POV camera with wide shots from two tripods. In the back, Chavah grinned stupidly wide all the way through.

Jackson stared open-mouthed. Lackland repeated a single quiet profanity again and again.

"Is this real?" Freeman managed finally. "It's not—this isn't some CGI joke. You really did this?"

"It's all real," Jessi assured her, "taken yesterday, and from this morning's observations, Kiba is doing fine so far. Chavah gets all the credit; all I did was talk her through the procedure."

"All you did was contribute years of veterinary education and experience," Chavah put in. "Hardly a thing."

The video ended with a final image of Kiba stretching through the rock window to look after Chavah.

"Why didn't you tell us you were making progress?" Jackson said. "Surely you didn't accomplish this in a day or two. We could have gotten a report?"

"We didn't want the pressure," Chavah said. "I mean, we felt enough pressure already. We wanted to be able to stop if necessary and—let's be honest, I'm an intern and I wasn't supposed to be training a dragon."

"Well." Jackson leaned back. "I thought I was going to have today's big announcement, but that will teach me humility."

"What's your news?" Lackland asked.

"The Kumano Foundation is awarding us the grant."

Freeman sat forward eagerly. "Really? That's fantastic!"

Jackson broke into a wide grin. "So a proper protected contact wall should be first on the new budget?"

Jessi looked back at the rock window framing Kiba's head and extended neck. There would always be a special significance to the stone wall, though. That shot was a fantastic image; it would be a good choice for the cover of their new dragon veterinary manual.

Laura VanArendonk Baugh writes fantasy of many flavors and non-fiction. She lives in Indiana and enjoys Dobermans, travel, chocolate, and making her imaginary friends fight one another for imaginary reasons. Find her award-winning work at www.LauraVAB.com.

MEGAN ENGELHARDT

SERPENT IN PARADISE

"Heavens, Harris! What a mess!"

I am a woman usually possessed of a level disposition but I turned a snarl on Zinnia. "A mess indeed! And who do you think made that mess? That fluffy beast of yours!"

Zinnia frowned.

"Strawberry?"

The cat in question poked its head around Zinnia's ankles and mewed at me.

"Yes, that—that monster has—look!" I gathered a small handful of paper and shoved it at Zinnia. Our previous case had generated an extensive paper trail. Compiling and organizing it all had taken weeks and now most of my work lay in shreds on the floor.

Zinnia picked up Strawberry and brushed its head. The cat favored me with another smug mew.

"I'm sure she didn't mean it," Zinnia began.

"I am sure it did!" I interrupted. "Really, Zinnia, I have put up with quite enough from that thing. First it trips me in the hall, then it attacks me in the middle of the night, and now this!"

"You two have gotten off on the wrong foot, it seems," Zinnia said. She set the cat on the floor and placed a soothing hand on my arm. "Don't take it personally, Harris, darling."

A look at the thing told me that these incidents were, in fact, personal.

"I wish Lord Brockton had not given it to you," I complained. "I understand that he is wooing you but why could he have not given you another gown or set of jewels instead of this hellspawn creature?"

"James knows I like animals."

My response was not polite.

Zinnia looked from me to the ruined pile of papers and tilted her head thoughtfully.

"You could use a rest," she said. "Let's have a retreat."

"There is so much to do—" I began.

"Nonsense. A bit of work from both of us will set your pile aright, and I have already finished the report for the Society. After our presentation to Her Undying Majesty's council we will have plenty of time for a retreat, I promise." Zinnia came behind the desk and took my hands. "Darling Harris, please say you'll come!"

I was able to delay my answer while Whist, Zinnia's butler and my sometime nemesis, entered with the tea tray. He surreptitiously kicked at the cat as he passed. We had our differences, but Whist and I were united in our hatred of Zinnia's newest acquisition.

"Your tea, miss," he said, offering Zinnia the tray.

Zinnia fixed my cup and handed it to me. It was a bribe, an obvious attempt to soften me up, but I am not one to refuse a cup of the genial beverage when it is offered.

The tea did its work, as did the sight of Whist removing the cat from the room at Zinnia's request. I settled back into my armchair and let the distant yowls and curses thaw my disposition.

"Very well," I said when my cup was empty, "I am mollified. Slightly."

Zinnia flopped into her own chair.

"Thank goodness! I don't like when you are cross with me, Harris, darling."

"You promised me a retreat," I reminded her.

"I did, and I will keep that promise. We shall go to Unukalhai."

"Where?"

"Unukalhai. The resort is brand new, frightfully luxurious, and it just so happens that James is the owner. He's been trying to get me there for months. I do feel I've earned a bit of a break from work, as well."

This I could not deny. Zinnia was an heiress, comfortably well off and a feature of the city's most prestigious social circles, but she was also a scientist with a sharp mind and an insatiable curiosity. Together we searched out strange, unique beasts all over the world and brought back what evidence we could. I have heard us referred to as "lady monster hunters," but that is not precisely accurate. Technically only Zinnia is a Lady; I have no such title. Also, we do not hunt—we do not injure or kill unless our lives are in immediate danger—and besides, Zinnia would never classify our quarry as "monsters." She adored every creature, great and small, beautiful and hideous, safe and deadly. She even liked Strawberry.

"What is Unukalhai like?" I asked, nearly persuaded.

"James says it's wonderful, secluded but with every amenity. There are hot springs, too."

I grimaced.

"Is there anything interesting to do?"

"I expect there will be a library somewhere. And if nothing else you can go wandering around the island and look for trouble."

"I never look for trouble!" I protested.

Zinnia sipped her tea, a wicked grin on her pretty face.

"No, but it seems to find you nevertheless."

As we stepped off the boat at Unukalhai I found myself entranced by the starkness of the beach, the plain marble statues that were artfully hidden among the scrub, and the looming resort in the distance. It was a cold beauty. I could appreciate that.

Resort staff waited for us at the end of the gangway. Young and attractive, they were the sort of people I would expect to meet at leisure in the City. According to James—Lord Brockton—who met us at the ship, these

Adoni and Dianas used their time at the resort serving as escorts and companions for the guests, making social connections that would serve them well later in life.

James begged off showing us around, citing a previous engagement, but motioned over a young lady.

"Helen," he said, putting a hand on her arm, "please show these ladies the resort. Take good care of them, now. I'm counting on you."

She flushed.

"Of course, J—of course, Lord Brockton."

I watched her watching him go and shared a glance with Zinnia.

"How wonderful to meet you, Lady Carmichael," Helen said, turning back, her smile matching Zinnia's in sharp politeness. "And…" She paused, waiting for someone to explain me. Zinnia came to her rescue.

"This is Miss Amaya Harris, my companion."

"Of course." The Diana dismissed me as unimportant and turned back to Zinnia. "My Lady, if you'll follow me, I will show you to your rooms."

We took the scenic route to our rooms. Helen led us all around the resort, talking incessantly about tennis courts and pools, breakfast on the veranda, romantic secluded gardens, and the large stretch of beach that was roped off for the resort's use. "To keep swimmers safe," Helen chirruped. "There can be some dangerous tides around the island."

I was relieved when we reached our appointed rooms and Helen left us to refresh ourselves. We let Strawberry out of the luggage and it prowled around the suite Zinnia and I shared. Large glass doors opened onto a sizable balcony. The hotel stood on top of a rise, keeping watch in a rather matronly way. Constant as time, its sound all around us, the ocean crashed and clashed against the shore. It seemed a splendid place.

"What a splendid place," Lord Tremare said. "Really, everything is just splendid." I sighed: he had repeated the sentiment three times and we were only on the second course.

We had been on the island for four days and had dined the previous nights in James's private quarters. Finally Zinnia put her foot down and demanded to mingle with the other guests. The company at table that night was Lord Tremare, Miss Holsopple, Mr. Bentley, and the three in our party. Lord Tremare was standard issue aristocracy, fully enjoying his late middle age and considerable wealth. I found him pleasantly dull.

"Have you been to the springs yet?" asked Zinnia in a valiant attempt to spark some conversation.

"I have been," ventured Miss Agneta Holsopple. "It was to ease my ailments but alas, I fear the miracle waters, like so many other miracle cures, will avail me not."

Miss Holsopple, wan and thin and the sort of woman who favored styles and colors that made her more so, had many ailments. It seemed she could speak about nothing else.

"Have you sampled the springs yet, Mr. Bentley?" I asked, turning to him politely.

Mr. Bentley did not provide an answer. Hunched over his plate, a vulture in shabby evening dress, he ate steadily. I recognized the determined pace of someone who did not always have regular meals.

"I tried the springs," Lord Tremare said. "Didn't care for it. Too blame warm."

"They are hot springs, sir," James pointed out. "They are meant to be warm."

"Full of minerals, I expect," said Lord Tremare. "Healthy stuff. Nature's bounty and all that. Still, too warm for me."

"It's dragons," said Miss Holsopple. Fluttery little hands clasped and unclasped at the hollow of her neck where rested, I now noticed, a dragon-shaped pendant. Her eyes glowed with a fanatic's light—easily recognized, for had I not seen it often enough in Zinnia's face?

"I beg your pardon, Miss Holsopple?" James asked.

"Dragons! I have heard that the springs are heated by the breath of a dragon that lives beneath this island. The spring flows past its lair and it heats the water with its fiery breath."

"What, out of the kindness of its heart?" I asked.

"Harris," Zinnia remonstrated. But Miss Holsopple shook her head.

"Oh, no. The dragon is not *kind*. But the rumors say it is somehow kept away from the island so we are perfectly safe. That's for the best, of course, but I would dearly like to see the dragon." She lowered her voice as if we were all willing conspirators instead of awkward dinner companions. "My spiritualist, Madame Zoloya, says I have traces of dragon blood in me."

I once had a cousin who was fully convinced that he was a foundling, a fairy switched at birth with a human child. Whenever he spoke of it I had to leave the room for fear of breaking into violence. I felt the same urge now.

"The notion of dragon-blooded humans," I managed through gritted teeth, "is a bit far-fetched."

"A bit?" Lord Tremare chortled. "Young lady, everyone knows there are no such things as dragons."

Zinnia allowed a faint smug look onto her face. We knew no such thing—in light of what we'd seen we would be fools not to think otherwise—but we did not feel it proper to enter this knowledge into the discussion. Mr. Bentley apparently felt otherwise.

"Lady Carmichael and Miss Harris might disagree," he said, looking up from his meal for the first time.

James bristled.

"I beg your pardon! Lady Carmichael is a highly rational thinker and—"

Zinnia laid her hand on James's arm to quiet him and smiled at Mr. Bentley.

"I will not say you're wrong, Mr. Bentley. I am curious what would lead you to think that of us, though?"

Bentley put down his fork and reached into his pocket. He handed a card to Zinnia, who read it aloud.

"Thornton Bentley, *Scientific Inquiry Quarterly*? I'm afraid I'm not familiar with that publication."

That was a lie. Whist had standing orders to procure a copy of each new edition from the newsstand around the corner. Much of it was bunk, but there were occasionally small pieces of interest and someone had taken to writing up brief reports on our expeditions. Bentley's smirk suggested the identity of the anonymous author.

"I've been following your career, Lady Carmichael," Bentley said, confirming my suspicion. "I'm pleased to be on the scene now just in case something exciting happens."

"Nothing exciting will happen, I assure you," Zinnia said.

Bentley cocked an eyebrow at Miss Holsopple, who was following the exchange with wide eyes.

"Care to give a statement about these dragons, Lady Carmichael?" he asked.

"I know of the existence of no dragons," said Zinnia, "nor did I hear anything about their possibility until tonight. I am here on a strictly social engagement."

"Don't encourage him," Lord Tremare said. "Men like that are to be ignored."

As we stood to take our leave after dinner James suggested that he and Zinnia take a walk in the gardens. Zinnia declined, explaining that I was overtired.

"Kindly keep me out of your wooing in the future," I hissed after we parted ways.

"But you are such a perfect excuse, Harris, darling!"

As always, she laughed away my glare. She knew I did not really mean it.

Once in our rooms Zinnia kicked off her shoes, undid a few of her hairpins, and sighed contentedly. She picked up Strawberry and accepted the cat's perfunctory tongue bath. "What did you think of Mr. Bentley? Rather bold of him to call us out like that. I liked him."

"The others certainly didn't. 'Men like that,'" I said, imitating Lord Tremare. Zinnia laughed.

"Yes, exactly. Men like *that*. You know, I rather think I prefer *that*." She petted Strawberry thoughtfully as we made our way out onto the balcony.

We do not often get the chance to just sit and enjoy an evening, chatting together for some time. And when we ran out of words it was pleasant to sit in the dark and listen to the faint music from the ballroom, the steady crash of the waves, the distant scream and large splash.

Strawberry darted to the edge of the balcony and hissed at the night. Her back arched, her ears drew back and her tail went as bristly as a pine.

We leapt up and leaned over the balcony, straining to see the shore.

"Perhaps it was just an enthusiastic merry maker," I said.

"Perhaps." Zinnia looked unconvinced.

We listened a bit longer but there were no more suspicious noises. The stillness returned. Strawberry reverted to her supine repose.

"I believe I shall retire, Harris, and leave those merry makers to their merry," Zinnia said after a time. "Will you stay out?"

"A little longer. I find the evening air refreshing. Take the cat," I said, and settled back into my chair.

Two mornings later, Zinnia woke me with a cup of tea and the day's gossip.

"You'll never guess what's happened," she said, handing me the cup and dropping onto the bed beside me.

"James proposed?" I asked.

"No, silly. There's been a disappearance!"

"Here? Anyone we know?"

I was hoping it was Strawberry.

"It was Helen, that young lady who talked us around the resort the first day. She went for a walk the other night and was never heard from again."

"Or at least by this morning."

Zinnia made a face and went on.

"They've scoured the whole island. They're getting up a search party to do it again, but it is not a large area, you know, so I expect if they didn't find her then, they won't find her now."

I sighed.

"I suppose you want to be part of the search party?"

"Certainly not! It wouldn't be appropriate. Imagine if we found the body!"

"But—"

"Besides, we have another appointment."

"We do?"

Zinnia nodded.

"We are meeting James in his office on the hour. Remember the splash and scream we heard?"

"Yes—do you think it was Helen?"

"Perhaps. It's our duty to share any information that might be pertinent, isn't it?"

I studied Zinnia. Her color was up and her eyes shone.

"A woman is missing," I said. "Try to contain your glee."

"Oh, very well. I will strive to be appropriately dour." She flounced off the bed and threw open the wardrobe. "Hurry up, Harris. We're going to be late."

James seemed preoccupied when his secretary showed us into the office.

"I am quite busy, Zinnia. You think you have information about this missing girl?" he asked by way of welcome.

Seeing that he was not going to offer us tea or even seats, Zinnia took the courtesy of hostessing onto herself.

"It is a pleasure to see you this morning, Lord Brockton," she said sweetly. "No need to stand, Harris, do take a seat. Lord Brockton, would you care for a cup of tea?"

She moved to the tray and began to pour three cups.

"Yes, thank you," James said automatically. "Zinnia—"

"Lady Carmichael, please. Now, here is your tea, Harris, and I'm afraid I have forgotten how you take yours, Lord Brockton."

This was a society insult that made James flush.

"One sugar and cream, please. Zinnia, I—"

"Lady Carmichael, please. There you are, then. Now, we're all comfortable? Excellent. Lord Brockton, I must tell you, your resort is delightful."

"Uh, thank you. Lady Carmichael, I apologize—"

"It is a shame about that poor girl, though. Missing, I believe? What a tragedy! How can they be sure she hasn't just ensconced herself in the library or taken a boat excursion?"

"Helen gets seasick," James said, giving in to Zinnia's implacable command over the conversation. "Her roommate Mary was with her until late that night. Mary retired around eleven. Helen indicated that she was going to take a walk and then retire herself. There is no evidence that her bed was slept in, and we have already searched the island once with no results."

"Poor girl." Zinnia sipped her tea. "I can't say I blame her for wishing to enjoy the evening. It was lovely that night. Harris and I took the air on our balcony. It was a beautiful, unspoiled evening. Well, until the scream."

James looked as if he wanted to say something but wisely kept his mouth shut. Zinnia was in no mood for interruptions.

"Yes, it was a girl's scream, wouldn't you say, Harris? And it was followed by a rather large splash. Of course we were concerned but as there seemed to be revelers on the beach and no further disturbance we assumed there was no trouble and went in to bed. Well, there was no reason to assume there would be trouble, was there, Lord Brockton? Unukalhai is supposed to be safe."

"Yes," James said "It is. But of course, accidents do happen."

"Well, we can but pray she is found unharmed," said Zinnia. "Lord Brockton, have any dragons been seen around Unukalhai?"

James choked on his tea.

"Dragons? No," he said when he had apologized and set down his cup.

"I see. Thank you for your hospitality, Lord Brockton."

Zinnia does a very good flounce when she has a mind to. I just stalk.

We left James behind in his office and entered the promenade that ringed the top floor of the main building. Zinnia's face was flushed and while her expression remained pleasantly neutral, a familiar exultation illuminated her eyes. She leaned against the rail and stared blankly at the couples meandering past us.

"There is something happening here," she said. "James is lying about something. What do you think, Harris?"

"I think we haven't been here long enough to know anything about anything. We arrived only a few days ago. That does not make us experts on the oddness of the place. James is your paramour, but that does not necessarily make you an expert on his truthfulness."

"He is hardly my paramour. But I have spent enough time with him that I can tell when he is lying."

"You have not been exactly truthful with each other, it seems," I pointed out. "As pertains to the nature of your relationship, for example."

Zinnia gave me a look.

"Harris, darling, you know I don't often bring up the difference in our stations. To me we are perfectly equal—if anything, you are a better person than me, pedigree or not. But in this matter I'm afraid you lack familiarity with the way things are done by men like that. It may not seem like it but James and I have an understanding. We know that our relationship is just a game, just something to pass the time. Neither of us expects it to result in a permanent arrangement. That is just how things work among people like us."

"She's right—the rich and titled do things their own way, and that way can make no sense to low folk like us."

Mr. Bentley, perched on a bench opposite the door to James's office, grinned up at us and doffed his hat but did not stand.

"Insufferably rude, I know," he said. "But you were speaking rather loudly and your conversation was so interesting."

"What are you doing here?" I asked.

"Waiting to see Lord Brockton. He does not seem too eager to see me, though. I've been kept out here all morning. I was just about to head to lunch. Join me, Miss Harris?"

"Thank you but no."

"Just like that? I'm hurt."

"You expected a different answer, given your profession?" Zinnia asked.

"Not really," Bentley said, shrugging. "But I thought it worth a try."

"And your boldness will be rewarded," Zinnia said. "Would you accompany us both to lunch?"

Bentley looked genuinely surprised.

"That's an offer I can't refuse. And one that makes me wonder why it was extended."

"You seem like a useful man to know," said Zinnia.

"Even given my profession?"

"Especially given your profession."

Bentley proved to be a pleasant luncheon companion. He refrained from asking any prying questions and answered all of ours frankly. He was, as we suspected, the author of all those articles detailing our expeditions. Once he had written for a more respectable publication, but some bit of unpleasantness had knocked him down the rungs until he landed at the *Scientific Inquiry Quarterly*. He did follow our movements carefully but coming to Unukalhai had not been his idea.

"I need money," Bentley said matter-of-factly, dabbing at his mouth with a napkin that probably cost more than his suit. "Unsurprisingly, writing for a small publication does not pay very well. I accepted an offer from a disreputable publisher to come here and see what I could see. They paid my way in exchange for a series of articles."

"About what?" I asked.

"Scandal," Zinnia said flatly.

"You could put it that way." Bentley saw our faces and put down his fork. "I know it isn't the most respectable avenue of income, but I'm pretty down on my luck. I had no choice."

"There is always a choice," Zinnia said.

He shrugged.

"That's an easy moral when you aren't worried about where the next meal's coming from. But not all of us inherited a fortune. Am I right, Miss Harris?"

I kept my mouth shut. I had seen hard times, too, before falling in with Zinnia, and if the only thing Bentley was forced to do in the lean days was become a gossip monger well, then, he could count himself lucky, indeed.

"I see," Zinnia said, keeping a cool tone. But I could tell she had softened toward Mr. Bentley. "Have another biscuit. So what muck have you raked up?"

"Nothing much yet. I'm just keeping my eyes open." He winked. "You ladies haven't heard of anything exciting, have you?"

"Well, there's the disappearing girl," I said.

"And Miss Holsopple's dragons," said Zinnia.

Bentley dismissed the second idea.

"That's not muck, that's dreams and cotton wisp," he said. "Some charlatan planted the idea in her head and now she sees the beasts everywhere."

"And Helen?"

"Is that the girl? That has some promise. Perhaps she was running away with her married, titled lover, or some such nonsense. Lord Brockton's the one with the information there, I expect, which is why I've been trying to get in to see him. No luck, though."

"And if it turns out to be nothing? Would your readers be interested in a simple disappearance?" Zinnia asked.

"Ah, well," he said, shrugging. "Maybe not. But I'm a reporter, remember. I'm drawn to follow a story even if my only audience is myself."

We parted amiably, with mutual agreement to inform the other of anything odd that came to our attention.

"Of course we won't," Zinnia said once we were back in our rooms. "But it may be a good idea to keep Mr. Bentley agreeable. We can always use another source of information. Now, Harris, I believe we should split up and investigate this girl's disappearance further. Would you like the hot springs or the beach?"

I chose the beach. I know my strengths and weaknesses, and people skills are among the latter. Investigating at the hot springs meant talking, asking questions without offending or accusing, teasing out bits of information. Investigating at the beach involved walking around and looking down.

Strawberry accompanied me in a tightly latched picnic basket. Zinnia had requested that I take the cat with me so it could enjoy some fresh air. The basket was not so tightly woven: undoubtedly enough air was getting in to fulfill my obligation. The scratches all along my forearms and hands made me disinclined to check and make sure.

"Miss Harris! Miss Harris, wait!"

Thornton Bentley jogged up and gave the briefest of nods in greeting.

"Out for a picnic, then?" he asked, indicating the basket hopefully.

"This is a cat," I informed him. "If you are hungry, I suggest the dining room."

"They don't reopen for another few hours," he said. "Oh well. Why do you have a cat in a basket?"

"I am exercising it."

"Cats need to be exercised?"

"Apparently. Good day, Mr. Bentley." I began to walk away.

"Hold up! I'll come with." He caught up and matched my pace, hands in his pockets, kicking at the surf, whistling a jaunty tune.

I shoved the basket at him.

"Carry this," I said, "and no whistling."

When not being aggressively annoying, Mr. Bentley was a pleasant companion and an interesting conversationalist. We walked together until we reached the heavy rope that marked one end of the beach. Large signs warned beachgoers that various dangers lay ahead, none of which the management of Unukalhai was responsible for.

"Shall we turn back?" Bentley asked.

"I often find, when barriers are in place, that the most interesting things are on the other side," I replied, and slipped beneath the rope.

"Miss Harris," Bentley said, "I think we shall be fast friends."

A mile from the rope the shoreline took a sharp turn and was hidden from sight. On rounding the turn I faced a strange vision.

At first glance in the dying sunset light it appeared that victims of a terrible shipwreck had been washed ashore—crumpled, vaguely human-like figures that made my heart clench. Even as we approached I could tell that my initial impression had been incorrect. It was with immeasurable relief that I kicked the bundle apart to reveal a black evening dress and a pair of stockings, sodden, ragged, and thankfully unoccupied.

"Doing laundry on the beach?" Bentley wondered, turning away to look for the culprit.

He did not have to look far. Some little ways down the beach, an old man worked at another bundle.

"Good afternoon, Mr...?" I said as Bentley and I approached.

"Natterly," the man grunted, still working away.

"I see you are..." It was impossible to finish the statement, for I did not, in fact, see what he was doing. Mr. Natterly took a small length of thin wood or reed from the cart next to him and attached it to a structure that rested on the ground. Next he wrapped a piece of old cloth around the structure, like one creating a papier-mâché mask. Another piece of wood, another strip of cloth—he completed a few iterations before I asked "I'm sorry, what are you doing?"

"Makin' un scrarecraw, aye?" he replied, accent thick enough that I had to squint to make out what he'd said. He was a real old salt, skin creased by the waves and hands knotted as the netting he draped over the structure.

Something tugged at my mind as I watched him work.

"There are no crops here," I pointed out. "And no birds in the sky to scare. And that doesn't look much like a man, at any rate, though I know there is often some stylistic license in the matter of scarecrows."

Natterly kept working, wood and cloth and wood and cloth.

"'s kets," he said.

"Kets?" Bentley asked.

"The scrarecrawn's no men. 's kets." He pointed to the basket, where Strawberry had begun to meow quite piteously. "Ket, aye?"

"Oh! I see. They're supposed to be cats! Well, I can't say they look much like cats, either."

The form taking shape in front of the old man had something vaguely catlike about it, now that I knew what to look for, but the other completed—I assumed—shapes on the beach looked nothing like cats, unless they were felines more nightmarish than Strawberry. Some were even beginning to fall apart, cloth coming slowly away to reveal the hollow frame.

There was that thought again, worming at my mind. Something about the cloth...

"You from t'springs house?" the old man asked. Assuming he meant the resort, I answered in the affirmative. "Naw sposed t' be here. Dangerous for 'en, off the springs house land."

"I can take care of myself, thank you," I replied. He had spoken more informatively than threateningly so I did not fear him. I was curious what he meant, though.

"Probab should no tell ye," he said when I asked, "but sunnone from up there should ken wat happens ere whilst dances 'n feasts opp 'igh."

The gist of his story, as best I could understand it, was that an ancient danger lurked in the waters off the island. To keep it away, large stone cat statues had been erected centuries ago. Lord Brockton and his people had destroyed the statues when they built the resort. Natterly, supposedly the only one who knew or cared about this danger, was making the scarecrows to ward off the danger, but it wasn't working.

"Come 'ere year 'n' year 'n' year, my mam did," he said. "Mam 'n' 'er mam and all back, come over to the island ev'ry week o' the warm months to decorate the scrarecrawn. They had the knowing. No girlchillen for her, so my mam told my wife how 'tis done, but both died o' the sweat fever twenty year now. Didn't think none o' it when naught was here, but now with the spring house and rich folk and dying, I's recalled o' my duty and here tis I, do what I can."

"People dying?"

"Oh aye, they no tellin' oop at the spring house? That girl just t'other night, a handful 'fore her, and some men came to death when the spring house were built."

"Was it the danger in the water?" Bentley asked. "What is the danger?"

"'s a serpent," the old man said, "all long and scales that lurks in the dark caves in the water. Sleeps 'o the day, but aught on the beach alone at night, well. Sneak oop to snatch 'em in the dark. Only twa things beast don't like: kets and fire."

From her basket Strawberry hissed. My mind finally worked free the thought that had been tickling it, the grit of a notion coalescing into a brilliant pearl of terrible realization.

Natterly made his scarecrow cats from strips of clothing, piled in his cart already torn. But the first pile I encountered on the beach had been a dress and stockings, whole and untorn.

"Helen," I said, beginning to turn back to where I had seen the clothes. Strawberry hissed again, scrabbling frantically at the basket.

There was the sound of rushing water. I may have screamed. I certainly ran, up the dunes, inland, as fast as I could.

Bentley and Natterly followed, but they were not fast enough.

At Bentley's yell I skidded to a halt and turned to see a huge head swing down, huge jaws thudding into the sand next to the old man. He scrambled away, heading up the beach toward me. But Bentley—

The creature's head was flat with a jaw that unhinged. Around its head were a number of tentacles. One of these wiggling appendages had caught Bentley and had him trapped within its coils.

Even as I ran back down the beach I was thinking through my options. I have been in many rough situations while adventuring with Zinnia and as such always carry a knife on my person. Unfortunately the one I bore at the moment was small—what Zinnia laughingly called my "evening knife"—and would not do much damage to the creature. But I drew it anyway, reasoning that some damage was better than nothing.

I avoided the flailing tentacles and reached Bentley.

"Harris!" he yelled. "A soft spot! At the base of the arm!"

I ducked as a tentacle passed over my head, jumped to the side as one thumped the sand beside me, and headed in, trusting in Mr. Bentley's observational skills.

My trust was not in vain. As the tentacle writhed I was able to see, at the point where the arm joined the body, a spot much lighter in color than the surrounding hide. It seemed to have more give to it, as well, perhaps to allow the tentacle its full range of motion. The spot was not large but it was large enough. I drove in my knife as far as possible and dropped to the ground. The tentacle holding Bentley released its grip and joined the others in flailing wildly in pain. Bentley ran and I followed, pausing only long enough to grab Strawberry's basket. The lid fell off when I jostled it and Strawberry's cries spilled out.

Instantly the dragon stopped.

Strawberry hissed and spat and, miraculously, the monster began to retreat.

"Kets," I said grimly. "Come, gentlemen. Lord Brockton has some explaining to do."

Zinnia was already in our rooms when we arrived. I introduced Mr. Natterly and Zinnia welcomed him graciously. She rescued Strawberry from the basket and stroked her while Bentley and I spilled out our tale.

"So, a sea dragon," she said. "Harris, you lucky duck, how did you manage it? And Mr. Bentley, what did you think of the serpent? Was it terrible?"

"Absolutely," said Bentley, but the gleam in his eye matched that of Zinnia in the midst of the hunt. "Terrible and beautiful. And fast! It was up out of the sea like a shot, a geyser of water falling like rain around it. It was—and I know it tried to eat me, but still—it was magnificent."

Zinnia nodded her approval. "And what do you have to tell us, Mr. Natterly?"

He looked up from the glass of spirits Zinnia had poured for him and shrugged.

"Beast dun like kets," he said.

"I do feel bad for the girl," Bentley said.

I nodded. "Helen must have wandered past the ropes the other night and been caught by the beast. She wouldn't have had the benefit of a feline companion to save her."

Zinnia was unconvinced.

"Yes, but what about her clothes? Unless the serpent can use its tentacles to peel a woman out of her dress and leave it neatly on the shore—"

"You're right." Bentley frowned. "Murder, then?"

"Perhaps," Zinnia said. "At least by neglect."

I understood what she was getting at. James had knocked down the original stone statues.

"Mr. Natterly," Zinnia said, "you say Lord Brockton somehow stirred up the creature when he was building the resort?"

"Oh aye, must'n done," Natterly said. He had Strawberry on his lap—the cat was submitting to his petting, puddled over his thighs. "Knocked down the scrarecrawn, did they no? No scrarecrawn, the beast's a-cummun."

Zinnia was silent in thought for a moment. Then she smiled brightly, so bright I was immediately on my guard.

"Mr. Natterly, you stay here. The rest of us will go visit Lord Brockton," she said. "We shall tell him all we know and see what he has to say."

When we left, I made sure I had my revolver, and that it was loaded.

James was back in his office despite the late hour. He looked almost relieved when we told him about the serpent attack.

"It has been a problem," he confessed. "I thought I had it under control, but lately it has been coming more often."

Bentley had not yet caught on. He said "Under control? How do you control a sea dragon?"

"We kept people away—roping off the beach, encouraging them to stay away from the shore at night," James replied.

Zinnia's face was thunder. "And you thought that was enough?"

"It just kept coming," he said.

"And Helen was your solution?" she demanded. "A sacrifice. You lured her down to the beach—you seduced her, didn't you? The poor girl thought she was heading for an assignation. Tell me, James, did you help undress her? Did you have the sea dragon eat her before or after you—"

"Enough!" James cried and threw open a desk drawer. But I was ready. I stepped up beside him smartly and had my revolver in his side before he could withdraw his own pistol.

"Hands up, please," I said. "I would hate to have to shoot you. It would make Zinnia cross."

A confession was not long in coming. Seeing that he was cornered, James revealed it all.

The island had been unoccupied for a long time before James (and his lawyers) pulled it from obscurity and purchased it at a good price from an obliging inheritor. The inheritor told him of the legend of the sea beast that had been passed down in his family along with the land and showed James the original stone cat statues. James hadn't believed a word of it and hadn't thought twice about knocking them down during construction. There had been a few accidents among the workmen, a few wild rumors that James quickly stamped on—until the night he saw the beast himself. Then it became a struggle to keep people away, and when that didn't work he thought to appease the beast.

"Appease it with a human," Zinnia chided. "How dreadful. Really, James, I never would have thought it of you."

"It was just one girl," James said. "I have spent a fortune building this place. It would have ruined me if anyone found out."

Zinnia advanced on James, her mouth a thin knife blade. She was a huntress by nature, her quarry whatever beast needed dealt with. Tonight, she was a fierce tabby, and James was the rat between her claws. She held him in her stare and then, when the tense moment had stretched nearly to the breaking point, Zinnia sat back and smirked.

"I will tell you what you're going to do," she said.

The fete went off without a hitch. It was a beautiful sunny day that ended with everyone in high spirits and two dozen cat statues lining the shore. When night fell huge bonfires illuminated the cats which stood guard on the beach. The masquerade lasted long into the night, and a few of the more senior and dependable Adoni made sure everyone returned straight to their rooms.

Zinnia and I sat on the beach and watched Mr. Natterly feed the fires.

"A Feline Fete," I said, and shook my head. "What silly people your class are."

"We do love a festival," Zinnia admitted. "Obviously I wasn't the only person to smuggle a cat here, and everyone was pleased to have a chance to show off their own fluffy little fellows. All day on the beach making cat statues finished up by a costume ball. It is ridiculous."

"And it worked," I pointed out.

"James has ordered the fete to be held every two weeks," Zinnia said, "all summer long. That should be enough to keep the beast away."

"Speaking of James…"

Zinnia patted my hand.

"Harris, darling, I can tell from your tone that you're cross with me. What have I done now?"

"That man is a murderer," I said, "and you've got him planning fancy dress! Surely you're not going to let him get away with it?"

"Of course not! I just needed his authority as owner of the resort to get the fete in order. Once things were in motion, I sent him off to the mainland guarded by Mr. Bentley. Justice deferred is still justice served, in this case, Harris, darling."

We stayed at Unukalhai for five more days with no further incidents. There were a few mysterious splashes during the day, and the cats that now openly promenaded the beach with their owners would occasionally stop to hiss toward the water, but on the whole it was a quiet week. Bentley sent word that James was safely behind bars, and that the running of the resort would be taken up by some nephew.

"I believe I shall write the young man a letter," Zinnia said as we walked to dinner on our final night. "There are some things he needs to know about a few of the finer points of resort ownership." She paused just outside the dining room. "Harris, I am sorry our retreat has been less than restful."

She did look apologetic and a little sad, standing alone in her dazzling gown, dripping head to toe with glittering jewels. I put my hand on hers. She turned to me and smiled—her eyes caught the sparkle of the stones and blazed.

"I think we shall come here again, Harris," she said. "We can check up on the nephew and make sure he's doing what needs to be done."

"Perhaps," I said. "And perhaps we can venture beneath the resort and find the source of the hot springs, as well. I have a theory…"

"As do I, Harris, darling."

I followed Zinnia into the dining room and to our table where Lord Tremare beckoned us. She was perfect, charming and witty, but I knew that beneath it all Zinnia was thinking fondly of a long dragon with a flat head and a Medusa's mane of tentacles, curled up asleep in the warm water caves below. That was Zinnia: always with one foot in two different worlds.

Conversation turned to people I did not know but whom Zinnia apparently did, Lords and Ladies and people with nicknames like Bunty and Hap. I let my mind wander.

I wondered if it ever tired Zinnia, being everything in every situation.

I wondered what it was like for these people, who knew nothing of the wonders that filled the natural world in its every nook and cranny. I wondered if they ever got bored with it.

I wondered if I would ever get bored of it.

I wondered, with suddenly sinking heart, if Zinnia would ever get bored of me.

And I wondered, as a set of sharp claws sank itself into my shin, whether we could leave that damned cat on the island. They undoubtedly needed it more than we did.

I kicked—there was a muffled squawk of a mew—Zinnia looked at me and smiled.

"She's staying here," she whispered, and poured me some fine champagne. My spirits rose with the bubbles in my glass.

Megan Engelhardt is a stay at home mom to four wild things. She lives just north of the Sasquatch Triangle of Ohio and writes in the margins of the day. Her work has previously been published in Asimov's, Daily Science Fiction, *and* Crossed Genres, *among others. She can be found at Aldi on grocery shopping day and on Twitter every day @MadMerryMeg.*

KEVIN COCKLE

TIA TIME

The water glass did what glass does when it's dropped from a sufficient height onto concrete: scatter shattered pieces, making an unpleasant noise in the process. I held Mike's gaze as he smiled, still ankle-cuffed to his chair, still suspending his glass-gripping hand in mid air for effect. I heard my security detail come to def-con 4 across the dimly lit room behind me, but I didn't give them the "go" signal. This was showmanship on Mike's part, not aggression. I had decided to let this play out.

"You remember your second law of thermodynamics," he said. I pursed my lips in silent response. "That'll be important later."

I don't know if Mike Donnelly was a genius, but he'd always been different. I'd known him peripherally from our Southern-Alberta-Institute-of-Technology days; got to know and like him better at Quantico-North. He was funny then, geeky by Bureau standards, irreverent, as comfortable with literature as he was calculus. He'd gone the forensic accounting/FINTRAC route; I'd gone straight counter terrorism, but when global markets had imploded in a way that made 2008 look like an honest mistake, we'd sort of come back into one another's orbits. Working out of Toronto, he followed the money; working out of Washington, I brought the guns. He provided the theory; I nailed down the solutions. We worked well together for two people who didn't have a whole lot in common. I never dreamed when all this started, that one day it'd be Mike in one of our CanAm east coast dark sites, and me conducting his interview.

He looked like shit; smelled about the same. Hair a tangled, ruddy-brown mess to his shoulders; beard a random growth almost to his chest. Eyes I remembered as playful, now haunted, twitchy. Looking over his Agency psych eval, I had seen that he'd been on the bubble for acceptability, but had been selected largely on his ability to see connections, make intuitive leaps others couldn't. He didn't profile cleanly; the more the tests tried to pin him down, the more the edges of him seemed to blur. A risky applicant in retrospect.

I could hear sirens in the distance; the muffled hum of a large city past night-darkened windows. I knew this was Mike's last chance to come clean in more or less civilized surroundings.

"Why don't you start with the server farm," I said. "Demolition seems to be a bit outside your skillset."

"You seen the skies lately, right? Kir-royale clouds. Sun like a gob of blood."

"Lot of forest fires out west, Mike. What're you gonna do?"

"Forest fires," he snorted.

"Mike…"

"You want to know why I blew up the Riemann hub, right?"

"For starters."

"Well strap in, Jay. 'Cause this is going to fuck you up."

Fair enough, I thought, and hit "record."

All right, so you know my team was attached to the IDA to establish chain-of-causation vis-à-vis the various derivative cascade effects that fueled the Meltdown. Standard forensics with a heavy-duty quant focus that led us to the Riemann AI network in upstate New York. You know I obtained a legal on-site warrant. You know I went in person to conduct interviews. You've seen my reports: so far so good.

Riemann Draco is interesting. They made money in 2008, scored again when Long Term Capital blew up in '98—hell—they even got attention from

Reagan's justice department by profiting too obscenely from the Savings and Loan debacle. Often fined, never convicted. They're masters at creating order out of chaos—always at the cutting edge of financial science and legality. This was not their first rodeo: they were good and ready for us before we got there.

Reimann's techs told a good, tight story. Their trading algorithm ecosystem had evolved past their control protocols, but it was winning—exploiting the very volatility it helped to create—so they let it grow. Same as every other bank: a lack of electronic oversight, but no criminal intent, yadda yadda yadda. It was 2008 all over again, at least from their perspective. They'd give us what we needed to recommend an expensive wrist-slapping, and they'd get back to business ASAP.

So, fine. But you know how I like old-school ledger analysis, right? Bricks and mortar accounting; real assets on the ground. I found paper statements that listed a lot of miscellaneous investment in an orphan mine up in the Catskills. Converted to a wartime bunker installation in the 1940s, subsequently bought up by a series of beneficial owners who ended up becoming Riemann Draco LLC in the 80s. A lot of sunk costs for an abandoned coalmine turned war surplus. What was an investment bank doing with such a thing on the books, and why was it not more transparently listed in subsequent financials? I love a road trip almost as much as I love dusty old ledgers and murky half-truths. Rented a jeep, went on up there to get eyes-on.

Beautiful country, Jay, the Catskills. Pine forest, low rolling mountains, clear blue lakes. I lost myself on that drive—figured I might go back on my own time one day, do some camping. You know the hours we were pulling in those first days after Goldman went under; this was like a vacation in the middle of my investigation. Not gonna lie: I knew I was being seduced by the open road, fresh air, scenic vistas. I didn't fight it.

So I get to the spot, and there's a little ghost-town/tourist bureau deal that hooks you up with maps or guides, gives you historical info—so on and so forth. Pretty girl at the desk—glossy black bob like a Bay Street broker; flannel shirt and jeans like a rustic co-ed; Persian features, Californian voice. Says her name's "Tia" and would I like a guided tour up to the mine site. No

I would not, but thanks anyway, right? I got this: it's an easy climb, and I got plenty of daylight. She did rent me a serious lantern and extra battery packs though, which I hadn't even thought about beforehand.

When you get up there, the mouth of the mine gives you new appreciation for the word "cavernous." It's not normal, man. You emerge from a pretty dense tree line and look up the rocky footpath, and this great dark maw looming over you looks like something out of a horror movie. Naturally I was thrilled, but seriously, you could fit a ten storey building in that opening. Wild.

Anyway—I head up, go in, and it's like subway construction from the 40s inside. That kind of design. Long oval hallways, whitewashed walls, descending staircases, empty rooms with open archways sans doors. It's pretty well maintained; rationally laid out—at this point, I'm not worried about getting lost. You ever see archival photos of the old Maginot fortifications? That's what I was reminded of.

Understand that I was already... compromised. That long drive where I kept telling myself the trip was critically important to the audit, that I was just being thorough? On some level I knew that was all bullshit. Didn't even think twice about the tourist bureau: why would Riemann have that? Or if not Riemann, why would the state have something set up for a private holding? You have to know that those questions never occurred to me then, only later. And they didn't occur to me... well. I'll get to that.

Lost track of time down there. Seriously. Every once in a while it'd dawn on me that my back and knees were getting achy from walking, but then I'd get distracted by some new armory, or brick-lined arch, or another descending spiral staircase. I'd check my phone and it would assure me that I really hadn't been gone that long. So I'd keep going, feeling, I don't know, mesmerized. Or something.

Never even thought to wonder at how pristine it all was. Aged, yes, but untouched by graffiti, no sign of previous visitors. Should've leaped out at me, and did, but only in retrospect.

Finally, I'm heading down a broad set of stairs, and the edge of the circle of light from my lantern illuminates someone's hiking boots and legs below me. 'Bout near had a heart attack, but as I edged forward, the light fell on the rest of the person: Tia, girl from the tourist bureau outside. She's just smiling up at me from the gloom, eyes shining weird like dimes in the sun. I'm still kind of shocked when she says "Welcome, Michael." Like she'd been expecting me.

Won't kid you, I was the opposite of smooth. Heart was in my throat, all I could do was frown and stare, couldn't think what to say. Eventually she just chuckled, shook her head. Then she said: "Brace yourself."

I paused the recording.

Mike had stopped talking, was just staring at the table top between us, so I cleared my throat, trying to convey impatience. He didn't look up, but he spoke in measured, I'm-perfectly-sane tones: "Jay, this next bit... I don't really have the proper words. I mean, there are no proper words, but I'll give it a shot. And you're going to think that I'm screwing with you, but I want you to sit there, and listen, okay? Listen right to the end."

He looked up then, just with his eyes, and I raised my eyebrows in the universal signal for "Continue." He sat back, tilting the chair onto the two rear legs for a moment until the chain caught, then rocked forward, glaring at me like Rasputin.

Should have stopped him right there. I often look back and wonder if that would have made a difference.

Instead, all I did was resume recording.

Suddenly, we weren't on that staircase anymore. Everything had changed. Instead of a World War II era bunker complex, I stood in this vast underground chamber with stalactites dripping from the roof, and mineral deposits in the stone reflecting light like jewels. Heat washed over me—blast furnace heat coming from some deeper level, and in the distance I could hear flowing water echoing in the immensity.

Huge monitors lined the walls, streaming numerical and visual data. Banks of servers hummed, illuminated by gigantic bronze braziers that threw light from burning coals. Somewhere there would be a massive generator powering the electronics, ventilation and cooling systems, making sense of the running water. Making sense of Riemann's capital investment. That was the thing: it did all make sense, if you didn't pursue the logic too far. An effort was being made to present the situation in a way I could rationalize. Above my head, catwalks spanned the distance, giving the whole thing the air of a Bond villain's lair.

Tia was gone. In her place, a... *the*... dragon leered. A Sumerian myth made flesh. No, Jay: let me finish. Colossal and reptilian; the great scaled head and fantastic bat wings. The endless, sinuous tail, and grotesque, nightmare talons. And the eyes: amber-coloured cats' eyes, filled with an ancient, monstrous intelligence. "I am Tiamat," it rumbled with a voice—I was made to understand, like the way you know things in dreams—fashioned by iris valves in the long throat to approximate speech. "'Leviathan' in your ancient texts. I am the abyss; I am the One." More of that "making sense" routine: a rationale for the voice; huge wing area to help dissipate internal heat; gill-like structures that would vent heat-expanded air to provide thrust for lift. The details all fit conveniently into place, giving me some kind of explanatory positioning. Convincing me of plausibility.

Then Tia was back, the girl, the human. Human except for the weird starlight where her eyes should have been. She held her hand out to me and I stumbled forward, recognizing in my enslaved gait that she'd been drawing me to her all along. Maybe for my entire life, the pull at first gentle, barely felt and only understood as a force after the fact. Like gravity at a distance, getting stronger as I got closer.

Her hand was blazing hot to the touch, and weirdly dry. Like snakeskin.

She walked me over to a bank of monitors. For-ex markets; commodity futures; stock exchanges; bond bids and yields; crypto-currency crosses. Complex stochastics spit out live rolling averages; Black-Scholes calculations updated and projected time values as data from myriad sources aggregated and changed. It was like a main line cut into the vein of global finance: news feeds and financial data propagating each other like electromagnetic waves. Tiamat was at the center of the Meltdown, the cause of it all. And Riemann Draco was one of the few beneficiaries.

Contrasted with the cold hard numbers were the vid feeds from all over the world. Scenes of food riots, armed border disputes, air strikes, carrier groups conducting tactical ops, protests being beaten down by armored phalanxes. The human expression of financial volatility. Tiamat was at the center of that maelstrom too.

"Do you get it?" She said, smiling up at me from just about the height of my right shoulder. A picture of Smaug—that dragon in *The Hobbit*"—lying atop an impossible mound of gold, forced its way into my mind, and yes, I did get it. Dragons loved concentrating and accumulating wealth, and in the 21st century, this is what a treasure room full of other people's gold looked like.

"You..." I struggled to speak.

"Indeed."

"This can't be real," I said. Part analysis, part hope.

"Sure it can. Because I'm back, baby. Or just about. That's where you come in."

"Just about," I stammered. "What do you mean, 'just about' back?"

"I can influence human affairs. Move economies, thanks to digital interfaces and corporate personhood. Cause signs and portents in weather and other natural phenomena. I can whisper into the ears of sensitives like Tolkien or Lovecraft—why do you think Tolkien's Smaug is so obsessed with money-supply? Why are Lovecraftian monsters always grotesque mashed-up wholes of things that shouldn't go together, rather than discrete parts? Me. I'm the inspiration. I was once contiguous with the cosmos, whole and indivisible. I am Cthulhu moving poets to madness in the dark.

"But only you, Michael, can see me in high res. How I've waited for you. Longed for you. Called for you. In perceiving me, you make me real again. Real-ish, at any rate. And, having made me real, you shall be my herald, preparing humanity for my re-emergence. You are the gateway, Michael, the Prime Perceptor. The Mind Shaper. Through you shall others see me, and in their seeing, shall I wax strong again. Or words to that effect. Big picture, Mike: I need you. Consider yourself blessed."

Mike had drifted again, staring past my right shoulder. I was just about to say how disappointed I was in his testimony, when he started speaking again, practically to himself. "E Pluribus Unum," he mumbled.

"Out of many, one," I translated.

"Now you're getting it," he said. I assumed he was referring to his "whole and indivisible" line, but it was safer not to get caught up in his reveries.

"There was more," Mike continued, "in the cavern, much more, but that bit was the big reveal. She took me to Maxwell's lab in the 1800s—showed me his notes for a derivation of what amounted to some kind of relativistic correction to Probability. It was related to his stats work in thermodynamics—never published—all pre-vector calculus, but brilliant, far as I could tell. And then it dawned on me. Jay, remember 'Maxwell's Demon'? That was Tiamat; she was there, fucking with him, pulling his strings.

"She showed me a vault in Princeton that contains hard-copy volumes of calculations—thousands of pages—working out the scatter-amplitudes for a single set of classified Feynman diagrams that researchers apparently refer to as 'blasphemous.' That I couldn't follow as neatly as Maxwell's speculations, but it doesn't matter: it's a work in progress. When they're finished, it'll be a description of the cosmic dragon herself, though they won't know it. Another sign, another portent.

"She knew I needed to understand her in terms of math. She was speaking to me in the language I had always used to describe reality. She was helping me to see her, and the more I saw, the more I could see. She was bootstrapping herself into our world through my perception.

"She showed me history she'd guided, taking me there with illusions as vivid as reality itself. I saw her create the petro-sorcery that allowed Byzantines to use Greek fire without setting their own ships alight. The same sorcery that would one day allow Standard Oil dowsers to locate the massive hydrocarbon structures so crucial to the shaping of our modern world. I was in the room when she whispered in Churchill's ear to switch the British fleet from coal to oil. A thousand little moves and trajectory tweaks and domino reactions designed in the end, to bring me to her. I mean, she was thinking in terms of genetic probabilities, maximizing the chance that something like me—something that could directly perceive her in our space—would be generated.

"The vastness of her intellect, Jay. The granularity she perceives. Do you see? It's 'Maxwell's Demon' in another reference frame."

"Okay," I said, nonplussed at his data-free performance. "Are you ever going to get around to the attack on Riemann's server farm, or..."

He turned his face towards me, and his eyes seemed to get a bit more present. He smiled a smile that was all irony and regret. "Yeah, well. When I woke up at the cave mouth, I thought only a few hours had passed, but it had been weeks. And at the bottom of the trail, there was no ghost town, no tourist bureau. Not gonna lie, I didn't take that news as well as I might have. I was not, shall we say, particularly resilient. Many of the ideas I came up with in that period were not the result of intricate planning and deep reflection. And it's true: blowing up the Riemann hub was one of those ideas.

"Understand, I thought that destroying the hub might disconnect her. I still thought that Riemann's quants were doing the dirty work, but it turns out they were basically monkeys taking dictation, doing the paperwork, managing the machinery. They didn't actually have advanced AI code: it was all Tiamat. And the worst part is, while I thought I was doing some enlightened destruction, the actual point of the operation turned out to be to attract the attention of the counter terrorism task force. To attract you. I didn't see the design until I was brought here. But now it's obvious. In our frame, that's how magic works. It shows up in our narratives, and all our narratives are shadows of some higher explanation."

"Still a little opaque to me, Mike. I'm an engineer, remember? I like a little concrete mixed in with my batshit theory."

"I'm the herald of Tiamat, Jay. I'm here to announce her presence. To tell her story and make you see."

"Hate to break it to you, buddy, but you haven't exactly convinced me that dragons are real."

"Yeah?" Mike's eyes got glossy as they welled up. With his left hand, he pointed down at the floor where he'd dropped his water glass. I glanced down on reflex.

The shattered pieces of the glass had randomly reconstituted, leaving the unbroken vessel standing on its base. Second law of thermodynamics came back to me in a torrent. I was looking at a bunch of Royal Flush draws in a row. And I was the farthest thing from a poet, or even a polymath like Mike. If I could see what I was seeing, anyone could; everyone would. Peggy, the kids, our folks. Everyone. Dimly, I began to see why Mike had been trying to get my attention in particular. Or more precisely, why something had been using Mike to get my attention, and put us in a room together.

A mean Hudson Hawk rattled the windows of the safe house with a thumping blast, carrying the sound of distant gunfire with it. More sirens, too; more of that sense of the city seething in the darkness. Things boiling hot, getting energetic. Getting ready to explode.

I tried to swallow but my mouth was suddenly dry.

"What're the odds, right?" Mike whispered. "I'm sorry you can't unsee that, man. It's Tia Time. Not gonna lie: this is gonna hurt."

Kevin Cockle is a speculative-fiction author with over thirty short stories appearing in a variety of anthologies and magazines. His novel Spawning Ground *is narrowly believed to have invented the micro-genre of "occult game theory," and was published by Tyche Books in 2016. In 2019, Kevin alongside co-writer Mike Peterson won AMPIA's "Rosie" award for the feature-film screenplay* Knuckleball, *breaking a persistent streak of long-list nominations, honourable mention citations, and other close-but-no-cigar metrics.*

WWC
2023

To Tony
All the best,
Kirstin P B

KRISTA D. BALL

FOR THE GLORY OF GOLD

All things considered, things were looking up for Miranda. A month ago, she'd lost her job with Orbit News. Thankfully, Miranda was an award-winning journalist and had a successful podcast with enough sponsors to cover her weekly station costs on New Sky.

And, honestly, that was great and everything, but what Miranda really wanted to do was write a book. Specifically, she wanted to write about the big races that made the move to New Sky—the station that now orbited the moon—and their role in the successful advancement of humanity.

Personally, she loathed the term *humanity*. How human-centric. However, no one had come up with a better term that everyone could agree upon, so humanity stuck.

She wanted to write the history of the station and highlight the importance of her own kind: trolls, orcs, giants. There was a small problem with that plan—it required her to interview the original founders of New Sky, the investors, and the administration team.

And *that* meant interviewing the Duchess of Toronto.

She couldn't remember the last time she was this nervous, which was surprising given that the entire reason Miranda was unemployed was because she'd outed the duchess' financial interests on her podcast.

A well-dressed woman stepped through a door and into the reception room. "The duchess will see you now."

Miranda immediately noticed the woman's jewelry. There was a ring with a different gemstone on each finger, both thumbs sported thick gold bands and delicate diamonds and emeralds decorated both her ears from lobe to the very top tip. Most impressively, she wore a choker of emeralds and diamonds that must have cost a lifetime's worth of wages.

The woman motioned for Miranda to follow her. When she turned, Miranda noticed the woman's high heels. The spike tips were gold, or at least gold-plated.

Miranda picked up her equipment bags, taking the time to distribute them correctly so that she could stand straight and not worry about them slipping off.

I am in the wrong profession, Miranda thought.

Miranda dutifully followed the assistant through a confounding maze of corridors, stairs, and doors. Miranda was growing sweaty and she wasn't even wearing metal-tipped spikes. She soon realized they'd been walking in a circle, slowly moving toward the middle of... something.

Finally, they arrived in a round, three story room. A surprised sound escaped Miranda, which caught the ear of the assistant.

"Everyone is awed upon their first visit." She motioned at the round table in the middle of the room. "Please, set your things there. The duchess will be seated in the gold and red chair, exactly in the position it is now placed. That will allow you to set up any lighting and cameras you wish to use."

"Am I permitted to take photographs of the room?" Miranda asked.

"Of course. However, the duchess will need your drive to be submitted for inspection. Any photos not permitted will be deleted from your device."

Miranda took a survey of the room. "Is there anything specific here you know I should avoid?"

"Merely anything that hints at our security. The safety of the duchess is paramount."

"Oh, of course. I have no interest in putting her life in danger."

"Excellent." She glanced at her watch. It was, of course, gold. "Her Grace will be with you in six minutes."

Miranda got to work setting up her equipment. Once the camera and lights were positioned correctly at the golden chair, she used her handheld camera to take some shots about the room.

And what a room. Everything was decorated in red velvets, and light filtered down through the skyline windows above. Of course, that was only an illusion; the room itself was in the middle of the station's administrative wing. She must have at least forty glow sprites living in the ceiling to create this kind of light. How in the world did she manage to convince them to work for her? How rich was she?

The amount of gold in the room risked bordering on tacky, but the rich fabrics, simple marble floor, and the proper amount of black and wood items somehow turned it down enough to go from tacky to opulent. In the far corner was a dragon statue, wings spread the entire width of the room, it heads throw back in a scream.

"It is magnificent, isn't it?" spoke a silky voice behind her.

Miranda turned around. She'd not heard the duchess enter. She put on her reporter smile and said, "Thank you for granting this interview, Your Grace."

"May I call you Miranda? Or do you prefer the entire name, Miranda third of her generation, Ottawa Clan?"

Miranda accepted the outstretched hand and shook it. "Miranda is fine."

"Then you may call me Rowena. Megan tells me you are writing a book about the station's creation." She motioned at the table. "Please, have a seat."

Miranda sat in her designated spot. She answered Rowena while pulling out her notepad and voice recorder. "My goal is to write a book about the station's creation, yes, with a focus on the role big races played in getting New Sky made."

"I have never considered myself among the big races," Rowena said.

"But you were the first non-human, major financial backer for the station. So I wished to talk about that, if you are willing, of course. Your... Rowena."

A smile spread across Rowena's lips. "You wish to know my history?"

"Is that... okay?"

She looked over her shoulder at the dragon statue. "Very. In fact, Miranda third of her generation, Ottawa Clan. I believe I shall give you more than just that."

"If there are things you need said off the record, please identify them. I can turn off the camera and the recorder and restart once you give the go ahead."

"Oh, no. Let us have it all on record. It is a stereotype, you see, that dragons primarily hoard gold."

Miranda glanced about the room and back to Rowena, cocking an eyebrow.

That made Rowena laugh. "Oh, we hoard gold, and silver, and platinum. And precious gems. And artwork. But, perhaps the thing we hoard most is knowledge. You see, in this age, brute force is gauche. Taking down an enemy with simply knowing more than him is the truest form of power."

"How many enemies did you have to take down to afford something like your New Sky investment?"

Rowena smiled. "Just one."

1830
London, England

"Gentlemen, what do you mean I cannot access my finances?"

Rowena was young for a dragon, it was true, but these men could not legally withhold her inheritance. There were rules, after all, both for the banks of the country and for dragons and the supernatural. She stood in the boardroom of the London Bank of England and stared at the four men seated across from her, hands folded. All heads turned to the man seated in the center.

"Legal papers have been filed against your inheritance."

Rowena stared between the men. "My father's will was concrete. This bank provided the lawyers, even."

"Perhaps you should not have been so trusting."

Rowena recognized that voice behind her. She bristled when he purposely walked so close as to brush against her arm, but she did not move. Benjamin, The Duke of Scotland, was a young dragon, too. Only fifty-something years her senior. Yet, in that time, he had amassed over ten thousand gold bars, and hundreds of thousands of silver coins. She'd never seen any of this, of course. Only rumors. But power and lifestyle in this place was fueled by the mere whispers of gossip.

"Your father's will allowed for the investment of your inheritance," Benjamin said.

She did not like where this was going.

One of the other gentlemen at the table raised a hand for silence. He smelled like pork that had sat in the sun for too long. Clearly human. "Miss Rowena, we invested your father's assets into the railway."

"Oh." That did not sound too terrible. Some of her own meagre wealth was tied up in industry. A gold bar in London Rail. A bar each in two cotton mills in the north, and another bar into the railway company that connected the mills to London Rail's lines.

That was most of her liquid assets. Everything else was tied up in her father's inheritance, which she had planned to invest into rail, steam, cotton, and maybe a couple of tin or copper mines down in Cornwall. She'd even heard about the potential for silver on an estate there that had fallen on hard times. She'd planned to make a trip there and if she could convince the elf who owned it to sell to her. Or, at least lease it. Silver was well ahead of tin and cotton.

"It was invested into the Scotland Flyer."

Rowena blinked. "I apologize, sir, but I have no idea what that is."

"It was supposed to be a grand new form of transportation between Edinburgh and London. Hot air balloon." The man turned to Benjamin. "It did not, shall we say, get off the ground. Apparently, air spirits are not easily bribed, unlike some other races, and refused to work for anything less than a comfortable wage, thereby making the ticket prices unachievable by the average man. And the wealthiest individuals still prefer their luxury suites in the trains for such a long journey."

"What does this mean?" Rowena asked. "How much of my money was lost in this venture?"

"Nearly all of it."

"Define nearly, sir."

The men at the table all turned to Benjamin. A small smile formed on his mouth. "Five bars of gold remain."

2019
New Sky

"Are you telling me he stole your entire inheritance?" Miranda asked.

Rowena lifted her index finger. "Five bars of gold were still mine."

"How could such a good businessman lose so much money?"

Rowena laughed. "I discovered too late that he was nothing but a conman. He used every tool at hand to destroy his competition, even going so far as to use his influence at the bank to purposely invest the good money of competitors into failing businesses to bankrupt them."

"Forgive my ignorance, but could you not do anything?"

She raised her hands. "I was but a young dragon with a five gold bar inheritance."

"Is that a lot? Sorry, I don't know anything about money in that time." Miranda giggled, and kicked herself for giggling even as the sound escaped her. "I've not even read Jane Austen."

"Oh, for shame! Jane was a lovely woman. She gave me my first silver locket."

"I'm sorry, what?" Miranda exclaimed.

"Jane Austen gave me my first silver locket."

Miranda's mouth twisted into several shapes, trying to form a dozen questions at once, until her brain forced her to spit out, "Why? How? When?"

"You left off who, what, and where, my dear." At Miranda's disappointed sigh, she said, "The Austen story shall have to keep for another interview."

Miranda deflated. It wasn't that she was an Austenite, but rather that she was interviewing someone with those kinds of stories. The kinds of stories that got her podcast paying patrons, that sold new articles and pitches, that could one day fill a book.

And, in the short term, would pay her rent.

"Ah, mercenary enterprise. I can see it in your eyes," Rowena said. She added just enough purr and smoulder to make it sound dirty and delicious. "I do love a woman who knows how to capitalize."

Miranda ignored the comment, even as she felt the heat rise in her cheeks. She hated blushing. Humans got this cute darkening of the skin, and looked like they'd just run a marathon or had had the best sex of their lives. Some of the big races also just darkened more of their natural tone. Her? She turned fresh cut grass green *everywhere*. She hated it.

Miranda made a point to look about the room, to distract that she was glowing like a meadow. "I suspect this cost more than five gold bars."

"Just a few."

"How did you get them?"

Rowena's smile was a little terrifying. "Cunning, my dear."

1925
Toronto

Rowena watched the dancers. They were good. Not just at dancing, but at teaching the Dragon's Head Hotel patrons. She'd bribed them to come from Chicago and New York, to live in Toronto for the winter and teach the Charleston. She'd also bribed a band from New York to play at the hotel five nights a week. The offer of room and board (a weekly stocked bar included), free railway tickets, and a weekly salary sure encouraged them to make the jump across the border.

She hated to use the phrase, but the hotel was a roaring success. She turned this dump into *the* place to be in Toronto, allowing her to now own forty-three percent in the Great Western Clipper railway, thirty-two percent shares in Montreal Railways, and twelve percent in the Halifax Great Rail Company.

She always liked trains.

She was a silent partner in eleven mining companies throughout Quebec and Ontario. One of those mines had large deposits of cobalt. The silver was more valuable, but she knew too well to keep her options opened. She planned to have enough gold bars in her basement to purchase that mine outright once the silver was abandoned, probably another year or two and she already had nearly enough to purchase her first gold mine. Specifically, New Scotland Trust Gold.

So when Benjamin, Duke of Scotland, strolled in through her door that night with his little gang of hangers-on, she knew it was London all over again.

Only this time, she was ready for him.

2019
New Sky

"Why didn't you just kick him out?"

Rowena looked offended. "My dear, you can't just kick out a duke. That would've been incredibly rude."

"He stole your inheritance!"

"Indeed."

Miranda stared at her. She knew, in the place where her brain normally existed, that she needed to be neutral in this, but damn, she was sitting across from the Duchess of Toronto, the story was now in Toronto, and it was killing her to know what happened. And, more importantly, if she could get the scoop, what happened to the Duke of Scotland.

"My dear Miranda, third of her generation. You cannot simply be rude in public. In those days, it would have destroyed a woman's reputation."

"Forgive me stating the obvious, but you are a dragon."

"And, I was a young dragon, without any real power. I was only Lady Rowena on the deeds. Anyone who was anyone had the title of lady in those days. Live long enough and you're bound to marry into some random baronet's family."

"You were married? You never mentioned that."

"Because thankfully he died after six months."

Miranda cleared her throat and asked, "How?"

Rowena's smile was a little scary. "A house fire."

"Suspicious?" Miranda knew she was pushing her luck, but she was also a reporter.

"I was in Paris at the time."

"Suspicious?" Miranda asked again. This time, she raised an eyebrow.

That made Rowena laugh. "Apparently, it was truly an accident. Unless, of course, you believe prayers to one's ancestors can make a kitchen explode. In that case, yes, it was suspicious."

"So why was the Duke in Toronto?"

"I never knew the entire story, if you must know. I do know the Great War had been tough on his finances, as it was everyone over there. I had escaped to Canada with my meagre holdings as quickly as possible after the incident, so I was mostly unaffected. However, he'd come to North America to make his next fortune. And found me in the process."

Miranda waited in the pause for as long as her professionalism told her was acceptable. Then she blurted, "And?"

"He stole my hotel."

1925
Toronto

"Well, well, well. Rowena. I had wondered when I would see your delightful face again."

She pushed herself up from her bar stool, well into his personal space.

Rowena took a long drag from her unlit cigarette, smoke billowing from the end. She rubbed her thumb across her gold index ring, the one that held her cigarette, and then blew the held smoke into his too-close face.

"I had forgotten about you."

"Surely you are not still sore about that little incident," Benjamin said. He had that same smile she remembered so well; the one that said he was about to screw her over.

"Would you like a drink? I have the best bourbon selection in the city."

"I prefer my beverages hot. Like a true dragon."

She shrugged. "Your loss. So, what brings you to my establishment? Business or pleasure?"

"Business is always a pleasure," Benjamin said. "Would you prefer to speak privately? I wouldn't wish to embarrass you in front of your patrons."

Rowena glanced about the room. None of her employees noticed the exchange. Benjamin's thugs, however, were drawing attention. "Is the orc muscle necessary?"

"They offer a certain…" He motioned vaguely in the air. "Aura. But, if they intimidate you, they are welcome to stay at the bar."

Rowena leaned over her shoulder. Catching the bartender's eye, she said, "Charlie? These gentlemen are my guests. On the house for them."

"Yes, ma'am."

Rowena gestured for Benjamin to follow her into the back rooms. They walked through the count room, where the proceeds from the gambling tables were counted and put into the safe. She waved at Godwinson, second of his generation, New York clan, and Just Johnny, the accountants that worked her books. Through the doors lay her office. She sat down behind her rather simple wooden desk, took off her cigarette ring holder, and crossed her legs.

"Now, what can I do for you?"

If anything, Benjamin had grown more arrogant in the last century. He pulled out a folded set of papers from his inside jacket pocket. "These are for you."

She read them. He'd bought out her hotel's silent partner. Her equal silent partner. She kept her temper in check when she asked, "When are you going to get over that I said no to you?"

"No one says no to me, darling."

2019
New Sky

"Wait, wait, wait! You said nothing about him being in a relationship with you," Miranda demanded.

"We were never in one."

"But you just said…"

"I had rejected him. My father supported my free will on the matter, and my right to make my own choices in life partner. After all, life is a very long time."

"Is that why he was screwing with you?"

Rowena shrugged. "I never really considered other options. Though, I suppose he could have just been an ass. Now, do you want the rest of the story or not?"

"Sorry, sorry! Go on."

1925
Toronto

Rowena folded the letter back up then handed it to him. "I thought the war had been hard on your hoard."

Benjamin accepted the letter and put it back into his jacket. "Thankfully, I have a few friends still who helped me find new investors. I believe this hotel will help me get back on my claws, as it were."

She put her smoking ring back on. She took another puff from the cigarette. This time, she blew three perfect smoke rings.

"There is a top staff meeting on Monday mornings at noon. We have lunch together in the dining room. I expect you'll be there?"

"Oh, I plan on it. Bring some changes to this establishment."

She smiled at him and said, "Oh, I look forward to tomorrow."

"I'll see myself out." Benjamin stood from the desk and turned around to face her. "I say, Rowena, you are handling this much better than the London thing. It's good to see you not taking business so personally."

"I am older and wiser, I suppose."

She waited until she heard the count room's door close. Then she stood from her desk, and walked into the count room.

"Did you boys hear everything?" Rowena asked.

Godwinson nodded. "Need me and Johnny to get it done?"

Rowena smiled. "Do it."

1925
Toronto
The Dragon's Head Hotel Dining Room
Monday Noon

Rowena waited alone in the dining room. She'd relocated all of the guests in the middle of the night, putting them all up at the King Edward Hotel, on her tab. The owner of the King Edward cut her a great price, especially since she was paying gold and not credit. The patrons were obviously upset about the move, but likewise mollified by the improved accommodations. She gave all the staff working that morning a week's pay and told them to lay low. Godwinson had been working all night to get everything in order, so Johnny said he'd take care of the rest of the staff and get their wages to them.

She propped the doors open and placed a chair in the middle of the dining room. A perfect view of the lobby entrance. There, she waited, puffing on her cigarette.

Benjamin strolled through the front doors and his self-satisfied smile didn't waver until he was halfway across the lobby's floor. He glanced about him and then back at her.

"What's this, darling?"

"Payback."

Benjamin's laugh sounded real, as if he didn't believe her. "Now, now. You are not wealthy enough to attack me. There are rules, my dear. New world or not, we follow the code."

She picked up the leather portfolio from the floor next to her chair and threw it. It landed just short of his well-made shoes. She smiled the smile of confidence and, for the first time, his flickered.

"What's this?" Benjamin asked, bending to pick up the documents. As he flipped through each page, his smile faded. Wood smoke filled the air. "This isn't real."

Rowena stood from her chair. She shrugged her shoulders to allow her stole to fall to the ground behind her. Slowly, carefully, she put one foot in front of the other, swaying her hips. "Who do you think has been propping up your mines? Your business ventures? Some troll you'd never heard of? Did you think to investigate him at all?"

Benjamin shook his head, furiously flipping through the pages now. "I have several investors. They can't all be you. I'd have known. I'd have heard *something*."

She didn't close her eyes when she began to transform into her true visage. Her wings came out first, slowly expanding across the entire dining room. "Godwinson's entire family have been excellent employees through the decades. And it's amazing how much people hate you, Benjamin."

"I am the Duke of Scotland still," Benjamin said. Smoke continued to curl about his figure. "Put away your wings, darling."

"You might prefer your drinks hot, but I prefer mine with ice, distilled down to their very essence."

"You can't take me, Rowena. Not here. We would destroy this hotel of yours."

Her body began the change, pushing her through the ceiling. "It'll be worth it."

And then she roared.

2019
New Sky

"Did you win?"

Rowena laughed. "Of course, I won. I had to pay for reconstruction. Two full city blocks were damaged or destroyed in the fight, but I like to think of it as a community project. Job creation, that kind of thing. It was excellent for my reputation. They even named a school after me."

"What happened to the duke?"

Rowena did not move. "I keep him close at all times."

Miranda's gaze shifted to the gold dragon statue and back to Rowena. She cocked an eyebrow.

"Never scorn a dragon."

Krista D. Ball *is an award-winning author of over twenty books, including the popular non-fiction guide* What Kings Ate and Wizards Drank.

BLAKE JESSOP

THE RISE OF THE DRAGONBLOOD QUEEN

Part One: Sarissa's last Spring

"*We hath nary a choice, sire,*" the chancellor said. He leant on a cane of carved ivory, too old to kneel properly before the king.

"There is always a choice," Sigmund said. Even kneeling, the knight was a big man, as unbending as an oak tree. He struggled with the high speech. "*I beg thee; allow me to command thy castle guard against the beast.*"

"*Thou art brave, sir knight, but unwise,*" the chancellor croaked. "*Sire, our army contends with the heretic Zenatans in the south. The dragon hath chosen a fateful moment to renew its war on thy house. Princess Sarissa must be sacrificed to foul Fafnaer, or the heart of thy kingdom will burn.*"

The princess, a sullen and intemperate teenager whom no prince had yet consented to marry, sat rigidly beside her father. For once, a minor note of panic had infiltrated her usually dour and demeaning voice.

"What shall we do, Father? Who will save me?" Sarissa said, stubbornly refusing to speak the language of kings.

The king and his knights and the chancellor all looked at each another.

Sigmund dragged Sarissa down to the cliffs by the water and set about tying her to a convenient tree. The castle loomed high behind her, and bells clanged and clamored from the wharfs below. Far across the bay, visible only as a shadow above the diamond shimmering of the waves, was the dragon's island.

"Let me go!" Sarissa yelled. She had run out of energy for wriggling, and her hair was loose from its ribbon and stuck across her eyes.

"This is my most shameful day as a knight," Sigmund said, "I have always… favored you, princess. I wish there was a way to save you."

"There is a way to save me, you giant wretch, do anything but this!"

In spite of her protestations, Sigmund lashed Sarissa efficiently to the tree and retreated as fast as chivalry would allow.

Suddenly alone, Sarissa squirmed briefly, then gave up. The rope was harsh and prickly through the thin fabric of her dress. Part of her still doubted the dragon was even real. She squinted at the distant horizon and huffed the hair out of her face. Nothing.

"Perhaps there is no dragon," she said, "perhaps terrible Fafnaer is just a myth."

Sarissa blew at her hair again, and saw a speck in the distant sky. She lost it in the sunshine off the waves.

The first herald of Fafnaer's arrival was screaming from the docks. The beast flew in low, and as the screams rose, so did he. Lost to sight for an instant below the lip of the cliff, the dragon shot skyward to blow the hair out of Sarissa's face in a titanic beating of wings.

Sarissa could hardly believe how big Fafnaer was. The dragon settled its claws on the edge of the cliff as surely as a giant bird of prey. Something shifted inside Sarissa. She had started her day sulking about the prospect of being married off to some snot-nosed prince or taking any more dancing lessons, but now those anxieties melted from her like dew at first light. The terror was merely mind-shattering until the dragon spoke, at which point it invaded her soul.

"Cowards, mice, traitors!" the dragon punctuated the words with gouts of flame that burned the leaves above Sarissa's head.

"I expected more," the dragon roared on. "King Reginn the sixth was much cleverer. He would at least have tested some new war machine on me. You surrender your daughter as meekly as sheep during the cull!"

A tiny spark of irritation cut through Sarissa's trembling.

"Stop yelling," she yelled. "I won't spend my final moments listening to you ignore me. My father already ignores me enough. Eat me and get it over with. See how much he cares!"

The dragon stopped.

"What did you say?" it rumbled in a lower voice, looking down at her.

"Eat me! All I am to my father is a burnt offering and all I am to you is a snack. I am utterly insignificant."

The dragon settled down on its haunches and squinted at her.

"You are indeed a little chit of no particular significance. If, for some reason I cannot yet conceive, I chose to listen, what would you say that I would find so very interesting?"

"If I told you what I really thought of you, my father, this kingdom, and your stupid war with my family, your scales would fall off. You worm. You fire-drooling old lizard. You corpse-breathed overgrown salamander."

The dragon looked surprised for a moment, then its great scaly brows gathered like thunderheads. Sarissa plowed on.

"I have so much scorn for your idiotic plan to vex my father than one language can scarcely contain it. *Perhaps thou wouldst prefer that I cursed thee in the speech of kings?*"

The dragon's voice held both the timbre and immediate peril of an earthquake.

"*Thou dasn't.*"

"*I dast,*" Sarissa yelled into Fafnaer's fearsome collection of scales and teeth. "*Thou smellest like a furnace full of unwashed undergarments! Thy scales art rusty and thy plans those of a drooling babe hoping to frighten his wetnurse!*"

High on the hill, the king averted his eyes. He had long since lost the sense of his daughter, and full though his mind was of the war in the south, he could not bring himself to look.

"Has it eaten her yet?" He said, slipping into the common speech.

"No, my lord," the chancellor replied, fingering the beads of an ornate necklace of state.

"What's happening, then?"

Sigmund shifted in his armor and looked through his fine Zenatan seeing glass.

"She seems to be begging for her life, sire."

"The poor creature," the king said.

Sarissa stopped to draw breath. The dragon had craned its neck down to listen to her tirade. He was as long as six ox carts laid end to end, scaled in deep red, and horned with ancient ivory. His breath smelled like a blacksmith's forge.

"Is that all?" Fafnaer said, lowering his great head to one side to scrutinize her with one giant, golden eye.

"Yes. I could probably think of more, but I'm going to get eaten first," Sarissa sniffed. "I'll never be a queen. I'll never fall in love. I'll never get to write any poetry or learn to dance. I don't even like dancing, but now I never will. I'll never turn eighteen and marry some poxy prince. Just eat me and get it over with!"

The dragon looked around the tree and up at the castle ramparts. There was a glint of glass.

"Convince me," the dragon said, "to spare you."

Now it was Sarissa's turn to look surprised.

"What? How?"

Fafnaer cleared his throat with a sound like a thousand brazier coals popping.

"What I meant," Sarissa said, "was how do you plan to defeat my father by eating me when you could just fly up to the castle and drown it in fire?"

"I do not seek just to kill him, Princess. I seek to torment him."

The girl gazed up at the dragon with something like pity.

"Why are you looking at me like that?" Fafnaer asked.

"If all you want to do is hurt my father, then you are as much his slave as I am."

Fafnaer looked at Sarissa for what seemed like a long time.

"Well?" the princess said, "are you going to eat me?"

"No," the ancient dragon answered, and gripped the trunk of the tree. Its claws sank into the wood and she felt the roots groan beneath her slippered feet.

Part Two: Sarissa's Fifteenth Summer

The flight to the dragon's island was a dark rush of wind and cold, because Sarissa kept her eyes closed the entire time.

After many frigid minutes, there was a gut-loosening sensation of descent. The dragon freed her from the ropes and cast the tree into the sea. His scales were smooth and warm against her skin. The air grew suddenly close, and Sarissa's feet were set bare upon the ground. Her slippers had long since fallen off.

"Open your eyes," the dragon said in a hot gust. "We've landed."

Sarissa did, and was struck dumb. She stood in a magnificent cavern supported by great pillars of stone. Some ancient people had built a longhouse in the cave, and the beams that once supported its walls still stood high above her head. Beyond that was the dragon's hoard. A shining mountain of gold and jewels, casks of wine and stacked rolls of hand-woven tapestry. Every imaginable kind of plunder leant against the cavern's walls.

"That's... impressive," Sarissa said. She saw the figurehead of a longship protruding from the hoard. The dragon slid by her like a colossal cat and curled itself amongst the broken oars with a huge creak. The boat was big enough to have thirty men rowing on each side. Fafnaer looked down at Sarissa from atop his kingdom.

"The taking of all this gold was amusing, but the hoarding of it is blander than you think."

Sarissa hugged herself and stared up at the dragon.

"Well, you've caught a princess," she said, "what is your usual procedure with royal captives?"

"I will keep you as a plaything."

Sarissa put her hands on her hips. Acid entered her voice, but when she spoke she felt angry rather than petulant.

"Oh, how lovely. Your munificence is as boundless as your hoard of gold. I can scarcely contain my joy at exchanging my life as a royal lapdog to become an overgrown cat's ball of yarn."

"You are the most ungrateful princess I have ever met. You have known luxury beyond what most could ever dream."

Sarissa let out an enormous sigh. "Then why has every moment of it felt like a cage?"

"Most riches are," the dragon said.

"You're the one sitting on a pile of gold," Sarissa said. The dragon snorted and puffed. It felt like being buffeted by air from an oven.

"Are you laughing?" she said.

"I am."

"Well, in that case I will not be a plaything."

"Are you certain?" the dragon said, and smiled a smile as glinting and cold as the sunrise at harvest.

Sarissa ran along the ancient ceiling beams and the dragon chased her. She wobbled and stumbled and naked terror lanced through her guts every time she slipped. The dragon hunted her from below, sending up little gust of fire from its nostrils whenever she started slowing down.

When she finally fell, screaming, the dragon caught her with surprising delicacy and put her down. She lay still and panted for a while. When she finally opened her eyes, she found Fafnaer looking down at her.

"Your beams are unsafe," Sarissa said, and the corners of the dragon's scaly jaw twitched. Sarissa realized a few things at once. Fafnaer was not going to eat her, for a start.

"And you have been very bored."

Living with the dragon presented complications. There was nowhere to sleep, and Fafnaer often ate nothing but rancid sheep and goats. Once she discovered that she would not be devoured out of hand, Sarissa started searching the dragonhoard for necessities. She found an ornate four-poster bed that must once have been the property of a queen, and made the dragon drag it over by a shimmering rock pool.

Each day she tried to think of new ways to occupy Fafnaer, who proved to be surprisingly subtle company when he wasn't in the mood for chasing her around.

"I'm bound to stop being amusing eventually," she said, "what happens when I run out of ideas?"

"I will return you before winter," the dragon replied. "I hibernate."

"I have to go back?" Sarissa hadn't thought about going home.

"Yes. Now, amuse me. Have you a singing voice?"

"I do, but my matron said it was raspy."

"Sing anyway."

So Sarissa sang, and stopped, laughing, when Fafnaer began humming along. It felt like being accompanied by a blacksmith's bellows.

"The matron was right," Fafnaer said when she ran out of songs, "you rasp, but your voice has personality."

Sarissa bowed.

After a week, Sarissa began to smell. She dug around the edges of the golden hoard until she found an enameled brass tub with clawed feet. The dragon seemed pleased with this project, and disappeared from the cavern to return with a huge armful of branches and small trees. He kindled a fire under the tub and waited expectantly.

Sarissa started to pull her grungy dress over her head, and suddenly stopped.

"Well?" Fafnaer said. "Wash."

"It is a well-known fact that dragons are lecherous, perverted monsters who love nothing more than the sight of maidenly flesh."

"You paid too much attention to your nursery rhymes. I am a dragon; I hatched from an egg at the centre of the earth itself. I feel no more lust for you than you would for a mouse."

Sarissa thought about that. Steam rose from the surface of the water and wafted into the air.

"Oh skies," she said, "what's the difference?"

She cast her clothes aside and stepped gingerly into the water. She emerged, after a long, blissful time, like a maiden from the pool.

"What is that?" She pointed.

"That is a tapestry woven from flaxen seeds grown at the farthest reaches of the known world. It was the personal banner of King Reginn the third, your great-great-great-great grandfather, and I took it from him at the battle of—"

"Please be quiet, oh mighty lizard," Sarissa said, "and give it here. I need something to towel off with."

Late that summer, Sarissa stood like a statue, chin cupped in one palm, clad in a long woolen shirt that had once belonged to a warrior who tried to kill the dragon in a bygone age. All around her were rickety representations of knights and queens and men at arms. On a board carved into the stone floor by Fafnaer's claws, the princess and the dragon were playing chess.

Sarissa walked amongst her pieces, and uncertainly shoved a rook a few paces forward, then started to shove it back.

"Leave that piece there," Fafnaer said.

"But I've thought of a better move," Sarissa replied. "I would not move it back if I didn't have to. These rooks are devilishly heavy."

"Once you stop touching the piece, the move is complete. That is the most ancient rule of the game of kings."

"I am no king."

"No excuse," the dragon said breezily, a little smoke curling from his nostrils.

Sarissa abandoned the rook to its fate. "Then how am I supposed to win?"

"You won't."

While her pieces fell with the inevitability of snow, Sarissa sighed theatrically and gazed at the vaulted ceiling. It had been a while since she ran the beams.

"Another game?" the dragon asked, placing a knight pinched delicately between two scimitar-like claws into a fatal position at her rear.

"No, I beg you to leave me to stew in my humiliation. I need sleep."

"You are improving," Fafnaer said, "not enough to win, but improving."

"I am trying to divine how you will use your queen," Sarissa said sweetly. She walked over to one of her knights. "This poor fellow looks particularly vulnerable."

The dragon reached out a great claw.

"I could defend my pawns, or take one of yours, or perhaps, as you suggest, take this knight."

His queen knocked the knight aside with a crash of steel plate. As the dragon spoke, Sarissa paced the edge of the board until her feet happened upon a tassel dangling from a tapestry affixed to one of the stone pillars.

"But I am hardly that foolish," Fafnaer continued, beginning to move the queen back. "You set this trap like a child. Now pick up your knight and—"

Sarissa grabbed the tassel and gave it a violent tug. The tassle was tied to a rope, the rope to another, and that one to a beam above the dragon's head. A weak and blackened log crashed down from above and broke one of the dragon's horns with a tremendous crack.

Fafnaer cast the beam aside and lunged toward Sarissa, who cowered against the pillar.

"That is a poor way to try killing a dragon!" His breath smelled like molten iron.

Sarissa quailed. Her imagination had not done Fafnaer's anger justice. Tears ran unbidden down her face.

"Explain yourself before I devour you!" Fafnaer roared. Sarissa trembled, but she had made her move.

"That queen must stay where she is if I am to win."

"What?" the dragon's anger ebbed fractionally.

"You've taken your claw from it."

"You dropped that beam on me," the dragon said, "so that you might cheat?"

"Of course I cheated," Sarissa yelled through her tears, "how else can I win? I'm sorry about your horn, and I'm sorry if I hurt you, but I have made my move. Now make yours!"

On the dragon's ancient, weathered face, a small battle played itself out. The forces of anger drew in his breath and loaded his throat with fire. Whatever opposed his rage marshaled his brow into a frown.

"That is admirably insane of you. I have eaten entire villages for less."

"I am not a villager," Sarissa screamed. "I am a queen."

The corners of Fafnaer's great jaws twitched.

"I see. I misunderstood the game we were playing. That was my error. Let me show you the move I should have made."

The dragon snatched Sarissa up in one huge talon and deposited her at the center of the chess board. Sarissa realized what was about to happen, and screwed her eyes shut.

"Dragon takes Queen," Fafnaer bellowed, and bathed the board in fire. Sarissa felt it lick all around her, felt the hem of her shirt whip around her hips. Her hair caught fire and her eyebrows smoldered. The dragon's terrible roar shook the air to pieces, and she stood rock still, each breath burning the inside of her lungs.

The dragon stopped, and Sarissa opened her eyes. She felt sunburnt and bits of her hair were falling away in pungent, crackling strands. She brushed at her tears and found that the fire had evaporated them.

"You didn't burn me."

"Only the skies know why," the dragon rumbled. Sarissa felt as if a weight was dropping from her.

"I think I do," she said, staring at the burning queen.

Part Three: Sarissa's Sixteenth Summer

"You have grown plump," Fafnaer said, dropping Sarissa lightly from one claw. From the other, he dropped a large bundle tied with rope. Having survived one summer with the dragon, this time Sarissa had packed.

"Oh skies," she said, "not you, too."

"You should mind your shape. Every part of you is a reflection of your will, from tail to nose scales."

Sarissa dragged the bundle into the cavern, glaring up at the dragon.

"I would, if it were not so infinitely boring to learn dancing and my pastry chef were not so talented. Now, make way."

The princess and the dragon did not play chess. Sarissa enjoyed recounting her winter to Fafnaer more than she thought she would. Her father had found a merchant prince who might consent to marry her, probably because he had never met her, and she had failed extensively in her preparations for a future betrothal banquet.

"I hate dancing. I'm clumsy. Dragons don't know any dark spells that can grant me mystical waltzing abilities, do they?"

Fafnaer thought for a while, then indicated a rack of ancient weapons that lay against one wall.

"No, but I can show you the secrets of the heroes who have tried to slay me with all these legendary swords."

Sarissa tried to imagine herself swinging a glaive and found she couldn't. "That's not what I need at all."

"Some of those heroes were very hard to kill. Their steps were complicated, and I studied them closely. How different can it possibly be? Besides, if I tire of you, you'll be able to put up a fight before I eat you. What say you to that?"

Sarissa thought about it.

"I'm warming to the idea," she said.

Every day Fafnaer made Sarissa disrobe and bind herself in the manner of ancient northern sword-maidens. He hunted sharks and Sarissa ate the diet of the warriors of the distant east. He rhythmically tapped the flagstones with his claws and made her prance and duck and weave, delighting in every moment of her discomfiture.

Sarissa soon lost any semblance of plumpness, and began enjoying herself. Her feet never felt graceful, but they began to feel sure. Fafnaer made her hold a broadsword rigid before her until her shoulders trembled and her fingers screamed.

"You will always be smaller and weaker, even if you only fight men and not dragons. You must learn to win regardless."

"That's easy for you to say," Sarissa said, regarding the dragon's massive bulk and terrifying claws.

"If you don't like your weakness, change it," Fafnaer said.

In mid-summer Fafnaer became increasingly irritable, and his attempts to turn Sarissa into the only warrior worthy of opposing him became cruel.

"I won't be much good to you if I die of exhaustion," Sarissa said. "Tell me what's wrong."

The dragon paused, and scratched at his scales.

"I'm molting," he said.

When Sarissa stopped laughing, she ordered the dragon to heat tubs of water. Sarissa scrubbed him with a succession of brooms until their bristles wore out on his scaly hide.

When the chore was finally done and Sarissa was wringing out her sodden hair, Fafnaer let out an enormous sigh. "That was excellent. Let us drink some wine to celebrate my new coat."

The dragon went rummaging around the treasure hoard.

"Wait," Sarissa called after him, "I can have wine?"

Sarissa awoke among her linen tapestries and wanted to die. Her head felt like someone had split it with a wood axe.

With a soft rustle, the dragon's pointed nose poked through the curtains of the ornate bed.

"*Art thou ready to face this vale of tears, noble lady?*" Fafnaer whispered. There was enormous mirth in his deep voice.

"*Perish, thou thrice-cursed wyvern. Thou corruptor of dignity and subborner of innocent maidens.*"

"Fear not, princess," the dragon said, mockingly, "we will practice, but I have run you a bath."

Sarissa practiced, and her head did clear.

"Why do you hate my father so?"

"Hold the sword until it hurts. Hold onto it until you your muscles scream at you to drop it."

It took a while, but the pain came.

"Do you want to let it go?" Fafnaer asked, by way of explanation.

Sarissa gazed up the shivering steel. She hated the exercise, but hated the idea of giving up more.

"No," she said.

"Indeed. Now show me the Von Falkenbach positions."

Sarissa's feet flashed through the steps, and as she twisted and spun the broadsword danced. She chased Fafnaer through the steps, and her blade caught the light like a fish twitching at the end of a line. She finished with a flourish that actually hit the dragon, who was incredibly agile for such a large creature. Fafnaer said nothing, and Sarissa beamed. Her face bragged as eloquently as any paean.

"Not bad, but hide your intentions. That is the first step to winning when no one expects you to."

Sarissa tried to arrange her features into a serious mien, and suddenly noticed the dragon's claw. Her face fell.

"I cut you," she said. A trickle of deep red dripped from beneath the dragon's scales to tap gently on the floor.

"It's nothing, I would have an enormous collection of scars, if I didn't molt," Fafnaer replied. "No, Sarissa. Do not touch the blood. It will burn. I'm fine."

Sarissa wanted to touch the dragon. He didn't move. She dabbed the back of her left hand ever so faintly against the wound, and withdrew it with a yowl. There was a dark, discolored stain on her knuckle. Smoke rose gently from it, and Sarissa cradled it under her other arm. She didn't cry or make a sound.

"I warned you," Fafnaer said.

When the summer ended, the dragon seemed a little forlorn.

"I have a gift for you to bring home," Fafnaer said, indicating a large, gilt mirror.

"I own a lot of mirrors," Sarissa said, long past being offended by the dragon's provocation.

The dragon emitted an uncomfortable rumbling.

"This one is slightly magical; knock upon its frame, and it will show the contents of another mirror, its twin."

"You want me to stay in touch," Sarissa said.

Part Four: Sarissa's Sixteenth Winter

Slumped at her mirror, Sarissa sank her teeth into a sweet roll and marveled at the quality of her pastry chef. She didn't miss much about rich, sauce-laden royal cooking, but the combination of caramel drizzle and candied walnuts made her feel cured of every ill she had ever suffered and possibly a few she hadn't.

She munched the perfectly browned confection and failed to decide what to do about her upcoming betrothal banquet. It didn't seem like a big deal, next to abduction by a dragon, but she didn't want to go, and couldn't decide if she should assert herself or just grin and bear it.

"Do sword practice and dance truly overlap?" she asked the mirror. The reflected Sarissa looked as unsure as she was. She decided not to attend, then changed her mind. She had grown used to having someone to talk to about serious things.

"This is silly," she said, and made up her mind for good. She knocked on the mirror. The glass became hazy, swirled, and in a few moments showed one large, scaly eyelid.

"I'm sorry to wake you," Sarissa said, "but I have a conundrum."

She explained her reluctance to the hibernating dragon.

"So," she said, "what would you suggest?"

Fafnaer's half-shut eye narrowed slightly, and the dragon's deep voice rumbled across time and space.

"Kill them all. Put them to the sword. Annihilate everyone you suspect and then eradicate the witnesses. Stun them with curses. Burn them. Take revenge on them until the fifth genera-"

"Thank you, Fafnaer," Sarissa said, hastily knocking on the mirror, "see you in the spring!"

Sarissa danced with the young merchant prince, and it wasn't all that bad. He seemed just as nervous and unhappy as she was.

"Just imagine you're learning sword fighting steps," she said, "and try not to step on my feet."

Part Five: Sarissa's Seventeenth Summer

The dragon was surprised when the princess arrived. She had grown taller and rather rounder, but the lean strength of the previous summer was still obvious in her steps. She seemed to have changed only subtly, but completely enough that the dragon couldn't help feeling he'd missed something. Her talk was still concerned with dancing and the prince and the ridiculous knight Sigmund, but all her questions were about the war that her father refused to end.

Fafnaer loved war, and was content to discuss it for days on end. Sarissa still practiced with the broadsword, and the dragon soon found that just a little training made her more than passable with a falchion as well, but they spent all their best hours recreating battles. Sarissa had learned a great deal from the merchant prince, whose father had not yet refused a possible betrothal, and was quite current on the disposition of the armies in the south. Each morning they constructed some new part of King Reginn's southern border with piles of gold for hills and inverted chalices for towns.

"I don't understand why neither my father nor the Caliph has attempted a winning move," Sarissa said.

"Decisive change is difficult," Fafnaer replied.

"That may be, but the coffers still drain and harvest after harvest goes unreaped while they tarry. My father should gamble everything on a final blow."

"Perhaps, but to draw out the infantry you would need bait."

"We have cavalry."

"And they have pikemen," the dragon observed.

"Then the cavalry would have to die," Sarissa said dispassionately.

"And why would they do that for you?"

That brought Sarissa up short. She thought. "I would be the queen."

The dragon laughed at her, a deep rumbling that rattled the coins. "That would work once, I admit, but that is all. Why would the sons follow you after you sacrificed their fathers?"

"I don't know. I don't know why they would ride forth to die for anyone. Why do they?"

The dragon, ever discontent with straight answers, said, "The real question is, why don't you know?"

The princess, ever more used to the dragon's philosophical musing, answered, "I suppose because I don't know why I don't know why."

"Exactly," Fafnaer said with satisfaction. "Have you ever seen a battlefield?"

"No," Sarissa said.

"Dress warmly and bring wine, then, we'll get there by nightfall. No, not a wine that you like."

Fafnaer landed and helped Sarissa down. Her boots sank wetly into the earth, though the sky was clear and no rain fell. A field of carnage swept out before her, with lines of men fallen like leaves tossed by the current and left upon the rocks.

With Fafnaer's wing beats stilled, Sarissa finally heard the battlefield, too. Carrion birds crowed, and there was an ebbing background murmur of moaning men. The smell of decay settled on the back of her tongue, as sweet and putrid as the scent of orchids.

Sarissa threw up, and discovered why she had the wine. She swilled it around her mouth to clear the taste of bile, and the alcohol lessened the whiff of death. She realized why the dragon insisted she bring a spirit she didn't like; she knew in an instant that she would hate the smell of it for the rest of her life. Marrow frothed from stumps, the wings of vultures flashed white under the moon, and men suffered the fates the manoevering armies had left them to.

Sarissa wandered the plain like a sleepwalker, sick to her soul, until something caught her at her ankle. She barely muffled a shriek. At her feet was a Zenatan pikeman, his belly lain open to the sky, looking up at her as though she were an apparition. Every fiber of her being screamed at her to run, to climb Fafnaer's flank and beat at his neck until he flew her away from there. She knelt.

The boy was dark-skinned and had a soft, new beard. He had been handsome, and was her age, or close to it. He said something she could not understand. She held his hand.

"Let me know when you're finished," Fafnaer said from behind her. "It's rare I get to eat a Zenatan. Their leather armor doesn't stick in the teeth the way plate does."

Sarissa stood after a while, and her face shone with tears.

"Will you fly me away from here, above the clouds?"

"You don't find me callous?" Fafnaer said, mildly surprised. He edged closer to the Zenatan.

"You're a dragon," Sarissa said.

"Flying high will not help you forget this," he said, lifting the dead soldier to his jaws. Sarissa didn't seem overly bothered by his chewing.

"I have been terrified every single time we've flown. I kept my eyes closed. I don't want to forget anything, but I do want to see something that will clear my soul."

The dragon swallowed.

"Climb on my neck," he said, and Sarissa did. They flew so high the fall stopped meaning anything, so high the clouds created a silver sea in the moonlight, and nothing in the world was the same. Sarissa shivered in her cloak, and didn't care, and her face shone slick with the dew of clouds.

Part Six: Sarissa's Eighteenth Summer

Sarissa lounged disconsolately in the bath. A lot had changed that winter. Her conversation with the dragon picked up where it had left off, even if months had passed between the words.

"There is no way to win the war without sacrificing the entire country to do it. It would honestly be better if you ate me, flew to the castle, and ate my father as well. He barely said two words to me all winter, other than to promise my hand in marriage to the merchant prince."

Fafnaer snorted lightly with one nostril to rekindle the logs below the tub and stared placidly at the bathing princess.

"What do you expect of a king? It is your fate to be raised by maids and tutors and matrons."

"And dragons."

That made the dragon pause.

"It does seem that way."

Sarissa enjoyed his discomfort. "Still, all you teach me is swords and tactics and how to conquer the unseen realms of the mind. I won't make much of a wife."

"I have played my role well, then," Fafnaer said.

Sarissa sloshed the water irritably.

"Please be serious. Don't you see this has to end? I'm eighteen. I marry this fall and that's the end of the Reginn line. Your feud with my father has no road left to travel."

"You think you know me very well, princess."

"Don't I?" Sarissa said.

They stayed silent for a while, and then Sarissa doused her head in warm water and scrubbed at her hair. She stood in the enameled tub, splashed around to rinse herself off, and stepped unselfconsciously out of the water to pad back toward her bed.

"I can't find King Reginn the third's towel," Sarissa said.

"Indeed," replied the dragon.

"Why are you looking at me like that?"

Fafnaer craned his long, scaly neck to scrutinize her.

"I lied, all those summers ago, so that you would get into the habit of disrobing. I have gazed upon your nakedness these passing years with the most lascivious enjoyment. Your nudity has been my supreme pleasure. *Art thou sure thou knowest me?*"

A blush spread from Sarissa's cheeks toward her neck. She weakly crossed one arm over her chest, to which the flush spread like a prairie fire.

"*Thou… slimy sky-forsaken salamander. Thou piteous creep.*"

The dragon laughed, deeply, as Sarissa wrapped herself in a sheet.

"I am a dragon, what did you expect?" Fafnaer said, and Sarissa began to laugh.

Part Seven: Sarissa's First Autumn

Autumn came, and this time when Sarissa sailed home Fafnaer admitted the parting was different. The princess packed her things aboard the best of the little boats adventurers had left behind without a word until she was ready to cast off. Fafnaer held the gunnels close to the rocks so she could step aboard.

"I want you to let me go," Sarissa said, "let all of this go. Let me get married and find my own way. Forget your feud with my father and his father and stay here. Things have changed, and you can change with them."

Fafnaer leant his head down, and Sarissa hugged his scaly snout.

"Very well," he said, "I promise. Sail home across the bay and be safe, the wind is picking up. There will be a storm."

Sarissa looked at him for a long time, and cast off. The dragon thought about what she had said far longer than he intended. She was right; the Reginn line would end soon, and everything would change. He looked across the bay at the distant shores, and spread his wings.

Some part of Sarissa knew, and she piled on sails until every scrap of canvas hummed and white water crashed against the hull.

High above, she saw the dragon fly by below the clouds.

"You stupid old lizard!" she screamed at the sky, and the prow of her little sailboat cut through the whitecaps like a sword parting silk.

Sarissa flew across the bay, but by the time she crossed it the wharfs were already burning. Every timber was ablaze and there was nowhere for her to land.

"You can't get rid of me that easily!" she yelled toward the castle, and hauled on the tiller until she was headed for the cliffs.

High above the cliffside battlements, the castle was in chaos. The wharves were burning and the dragon had crashed through the gates into the keep. At least one ship had already been seen to steer away from the conflagration, only to dash itself upon the rocks.

"We should go up there, or down to the docks," one of the guards said.

"We bloody well shouldn't," his companion replied, "I like living, and this is our post. Wait a second, look."

A hand appeared over the cliffside parapet clad in shredded lace and daubs of blood and grit. A disheveled girl climbed over the lip and lay gasping at their feet.

"Now see here, miss—"

Sarissa rose to her feet.

"Out of my way," she said.

Belatedly, the guards recognized her.

"My lady, let us—"

"Kneel!" Sarissa bellowed.

The two men both dropped as though they had been shot with crossbows.

"Thank you," she said, and ran up the hill.

Racing up the last set of stairs to her father's audience hall, Sarissa heard men cheer. She smelled smoke and heard steel ring and knew that despite everything, she was too late to mend the world.

The hall looked like a battlefield. The chandeliers had been torn from the ceiling, tapestries were on fire, and the flagstones were slick with blood. Fafnaer lay in the centre of the room, breathing heavily. A great hole in the roof showed how he had made his way in.

Sarissa stumbled along the dragon's flank and tripped. Fafnaer was held down by a thick tracery of ropes and hooks. King Reginn must have come to the same conclusion the dragon had, and prepared. When she finally reached the dragon's head, shocked faces turned to meet her.

Up on the dais the king sat on his throne. Beside him were one of his generals, and a tall Zenatan emissary. The boy prince and the chancellor were there, too, and before them all knelt Sigmund.

"I have dealt this blow," the knight said, and started again, "*I hast dealt this fell swoop in thy name, oh king.*"

Sarissa slid to a stop by Fafnaer's big head. The dragon was still breathing.

"Are you all right?" she said.

"No," Fafnaer grimaced, "the knight's sword arm is better than his grammar."

Sarissa's blood chilled. She looked back at the dragon's huge body. None of his wounds looked fatal, until she saw the hilt of Sigmund's sword. The blade was buried at the base of Fafnaer's neck, struck downward toward his heart. The dragon shivered in pain.

"My lady," Sigmund said, finally noticing her, "do not touch the beast, its blood burns."

Sarissa ignored him, sat down and leant against Fafnaer's cheek, sobbing.

"This is what I wanted," the dragon said.

"Fool," Sarissa said, then, with perfect inflection, "*thou most infinite fool.*"

"Perhaps, but I did listen. You were right; the time for this kind of thing has passed."

"I still need you," Sarissa said, simply.

"No, you want me. That's different. You do not need me anymore than you need him." The dragon's eyes turned for a moment to the king, then back to Sarissa.

"Then stay alive a little longer, if you can," she said, "and watch."

"Leave her be," the king said, as the merchant prince took a step forward.

The princess slumped to her knees in the pool of blood below the great wound. She put both palms on its flank, and dragon blood coursed over her hands. There was a faint, distant sizzle.

"My lady," Sigmund said, and took another step toward her.

The princess hid her face in her hands and leant her forehead against the dragon's side. Her chest heaved, and the knight felt a pang of pity.

On the dais, the merchant prince took a step back, and no one noticed.

Sarissa felt the dragon's blood scar her skin, felt it burn away her entire self and leave something new behind. Neither the vast sky of stars nor the bay below were as wide or deep as her anger, as her loss, as the gulf full of things she would be forced to leave behind. She felt the fiery, hollow emptiness of rage not in her mind, nor in her heart. She felt it in her soul.

With a cry borne by the infinite weight of her grief Sarissa dragged her fingers down her face. Fafnaer's blood burned long marks into her soft skin, war paint that would never fade.

She stood and grasped Sigmund's broadsword with both hands. The dragon's heartbeat quivered through the steel. It beat steadily, painfully, rhythmically, until in one graceful stroke Sarissa pulled the blade free.

Fafnaer roared, and heart blood gushed from the wound to coat Sarissa's arms and send a glittering ruby arc spattering through the air. The dragon coughed flames, shuddered, and lay still.

Sarissa stepped lightly past the dragon's snout and strode toward the knight.

Sigmund opened his mouth to say something, and Sarissa spun past him in a crouch and scythed the red sword across the backs of his knees. The knight fell. Sarissa finished the spin and brought the blade around in a sweeping arc that kicked sparks from the stone floor. The stroke separated the knight's head from his shoulders as cleanly as a seamstress cutting ribbon.

Everyone in the room took a step back, except the king, who pushed into his cushions. Sarissa strode inexorably onward. The chancellor hobbled forward on his cane, and Sarissa cut him down without ceremony. As she mounted the steps to the throne, she met the eyes of the merchant prince. He was taller, and the rapier at his waist sat comfortably for a change. His hand was on the hilt.

"Do you have anything to say about this?" Sarissa asked. Her eyes shone like falling stars in a black and fractured sky.

"No," he said, "not a thing."

Sarissa turned from him and started back up the steps.

"One thing, actually." The princess turned her eyes back to him. They were the eyes of a madman or a monster. The eyes of a dragon.

"Yes?" she said, dangerously.

"May I call upon you again, my lady?" he said, and swallowed. For an instant, the old Sarissa came back. The girl he'd danced with. The girl who had listened to him, and showed him where to put his feet.

"Yes," she said, distractedly, and turned away to face her father. She hefted Sigmund's blade, tested its weight. The king spoke.

"How dare you?" he said, his voice taut with rage.

"Address me in the high speech. People will remember these words when I am queen."

"No one will recognize you," the king said.

"They will," his daughter said, "when I give them a reason to."

Finally, the old king heard her. He switched to the old tongue, barely realizing he had.

"Art thou insensate? That dragon hath corrupted thee, daughter, poisoned thee. He hath tainted thy sense of right and duty."

"Thou sharest that honor with him, father, but he hath gone, and soon thou shalt follow him wherever goest fools."

Sarissa said the words, and was sure of them. Hoped some vanishing part of the dragon might hear them. She didn't know how long it took to die.

"Prithee, sit. Enjoy thy throne. Thou shalt never leave it, for thou hast killed that thing I loved and I cannot stand the sight of thee nor of him. I shall wash thy lands clean of thee, and my soul of thee, and this realm shall have a queen anon."

The sword did not tremble. She watched her father listen, really hear her, and disbelieve.

"Thou dasn't," he said.

"I dast," Sarissa said.

The blade was hot with dragon's blood. Sarissa transfixed the king on its tip and drove it though him, through the thick wood of the throne, until she could lean over the hilt and her nose almost touched his. His eyes were full of surprise, and Sarissa found hers blurred with tears.

"Now is a fine time to be shocked," she said softly.

"Why?" the king gasped. Little wisps of smoke drifted from his daughter's face. His vision was going grey, but he could smell the burning of her skin. Saw that the dragon blood had soaked into the lace at her wrists. It would leave a pattern there.

"My weakness bothered me," she said, "so I changed it."

Sarissa waited until her father went to join the dragon, and the world waited with her. At length she straightened, leaving the sword where it was. She tugged the royal circlet from her father's bent head and placed it atop her own. The white gold shone against the rusty ochre of her dragonburnt skin.

"Now," she said to the prince and the generals and emissaries and the nobles, "shall we end this war and restore some sense?"

As one they nodded, and the wise among them knelt.

Blake Jessop is a Canadian author of sci-fi, fantasy and horror stories with a master's degree in creative writing from the University of Adelaide. You can read more of his supernatural speculative fiction in the Winter 2020 edition of the Mad Scientist Journal, or follow him on Twitter @everydayjisei.

CANDAS JANE DORSEY

A NIGHT IN THE PHILOSOPHER'S CAVE

She woke in the usual darkness, alerted by the click of claws on rock and the sound of her own breath. Took her sword tiredly from its scabbard.

"Are you finally ready?" said a tired voice from the corner.

"Again?" she said. "Again?"

"Yes, again. Are you ready?"

"Why don't we do this in the light this time?" she said, and from the other corner heard a chuckle.

"Because I am a being of the darkness beyond the darkness of the pit," said the voice.

"Oh, don't eat that, city boy," she said, "it's horseshit."

This time it was a laugh. She pulled some of the dry, compacted, slightly humus-y straw into a heap, and struck her shield-edge against the stone beside it a couple of times, until a spark larger than the rest lit the heap. She lay on her stomach to blow on the tiny flame, and felt another warm breath stir the air from the other side of the fire. The beast was helping her nourish the flames.

"You blow, I'll get some real fuel," she said, and her hands, much more suited to the task than the beast's curved claws, pulled more straw into a heap and fed it to the flames.

The fire woke a little more. "It won't last long like that," said the beast, pushing more straw from its corner into the flames with impervious fists and tail. Its fists were five-clawed, like hers, gold as the sunset and large enough now that they could have caged her torso, were the beast so inclined.

"You've grown," she said. She looked around for more fuel.

"I always grow," said the beast. "It's our curse. If nobody kills me, I'll grow until I can't lift my own bones. It's annoying."

The cave had grown too. She knew from the shape of the striations on the curved shell of it that the bored beast enlarged it in its spare time. She laughed. "Some days I can't lift my own bones either. It's not annoying, it's entropy. But today's a good day. More or less. I survived the dream again."

Over in the corner, the broken handles of the weapons of warriors gone before were swept into an uneven heap as high as her ribcage. She limped over and began to drag an armful of them toward the fire.

"Hey," said the beast. "I was saving those."

"For what?" she said. "A museum? In here? You're supposed to eat everybody who comes here. Who'd see it?"

"Point," said the beast, and reached above her head for a spear haft. The golden points decorating its arm clattered, and combed her long hair on the way past.

As she put a couple of mace handles on the flame, the beast turned the spear handle in its front claws. "I remember this one," it said, "fought like a demon. Cheated really. Gave me this," and it raised its scarlet-plated hip to show her a long, puckered line, green with scar tissue, across a wrinkled haunch.

"Pretty good one," she said. "Takes heft to hew those scales. What did you do to him?"

"Oh, I let him go, of course," said the beast, "but I ate his right arm first. Had to, really. Couldn't let him think I was getting soft."

"But you are," she said.

The beast roared and reared up in the darkness beyond the flames. She saw iridescence gleam on silver belly scales, and the fierce eyes with their own banked golden glow blinked and glared down from far above her.

She continued calmly to feed weapons to the flame. She laid aside a good yew longbow, not yet old and brittle, because it would be a waste to burn it, but she made sure to toss it outside the cave mouth, so as not to give the wrong message.

After a moment, the beast backed off into the corner again, came down with a thump on all its golden feet, flat as a flung cat, but it continued to grumble, like a closed kettle coming to the boil.

"How pretty your belly is," she said. "I wish we had something to drink."

The beast still grumbled.

"Oh, give over," she said. "We're both old. Older than we used to be, anyway. So what? We're smarter. We can still show the young ones a thing or two."

There was silence beyond the rim of light. A great ruby and gold and copper and verdigris coiling and uncoiling, smooth, and its sound as if a bag of coins was dragged behind a horse, which was a thing she had seen, though the bag was tied to the belt of a dead man (who hadn't been dead when his long, bouncing career through a foreign forest had started).

After a long while, she said, "Well, if they'll let us, of course."

The beast rumbled, but this time it was a wry sort of rumble, and after a moment it untied itself and flowed into the firelight again, and, arranging itself with belly turned to the fire, drooped its head until its cheek rested upon one front claw. Its tail still lashed slightly. "Look out for the fire," she said sharply, "you'll burn your tail."

"I'm part salamander," said the beast. "It'll be fine." But it tucked its tail around a rear haunch, extinguished the slightly-smouldering molten-gold tip under a slightly over-rich roll of scaly blood-red hip.

"I've got some cave-water," said the beast. "Over in that corner, a spring and a pool. You could probably drink it out of one of those old helmets."

"Most of those have skulls in them."

"Find an old one. It'll be clean by now." So she did.

"Tell me a story," she said after a while.

"You first this time," said the beast.

"Fine," she said. "Let me tell you how I met my—"

"Oh, another 'first lover'," said the beast. "'How we met' stories. It's what all the humans want to tell. What about us beasts that have to live alone? Don't you think we get sick of all this breeder talk?"

"I never bred," she said sharply, "and I was going to tell you who my father was. At last. Too bad for you. I'll tell you about the first thing I stole, then."

"I thought you were the honest hero in this scenario," said the beast dryly.

"Oh, come on," she said. "Do you think anyone gets to our age without stealing something? A slice of bread, a piece of candy, a trust, a lie, a gold coin from the trough in front of a tavern's counter? A heart?"

The beast turned its long head and delicately, with the small row of front incisors between its fangs, scratched and rearranged at its isinglass ribcage until several ruffled scales were smooth and aligned, then raised its blunt snout, lip still pushed upward by its teeth's rummaging, and shook its head like a dog until its face returned to its inscrutable norm.

"What do you do all day in here?" she said. "Besides—" she gestured at the curve of wall-into-ceiling "—renovations?"

"Scratch and snort, scrabble and sniff," it said. "Never mind. Go on with my story."

"Your story!" she said. "My story, rather. Telling it to you does not make it yours."

"Giving it to me, you mean."

"Where I come from," she said, "the stories of a teller still belong to the teller."

"But you know," said the beast, "you and I have been doing this for so long, we're starting to forget whose stories are whose."

"That's true," she said, "but this one is different. There's no doubt whose story this one is."

The beast hooted its bellowing laugh. "So it's not the one about the dragon and the scorpion!"

She grinned and shook her head. "No, not this time. I've never told you this one."

This happened a long time ago, before I was a dragon-killer. *(The beast across the fire harrumphed, and the storyteller chuckled.)* Well, it was truly before I was much of anything. I was still chewing with my baby teeth, and holding on to my father's skirts, had barely even learned to call him father and to make fire, when it first began.

It was a sunny day in late spring. Where we lived then, beside the sea, spring came earlier than it does here, and there were fields and fields of rhododendrons and azaleas in those low mountains that won't grow up this high. The slopes and valleys were fiery and showy with them, and they were magnificent, though I took them for granted.

One day, as I played in the garden before my father's house, a great white horse bore a beautiful rider to my door.

(What kind of horse, asked the beast?

(Big. White, said the warrior. You know.

(The kind they call a destrier?

(I guess so, she said. Why do you ask?

(I ate one of those once, said the beast. Never mind that now. Tell on.)

On the horse was a beautiful rider, hard and smooth and weathered, with wild hair, black or brown—I can't remember, it got white later, but this was earlier—that blew in the wind. The warrior wore silvery-grey armour and was dressed all in white.

(Was it white samite? asked the beast. I had some of that once. Nasty slithery stuff. Felt wet in my mouth.

(I have no idea what white samite is, she said. Shush, or I'll never get on.)

The rider spurred the horse up the steps and into our house. I saw blood on the horse's white belly. Then the rider slew my father, with one mighty blow of a long and already-bloody sword. My father's head was split to his jawbone, and brain and blood flew all over me.

I ran away to the shrine where the swords and daggers lay on their ceremonial rests, and I pulled the matched swords down.

My father had always told me that the swords hung there because the day of the sword was gone. That using them would be stealing war from the era of peace. I had promised not to touch them until he gave me leave. So that was my first theft, and I broke a promise to my father. And anyway, the swords were too heavy for me to wield. I was only a child.

I dragged them away into a corner, while the white rider rode after me through the paper walls of the house. The great head of the horse burst through wall after wall, then the wall shattered below, around its great chest, and finally the paper peeled away to the sides as the rider's body sliced through. Sometimes for variation the rider set the horse rearing, and its hooves sliced a long slitted door which would curl away from itself and then after a moment the white rider would widen it.

It was a large house, built around a courtyard with a sand garden and another courtyard with a water garden.

(Your father was a scholar, said the beast.

(Shhh.)

My father had been a scholar. Now he had been forced into retirement. And I had to plan for my future in the seconds of safety before each wall behind me burst and I had to retreat again.

It all took on a kind of heavy rhythm: run, stand, break, run... finally I had come round in a great figure eight, like the sign for infinity, and I was back in the entrance hall with my father's body. He lay splayed on the tile floor, his head as cloven as his hooves, and less neat. I stood beside his body again and shivered, grasping in my arms my daishō, which rested tip-down because they were too heavy for me to even lift. I'd had to drag them, and their sheaths had left furrows in the matting as I fled, which led to me like the rills of irrigation, bringing my killer to me as inevitably as spring water.

The rider's sword-tip pierced the last wall almost gently and sliced down to the level of my heart—low, I was small—and almost gently one hoof of the white horse probed through and tore the rice paper down to the ground. The horse and rider slid through like a ghost, so slowly that the paper made no ripping sound as the opening widened.

I looked through the high front door, through the carved frame unscathed by the rider's entry, and considered running out into the sunlight. But I was exhausted and racked with weeping, so I decided to make my stand by my father's body. Holding the swords before me, a double version of my father's staff, and the only thing that kept me upright, I stood as tall as I could and faced the enemy.

The white horse pranced up to me slowly, as if in dressage, and the rider looked down.

"So, the stolen child defends the thief," the rider said. "Do you not want to come home?"

"This is my home," I said, with only a slight waver in my voice.

"This is your prison," said the rider, "and I am your rescuer. Your saviour."

"You killed my father. When I am old enough I will learn to use the swords and I will kill you."

"Well, then, we had better make sure you get old enough," and leaning far down, off the side of the horse like an acrobat in the riding circus, the rider grabbed the swords and lifted them up—and me with them. The three of us were tossed across in front of the saddle. "Hold on." said the rider, and turning the horse in its own circle, and spurring it, the rider urged it from the shady house.

The last glimpse I had of my father's body and my father's house was under the white-clad arm and around the white-clad waist, three-quarters upside-down, and then I was desperately clutching the swords with one hand and the pommel of the saddle with the other, as the horse seemed to fly along the road away from the house, through the rhododendron garden down the azalea-lined path, and out into the bright hard world.

The bright hard world, it appeared, was also lined with huge rhododendron forests, blooming in the sunlight. I had never been out of my father's garden, for he forbade it, and indeed had me hide when tradespeople delivered goods or visitors came to consult him. "It is easy for a child to be stolen away," he said, "to the great grief of the parent. I would not want to lose you." Now, I was indeed stolen, but the great grief was mine, and the loss also. My father, wherever he was now, had attained the calmness of death, which we mortals seek to find in life, and so often fail.

I was not calm, and I wept and screamed at the heedless blossoms, kicking my unshod and uncloven feet against the horse and rider—until a thought struck me. I thought that I, alone, defenseless though I had swords because I could not lift them to wield, might just as well be dead.

I had been told by my father that chewing as few as two rhododendron leaves could kill a child. So I flailed out with purpose as the horse pushed through a narrow defile, and that night, I huddled alone beside the warrior who had captured me until I heard the deep slow sleep breathing, then I crept away from the bedroll with my few leaves. I held them in my hands, trembling with fear at the thought of death, then slowly raised them to my mouth.

"If you eat those, and the folklore is true, you will not live to kill me," said the warrior quietly. I looked up with a start to see that the great blue eyes were open wide, though they looked dark in the light of the moon. "If you do not eat them, I will keep you by me, and train you, and tell you who you really are, and then, if you so choose, you may kill me once you have the height, the skill and the strength to do it well."

I nodded, and threw the leaves away.

"Scrub your hands with the washrag from dinner," said the warrior, "and go back to bed."

I did, but I lay a long time in the gilded darkness, restless and afraid. The moon moved from directly above us across the sky of the clearing and hid behind the black-blossomed forest beyond.

Even longer after that, the warrior spoke. "I am sorry I killed him. I should have let him live, to tarnish before your eyes as you discovered the truth. Now he will always be your hero. Your scholar hero, guarding the three stolen swords."

"There are only two," I said under my breath.

"Your name means The Sword of Your Mother," said the warrior. "Now go to sleep." And, to my later surprise, I did.

After she had been silent for a while, the beast rumbled as if it were clearing its throat politely. When she said no more, it said, "What happened then?"

"Oh, the usual," she said. "I grew up, I learned to fight with the daishō..."

After another pause, the beast said, "I think I ate that rider. Anyway I ate a warrior who looked like that. Big, attractive to the point of arrogance, mean, rode a white destrier, white samite, the whole nine yards. Literally."

"No, you didn't," she said.

"How can you be sure?"

"Because I killed them. Years later of course, and after all the usual palaver. I clove their head in twain, right down to their jawbone. Brain and blood flew all over me."

"Curiously specific form of death."

"Oh, obvious as hell, and twice as boring. That's two rôle models I had who died that way."

"Was either one your real parent?"

"Probably not. They all lied. Who the hell cares? All these breeder stories, if they aren't about lovers false or true, they're about parents and children betraying each other."

"I've noticed that. Most evil is much more impersonal in the world than in the stories."

"I've noticed *that*."

"Did you feel better after? I sometimes feel better after."

"Not particularly. How did you feel when you let the one-armed hero live?"

"Not better." After a pause, "but not worse."

"There it is, then."

"Do you have any food left?"

"A bit. Well, not really."

"I'll go out and get us a calf if you want."

"Make it a sheep and I'm all in."

While the beast was gone, she made a torch (from a hardwood staff wound around with some mildewed clothing that its hero wouldn't be needing any more, which came pre-pitched with essence of mummy) and wandered around the cave. There was a whole new annex since she had last fought there, and it was full of shed scales. They were beautiful in the torchlight: red as fire, gold as sunset, pink and iridescent as sunrise. A few were as small as her palm. She picked out a number in a range of sizes, and brought them back to the fire.

When the dragon returned, she said, "Can I have these? I could make some kick-ass armour out of these."

The beast nodded, mouth still full of wool. It spat out the sheep by the fire. "I hate these things," it said. "It's so much trouble to get the matted wool out of my teeth after I get the meat out."

"I'll skin it," she said, and did, efficiently and quickly. She had been farming for a while, a few years ago, and some things you don't forget how to do. She chopped off a quarter with her sword—all that work with the clove oil and the soft rag had to be good for something—and impaled the meat on a spear. "Cooked or raw for you?"

"Raw." The beast held the spitted meat into the fire, rotating it slowly as if they sat in a great hall's kitchen—which in a way they did—until it was done. Then she ate her cooked meat and the beast ate the raw carcass, crunching its bones, gristle and fat into grit that would later feed its internal fire, if needed.

This took some time, and during that time, she told the rest of her story.

Then it was the beast's turn. She dozed through part of it, but woke politely near the end to listen to the final exchange of riddles and witticisms.

"What happened then?" she asked.

"I ate him."

"Why did you do that, after he answered your riddles and everything?"

"It's my nature," said the beast.

They laughed, because they both had told that old story to the other, at one time or another.

The fire had burned down some, and she thought they probably should save the rest of the weapons until later. "Well, my friend," she said.

"We're enemies," said the beast.

"At our age," she said, "anyone who's still alive is a friend."

The beast nodded. "Because we're the only ones who know what we know."

She smiled, reached across the low fire, and the beast reached out too, and their nailed fingers touched briefly in the safe warmth rising from their shared flame.

"What now?" she said after a moment.

"Let's go out," said the beast. "We can sleep later."

"All right," she said, and leaned on the beast's forearm to help lever herself up to her feet. They turned toward the cave mouth, her hand still on its wrist, and went up.

While they had talked and burned their history, the sun had risen, and when they went out of the cave, it was full daylight.

They stood on the lip of the cave, looking out across the vast country, their shadows stretching long and sharp and dark behind them into the cave.

"I will eat you one day," said the beast.

"Of course," she said. "It's your nature."

"But not today."

"And I will kill you one day," she said.

"Of course," said the beast. "It's the way of things."

"Or anyway, it's my job," she said. "But not today."

When she woke later from her familiar nightmare of death and the void, the old fighter beside her stirred, and squeaked a querulous sound of disturbance. She put a gnarled hand on his muscled shoulder.

"Shhh," she said, "go back to sleep. It was just a dream."

Candas Jane Dorsey is an internationally-known, award-winning Canadian author, editor, teacher of writing, and literary community leader. Her latest book, ICE and Other Stories, *came out from PS Publishing, England, in 2018, the same year Dorsey was inducted (not indicted!) into the Canadian Science Fiction and Fantasy Hall of Fame and also was the subject of a festschrift anthology,* Prairie Starport, *edited by Rhonda Parrish. A new mystery series is upcoming from ECW Press in 2020 onward. Many years ago, a student of Dorsey's wrote a Plato's Cave story and the set-up stuck in her mind, so with his permission to riff off his set-up, she started to develop her own rather different cave tale, and finished it years later for this anthology.*

Thank you for reading

HEAR ME ROAR

We would appreciate it a great deal if you would leave an honest review on Goodreads and wherever you purchased this book.

Your stars and a couple sentences mean the world to us!

Truly.

The importance of reviews cannot be overstated—they often make the difference between a book's success or its utter failure.

Always Be The First To Know!

Whether it's a new release, a call for submissions, cover reveal, super sale or I just want to share a new story I've written, you will always be among the first to know if you sign up for my newsletter.

I promise to respect your privacy and your inbox. I will only email you when I have something exciting to share, probably about twice a month.

Subscribe now and you'll receive a free download of my award-winning post-apocalyptic short story, "Starry Night" as a welcome-to-the-newsletter present!

Subscribe to Rhonda's Mailing List!

http://bit.ly/StarryStory

ALSO AVAILABLE FROM
POISE AND PEN PUBLISHING

26 APOLCALYPSES—ONE FOR EVERY LETTER OF THE ALPHABET!

READ IT FOR FREE

AT ALL YOUR FAVOURITE ONLINE DISTRIBUTORS!

http://www.poiseandpen.com/publishing/alphabet-anthologies/a-is-for-apocalypse/

ALSO AVAILABLE FROM
POISE AND PEN PUBLISHING

26 STORIES EXPLORING THE CONCEPT OF BROKENNESS—
BROKEN HEARTS, BROKEN DREAMS, BROKEN PEOPLE—THAT
SOMEHOW MANAGES TO NOT BE DEPRESSING!

http://www.poiseandpen.com/publishing/alphabet-anthologies/b-is-for-broken/

ALSO AVAILABLE FROM
POISE AND PEN PUBLISHING

STORIES WHICH BLEND REALITY WITH FANTASY, MESH SCIENCE FICTION WITH MYSTERY AND MIX HISTORY WITH WHAT SHOULD HAVE BEEN.

AVAILABLE AT ALL YOUR FAVOURITE ONLINE RETAILERS!

http://www.poiseandpen.com/publishing/alphabet-anthologies/c-is-for-chimera/

ALSO AVAILABLE FROM
POISE AND PEN PUBLISHING

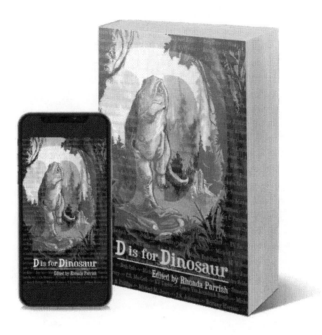

DINOSAURS BOTH LITERAL AND METAPHORICAL RAMPAGE THROUGH THESE TWENTY-SIX FANTASY, SCIENCE FICTION, AND HORROR SHORT STORIES

D IS FOR DINOSAUR
FIND IT ONLINE NOW!

http://www.poiseandpen.com/publishing/alphabet-anthologies/d-is-for-dinosaur/

ALSO AVAILABLE FROM
POISE AND PEN PUBLISHING

TWENTY-SIX DARK FANTASY, HORROR AND SCIENCE FICTION STORIES EXPLORING THE VARIOUS SHADES AND FLAVOURS OF EVIL

E IS FOR EVIL
FIND IT ONLINE NOW!

http://www.poiseandpen.com/publishing/alphabet-anthologies/e-is-for-evil/

Also Available from Poise and Pen Publishing

If you think fairies are sweet and sparkly, you don't know fairies. Twenty-six fairy stories that will challenge how you think of the fae.

F IS FOR FAIRY
Find it online now!

http://www.poiseandpen.com/publishing/alphabet-anthologies/f-is-for-fairy/

RHONDA PARRISH ANTHOLOGIES

Available Now

A IS FOR APOCALYPSE
B IS FOR BROKEN
C IS FOR CHIMERA
D IS FOR DINOSAUR
E IS FOR EVIL
F IS FOR FAIRY

FAE
CORVIDAE
SCARECROW
SIRENS
EQUUS

MRS. CLAUS: NOT THE FAIRY TALE THEY SAY
TESSERACTS TWENTY-ONE: NEVERTHELESS
METASTASIS
NITEBLADE MAGAZINE

FIRE: DEMONS, DRAGONS AND DJINNS
EARTH: GIANTS, GOLEMS AND GARGOYLES
AIR: SYLPHS, SPIRITS AND SWAN MAIDENS

GRIMM, GRIT AND GASOLINE
CLOCKWORK, CURSES AND COAL

HEAR ME ROAR

SWASHBUCKLING CATS: NINE LIVES ON THE SEVEN SEAS

Made in the USA
Middletown, DE
04 October 2020